London-born Catherine Andersen has lived and worked in several countries throughout the world, including Canada, Norway, Denmark, Holland, Sudan, Saudi Arabia, in the Eastern Province on the Arabian Gulf, and Jeddah in the Western Province on the Red Sea.

She has travelled with her husband, a Danish engineer, and wrote this book whilst accompanying him in a two-year work assignment in America. They actually lived in a two hundred-year-old converted Presbyterian church in the small New Jersey town of Asbury, which having changed very little from when it was settled, provided the inspiration for this novel.

THE HETHERINGTON FAMILY

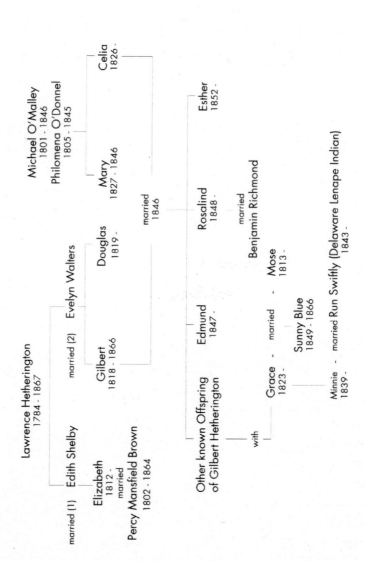

Lawrence Hetherington
1784 - 1867

married (1) Edith Shelby

married (2) Evelyn Walters

Michael O'Malley
1801 - 1846
Philomena O'Donnel
1805 - 1845

Elizabeth
1812 -
married
Percy Mansfield Brown
1802 - 1864

Gilbert
1818 - 1866

Douglas
1819 -

married
1846

Mary
1827 - 1846

Celia
1826 -

Rosalind
1848 -

Esther
1852 -

married
Benjamin Richmond

Other known Offspring
of Gilbert Hetherington

Edmund
1847 -

Mose
1813 -

with

Grace -
1823 -

married

Sunny Blue
1849 - 1866

Minnie -
1839 -

married Run Swiftly (Delaware Lenape Indian)
1843 -

The Hetherington Women

Part 2

FOR PAT...

A friend whom I have always treasured.

I hope your expectations are happily fulfilled in this conclusion to my tale.

"Paddy"

Catherine Andersen.

OCTOBER, 2014.

By the same author

The Hetherington Women Part 1 (2014)
ISBN 978-1-84897-449-4

Catherine Andersen

The Hetherington Women

Part 2

Olympia Publishers
London

www.olympiapublishers.com
OLYMPIA PAPERBACK EDITION

A CIP catalogue record for this title is
available from the British Library.

ISBN: 978-1-84897-450-0

(Olympia Publishers is part of Ashwell Publishing Ltd)

This is a work of fiction.
Names, characters, places and incidents originate from the writer's imagination.
Any resemblance to actual persons, living or dead,
is purely coincidental.

First Published in 2014

Olympia Publishers
60 Cannon Street
London
EC4N 6NP

Printed in Great Britain

To Kjeld, my husband, my heartfelt gratitude for the unanswering love and support he has given me.

Also to my good friend, Josephine, without whose enthusiasm and encouragement this book would never have been published.

Lilybee 1866

One

Edmund sat on the wide verandah staring out at the North Carolina landscape; he found it pleasant to sit there day after day enjoying the peaceful atmosphere. He was quite unaware that his aunt Lilybee had joined him and was watching him with concern. In her hand she held the letter she had just received from her brother Gilbert in New Jersey, informing her that his daughter Rosalind was to be married and extending an invitation for her to attend the wedding. At the same time, he urgently requested that she bring Edmund with her as his sister was adamant the she would not marry until her brother could come to the ceremony.

Lilybee had long since realised that Edmund found it difficult to communicate with his father and was, therefore, reluctant to return to his home in the North, but she also realized that this young man would have to be coaxed into resuming a normal life eventually. She had tried several times to persuade him to return home, but without success. Even when his mother had written to him, telling how much she and his sisters missed him, he had refused to consider it. Maybe now, she thought, his sister's wedding was just what was needed to encourage him to take the necessary steps to join his family once again. After all, he had been with her now for over a year and a half, trying to come to terms with the appalling injuries he had suffered in the war. She painfully remembered the night that he had been brought to her door long after dark in an old wooden cart, more dead than alive; in truth she held out no hope of his recovery, so badly injured was he. The makeshift dressings binding his wounds had been scarlet with his blood and it had saturated the rags on which he was lying. He had been scarcely recognizable and the sight of him had horrified her, but even so she had somehow managed to compose herself and arouse the servants from their beds, then together they carried him into the house. She would never forget how she had felt as she stood watching this young boy's life ebbing away, nor would she ever forgive her brother Gilbert for forcing his son into that shameful and disastrous war.

"Edmund, I have just received a letter from your father my dear."

The boy looked round and nodded his head. It was evident that he was not really interested. Fingering the letter apprehensively, Lilybee sat down.

"He tells me that your sister is betrothed to a Henry Youngman, but she will not consider setting a firm date for her wedding until you are well enough to attend. Your father seems most anxious for you to go home as soon as possible, so will you not consider it my dear boy? It will be a joyful occasion and one I am sure you will not want to miss. Just imagine how happy Rosalind will be to know that you are able to attend her wedding, and your mother too will be overjoyed at seeing you once again. Won't you think of them and try to make the journey for their sakes? I have also been invited so we could go together. What do you say?"

Edmund remained quiet for a few moments, his elbow propped on the arm of his chair, his hand pressed against his forehead. "No occasion could be joyful in my father's house Aunt," he said sadly, "But of course I should attend Rosalind's wedding. Nothing would give me greater pleasure than to see my mother and sisters again, but I doubt very much that Roasalind has had any choice in the matter of her marriage to Henry Youngman. He is old enough to be her father and I can well imagine exactly why she has been betrothed to him. I know my father and I also know that my sister would never have chosen to marry that man. It is obvious that my father has arranged this alliance to benefit himself in some way. It is probably to further another of his underhand schemes. Everyone knows that Henry Youngman is an extremely wealthy businessman, so it is blatantly obvious that father must be manipulating him by promising Rosalind's hand in marriage. It is so typical of him; he cares nothing for any of us. You are right Aunt Lilybee, it is time for me to return to New Jersey, so perhaps you would be kind enough to write to my father and tell him that I shall be returning, for I am longing to meet my mother and sisters again. I feel that they may need my support, as they cannot be in agreement with this forthcoming marriage."

*

Lilybee felt a surge of relief at Edmund's decision to return home but at the same time she was deeply saddened at the thought that he would be finally leaving 'White Lakes'. She would sorely miss her nephew after having him with her for so long. It had been such a comfort for her to watch him gradually regain his strength through all those months when she and her maid, Grace, had nursed him night and day. There had been times when she felt sure that they would lose him, particularly when the wound to his leg had turned gangrenous. Finally, they had found a doctor who had advised the immediate removal of the rotting limb and he had amputated Edmund's left leg on a hastily prepared operating table in her own kitchen.

It had taken two of the strongest slaves to hold him, and she still marvelled at how she and Grace had managed to assist in the gruesome ordeal without fainting away. It was probably due to the young doctor's professional handling of the emergency situation. He was obviously experienced in operations of that nature; in fact, he told her he was about to rejoin the Confederates in a day or two, when he received his new posting. They had been lucky to find him at all, as he had been treating injured troops in the battlefield for the past two years and had been visiting his family for a short furlough before being posted to a different location.

*

Having to nurse Edmund back to health, both physically and mentally, had also helped Lilybee over the worst heartache she had ever experienced, for when Edmund was brought to the plantation, she was also informed that her own dear husband had been mortally wounded in the same battle that had almost killed the boy. They had been fighting on opposite sides, her husband under General Lee and her nephew under General Grant. Was it conceivable that families could fight one against the other in such a futile war? How had it all come about and of what benefit had it been?

*

Lilybee hurried into the library, anxious to pen a reply to her brother Gilbert. She sat down at her desk and as she did so she ran her fingers lovingly over the surface of the beautiful little Davenport; it was one of the last gifts her late husband had given her and she treasured it above all others, particularly as its delightful little pigeon-holes were crammed full with letters he had written to her during their two long years of heart-breaking separation. How they had adored each other, and in those letters he constantly reassured her of his love. It was almost as though he had known that he would never be coming back to her again. She brushed a tear from her cheek and reached for a sheet of notepaper. It had never been easy for her to tell her brother anything and now her task seemed almost impossible as she struggled to find the appropriate words to describe Edmund's delicate state of mind. How could she begin to explain the problems that beset her nephew, to a man so devoid of sympathy? That he was the boy's father was completely irrelevant, for she knew him to be totally lacking in kindness and understanding. She feared that irreparable damage could be done to the boy if he were not handled with the utmost care, and as the relationship between father and son had never been a particularly good one, this would certainly aggravate Edmund's condition. She pondered over the problem for some time, then decided that the best course of action would be for her to wait until they came to New Jersey. Yes, that is what she must do. She would have the opportunity to talk with Celia, his mother, upon their arrival and between them they could decide how best to ensure that Edmund was protected from his father's interference. She almost wished she could avoid seeing him herself, but at the same time knew that it would be impossible for her nephew to undertake the journey unaccompanied.

Lilybee took up her pen to inform Gilbert of her acceptance and carefully avoided mentioning too much concerning his son's condition but she pointed out that they would not attempt the journey North until the winter was completely over, as Edmund was not strong enough to endure the stress that such conditions might impose. She had determined to take Grace with her, so that they might continue to care for the boy until they felt it was safe to leave him. She would now have to inform her younger brother, Douglas, because he relied very heavily on her in the day to day management of the household and the domestic slaves, and she knew he would not be pleased to hear that she planned to be away for some length of time. Nevertheless, she had made up her mind to go and she would not allow him to dissuade her.

*

Very little time elapsed before word came back from Gilbert in New Jersey, informing Lilybee that as soon as she felt the weather to be fair enough, then Edmund should return home. He told her that he was pleased to hear of her decision to attend the wedding, and that Rosalind would not set a definite date until her brother and aunt arrived. However, it was anticipated that the happy day would definitely take place in the Spring, when the weather improved, so he urged her not to delay for too much longer.

What a perfect time for a wedding thought Lilybee, as she went in search of Edmund to acquaint him of his father's reply, but she felt none of the joy normally associated with such an occasion. Instead, deep within her heart was a feeling of foreboding, which she could not explain.

There was much that she must do to prepare for the forthcoming visit, and as the Spring was not too far away, she decided to set about those preparations as soon as possible. For a start she would have to appease her brother, Douglas, for he had not been too pleased when she had first mentioned her proposed trip with Edmund, but nevertheless she was not to be deterred. It was high time, she decided, that Douglas shouldered more responsibility. In fact, she often wondered how he spent his days, as Ralph Clayton, the overseer, managed every aspect of the running of the plantation and had done since the death of her beloved husband. Although she had never liked the man, she had to admit that he knew his business well. A definite system of rules was involved, together with orderly regimentation, and on large estates, the fulfilment of these rules fell to an experienced overseer, who had general charge under the authority of the planter. His function was that of manager or steward, and he supervised the planting, cultivating and harvesting of the crops. He also had to be conversant with specialised forms of agriculture and capable of mastering the intricate details of cotton culture.

To the slaves, the overseer was the 'master's left hand', he rang the plantation bell and kept his eyes fixed on them, meting out harsh punishment whenever he saw fit. Ralph Clayton had been just such a man when Lilybee and her husband had first come to 'White Lakes'. He had worked for the previous owner for quite a number of years, so Percy Mansfield-Brown had been grateful to retain an overseer of his experience. From the outset, Lilybee had not taken to him and it was not only his appearance that she found so objectionable. He was a tall, lean man with flinty-blue eyes, which seemed to be perpetually hooded by his half-closed eyelids. When spoken to, he always gazed into the distance, as though wrapped up in thoughts of his own. It was virtually impossible to have a conversation with the man; he growled rather than spoke when replying to a question. His manner was arrogant, his demeanour severe, and Lilybee was well aware of how greatly the slaves feared him; and yet her younger brother seemed to spend a considerable amount of time in his company. She had never understood what it was that Douglas saw in him, what he found so fascinating about men like Ralph Clayton and his brother Gilbert.

Being fully aware of his weakness of character, she had not been unduly perturbed when he and Gilbert had parted on their arrival in this country. When Douglas had chosen to come to North Carolina with her and Percy, she had held out the hope that, maybe, now his own character would have the opportunity to develop, untainted by the evil influence of his sibling. Her hopes were soon to be dashed however, when it became apparent that he had taken up with their very own odious overseer.

Over the years, she had tried on many occasions to dissuade him from such an undesirable association, to no avail, but after her latest warning, at the beginning of the winter, she was determined to remove Ralph Clayton from his life – come what may. She believed that Douglas had been making a serious attempt to learn all that was necessary in the day to day management of a large estate such as 'White Lakes', and although it was taking him longer than she had envisaged, she was not overly worried because she knew that the man she hated would soon be gone forever. Now though, she had to accept that his departure would be delayed again, for her brother could not manage alone whilst she was away. In fact, she had reluctantly decided that her form of appeasement would be to extend Ralph Clayton's stay. She had the greatest misgivings, but she had no other choice. In what other way, she asked herself, could she possibly induce Douglas to run 'White Lakes' in her absence? For the time being she would have to let the matter ride, but things would be different when she returned – indeed they would.

Two

The day finally came for them to leave, and amid great excitement and the warmest of farewells, Lilybee, Edmund and Grace were driven away to meet the stage. They set off on their journey with decidedly different sentiments, and the time it would take them to reach their destination was to afford the opportunity for thoughtful reflection.

Grace felt that she must surely be dreaming, it was impossible for her to imagine that after all the years of heartache and longing, fearing that she would never see her daughter again, she was now to be reunited with her. Her spirits were soaring; so much so that she even dared to hope that it might one day be possible for her to see Mose and Sunny Blue again. The very thought of seeing Minnie had filled her with renewed optimism.

Edmund on the other hand, could sense panic welling up within him; it was engulfing him, making his heart race. His initial pleasure at the thought of being reunited with his dear mother and sister again, was now completely overshadowed by the thought of an encounter with his tyrannical father. Why, oh why, had he agreed to come he wondered.

For Lilybee too, the trip would be filled with emotion. She was longing to see her sister-in-law and the two girls once more, although the same could not be said for her brother. She could hardly bear to contemplate her meeting with him, for her loathing of him had grown beyond reasonable limits since she had come to learn of his cruel treatment of his family. Was it so many years, she asked herself, since her last carefree visit, when she and Celia had taken their wonderful trip into New York? What changes would have taken place, and how she wished dear Percy was here to accompany them now.

*

Once under way they settled down and retreated into their own private worlds, and as the coach rattled and bumped along, its occupants drifted off into fitful sleep. All three of them, in their dream-like state, found themselves drawn uncontrollably backwards in time.

For Edmund, the sound of the horses' hooves hammering on the hard ground, accompanied by the creaking and groaning of the coach as it swayed from side to side, became reminiscent of the war scenes which were indelibly etched in his memory. In his disturbed sleep, those same sounds once again revived the horror of the battles he had seen fought between the Confederate and Union armies, horrors which would return to haunt him for the rest of his life.

His first heartache had come with the sad parting from his mother and sisters on the day he had been forced, by his father, to march with the hundreds of volunteers and enlisted men from all the small towns throughout New Jersey, towns like the one in which he had grown up, but his overwhelming sadness at leaving those he loved had soon become submersed beneath the unimaginable scenes of massacre and destruction that he witnessed day after interminable day in the fateful war.

In that spring of 1863, President Lincoln once again called for more men to take up arms in the battle of North versus South. Their courage was outstanding, for they were not fighting men, nor well-trained soldiers, disciplined in the art of warfare, but farm workers, saddle makers, mill hands, textile workers, pedlars and the like. They were to perish and die in their thousands, and not always in illustrious battles. Tragically many of them were to die from starvation and disease, brought about by the severe shortage of adequate food and medical care.

On their first day, the raw recruits had been marched until they dropped and then, within six days of recruitment, every man took his oath of allegiance before either a magistrate or a regular army officer. After that they were mustered into a unit for six weeks' training, which was designed to transform then from civilians to soldiers. The training was not too well organised, in fact it was not in the least bit professional. It consisted of little more than teaching each man his left foot from his right and how to march in a straight line. In the initial days of recruitment, the soldiers had no uniforms and no weapons, so they had to perform their drill with wooden muskets or broom handles. Edmund was not the only one who found the whole process distasteful and degrading in the extreme; a good many of them had their illusions shattered when they had come face to face with the harsh realities of war, and for the soldiers of New Jersey those harsh realities could not have been more apparent than they were in the Battle of the Wilderness, where they fought and died so valiantly. In all, forty percent of New Jersey's men, between the ages of fifteen and forty-four went to fight for the Union army, the cream of its menfolk, in the very prime of their lives.

Edmund wrote twice to his mother during his days in the training camp, assuring her that he was fit and well, but longing for the war to be over. He had not wanted to join the army, and the art of warfare was of no interest to him.

It was not long before his unit received orders to join the troops of Major General George G. Meade. The men were issued with uniforms, flannel sack coats and trousers, flannel shirts and drawers, stockings and boots with leather stocks and great-coats. Thankfully the quality of the uniforms had now greatly improved, but at the beginning of the war they had been made of 'shoddy' which consisted of the refuse stuff and sweepings of the shop, pounded, rolled, glued and smoothed to the external form and gloss of cloth. Scandalous reports had circulated of how, when the first rainstorms soaked into it, the men found their clothing, overcoats and blankets scattered to the wind in rags, or dissolving into their primitive elements of dust. The supply contracts had come under immediate review, and drastic improvements carried out, so that the quartermaster received fewer complaints thereafter. Once they had been kitted out, the troops were transported to their battalions, whose numbers were continually depleted during the savage battles.

On the 1st July, Edmund found himself in Pennsylvania, where he was to become embroiled in the most terrible battle of the war. He was to fight with General Meade's Army of the Potomac at Gettysburg. This true military leader had replaced Major General Hooker; President Lincoln felt that, in his hands, the nation would be safe. His trust was well founded, for his chosen commander procured a resounding victory for the Union army. Both sides suffered crippling losses, and Meade was bitterly criticised for failing to pursue Lee's troops when they retreated, but he felt it more important to bury the dead who lay all over the battlefield, for as far as the eye could see; to tend to the wounded who had fought until they dropped, and to give those who had survived the ghastly slaughter, time to recuperate. He felt justified in his decision, for the Confederates had sustained such serious losses that they would never again be able to mount a major offensive. Nevertheless, he was, eventually, to be replaced by Ulysses S.

Grant, who at that same time had brought about the capitulation of Vicksburg in Mississippi.

Edmund survived his first taste of combat and miraculously suffered but a few minor injuries, which soon healed. His mind, however, was in absolute turmoil, he could not bear the thought of further fighting. He wanted to escape from it all, run away and find a peaceful, quiet place where he could forget all the horrors that he had witnessed during the past week; first the blood-curdling noises of the battle themselves, then, in the aftermath, the macabre spectacle of the thousands lying dead and wounded, who must be retrieved, then carried to field hospitals, or quickly buried. He had moved as though in a dream, unable to think for himself, following the orders that seemed never ending. He was unaware of what he was doing or why. When the time came for rest, he fell exhausted and slept uneasily. It was as though he had become part of a terrifying nightmare from which he was unable to escape. Almost without realising it, he had travelled down to Virginia with the Army of the Potomac, where things remained quiet for a while, but then he found himself on a train travelling westward; a train full of soldiers, bound for yet another battlefield. Fortunately, his involvement in the Battle of Chattanooga was not too prolonged and his regiment returned to the east once again.

The spring of 1864 was to herald the start of the Virginia Campaign, when the Army of the Potomac would once again engage Lee's confederates. Their aim was to advance through Virginia and seize the Southern capital of Richmond. Grant's decision was to cross the Rapidan River and make his way through the wilderness, where the Army of the Potomac had been so severely defeated less than a year earlier. Before he had time to reach open country, Southern troops made their attack and by the very nature of the terrain, the battle that ensued was to become yet another disastrous debacle. The dense wood areas rendered it impossible to formulate orderly plans for the assaults, with the result that the men fought recklessly, very often hand to hand, and the death toll grew alarmingly. Both sides inflicted appalling punishment on one another, with no obvious advantage being gained, and their numbers were savagely depleted during the forty days of fighting through the Wilderness to Cold Harbour.

The replacement of men was never as much of a problem for the North as it was for the South, and Grant was undeterred by the recent fearful slaughter, knowing that he could constantly replenish his fighting force from the reserves who were being held near Washington. His reckless insanity sent horrific shudders throughout the Northern states, and his men were convinced that they faced certain death in obeying his fatal orders. Many of them, when forced to make a suicidal attack, wrote their names and addresses on strips of paper and pinned then to their coats, so that their dead bodies could be identified after the battle.

Edmund followed all the others blindly into combat when Lee and Grant met near Mechanicsville, at the battle of Cold Harbour. Grant, once again, ordered a massive frontal assault upon the enemy, and the fighting was to rage from the third to the twelfth of June. It was bitter, bloody slaughter, during which the lives of thousands of men were, once again, laid to waste. The ferocity of the battle, the inhuman savagery, shocked and horrified Edmund and deplorably, as in the past, neither side had gained an advantage. Even Grant himself acknowledged that it had been a ghastly mistake. Despite all this, and in the face of mounting criticism, when confidence in him was fast eroding, Grant followed his chosen strategy. He decided to move his army to the south of the James River, where he hoped to cut off the Confederate capital of

Richmond. To do this would mean besieging Petersburg, but Grant fully realised that if he could capture this city, then Lee's army would be isolated in Richmond, and he would be forced to surrender.

*

In the first few months of 1864, Ulysses S. Grant had been extolled as a hero; he had been given command of all the armies of the United States, and the rank of lieutenant General has been bestowed on him. He had never been an ambitious man, and the honour acutely embarrassed him, especially as it had only been bestowed upon one other American officer in the country's history, George Washington. Now though, his butchery was engendering continual miscontent throughout the North, and because his actions were steadily backed by President Lincoln, whether they be good or bad, that fine gentleman's chances of being re-elected were in dire jeopardy. In fact, the democrats nominated General McClellan for the presidency in the coming elections, and drafted an election platform demanding an immediate armistice, with no mention of slavery. Morale was at its lowest ebb, yet still Grant was convinced that the end of the war was in sight. He was adamant that his war of attrition would eventually bring about victory for the North. To this end he began his assault on Petersburg. It had taken him only four days to move the whole of his army across two unbridged rivers, the Chickahominy and the James, a remarkable feat, requiring engineering skills of the highest order, but by the Seventeenth of June, the men were once again on the attack against the Southern defences at Petersburg. The Confederates, fully realising how near they were to overall defeat, were not to be ousted. In desperate resistance, and against enormous odds, they managed to hold their positions. It soon became apparent that this was to be a long and drawn out siege, and both armies resigned themselves to settling into their entrenchments, the Union forces under Smith, Burnside, Warren and Hancock, and the Confederates under Beauregard and Lee.

Throughout the remainder of June and most of July, there was complete deadlock, then towards the end of July, the 48th Pennsylvania Veteran Volunteers, comprised mainly of coal miners, took part in a skirmish against the Confederates. Having accomplished nothing, and realising the futility of their situation, one of the miners angrily commented that it would be far more effective if they dug a mine shaft below the enemy's fortifications, and blew them sky-high. Army engineers at first scoffed at the idea, but eventually it was put to General Burnside, who in turn took it to General Grant. His approval was obtained and the 48th Regiment set to work to dig the shaft.

By 30th July a five hundred foot tunnel had been completed, and eight thousand pounds of powder deposited in it. It was planned that an attack should take place when the charge exploded. Initially two brigades of black troops were chosen to lead the assault, but this idea was soon quashed by Grant's advisory staff, who pointed out that it would not be politically expedient to sacrifice these particular men. The black troops begged to be allowed to lead the assault, but Grant would not change his mind, they had to content themselves with being held as reserves. It was decided to touch off the fuse at 3:30 on the morning of 30th July, and everybody stood at the ready. Nothing happened. Then after an interminable wait, two soldiers of undeniable courage were sent into the shaft to discover that the fuse had gone out. It had to be re-lit and was finally detonated at 4:45 am.

Edmund had never before witnessed such carnage. The spectacle of destruction filled him with terror and sickening revulsion. It was as though a gigantic mountain had suddenly erupted before his eyes. The dawn sky was alive with grotesque, darkened shapes, strangely silhouetted by the ferocious red flames that leapt high into the air. The palls of acrid smoke eerily billowing above the gouged earth. Even worse were the agonised sounds that rent the air, screams of injured and dying men, the fearful noise made by wounded animals, hurled sky high by the blast, then plummeted to earth to become part of the hellish, tangled mass of dismembered bodies, strewn everywhere by the blast.

Suddenly Edmund was jolted into action by the shout, "CH... AAA... RGE!" and he was swept along in the massive surge of Union troops, towards the gruesome, forbidding crater which lay before them, some thirty feet deep and one hundred and seventy feet long.

At first, the Confederates were in a state of shocked confusion and a Union victory seemed assured, but when they reached the crater, the Union troops stopped dead. They halted their advance and remained huddled inside it for protection. As more and more troops advanced from the rear, and none of them felt willing to move forward, panic ensued. When the Confederate troops began to recover, they gathered at the top of the crater, unable to believe that they now had the most advantageous position from which to fire upon their attackers who were completely trapped. Aware of the mayhem, by seven o'clock in the morning, Burnside decided to send in the reserves. The black troops charged through the milling troops in the crater. They reformed on the other side and launched their attack upon the Confederates. The engagement was furious in the extreme, particularly when the Southern soldiers found themselves to be confronted by blacks. Then their fighting became frenzied, hand to hand, and at close range.

The two brigades of black troops, who fought so courageously, suffered the greatest number of casualties, which immediately brought an outcry from citizens and politicians alike. Grant was once again reviled for his actions, and he was later to acknowledge that the Battle of the Crater was the saddest affair he witnessed throughout the entire war. According to official reports, this sorry failure cost the Northern army almost four thousand men, killed, wounded and missing. This number was to include one Edmund Hetherington, and his injuries would ensure that he could never fight again.

Once the crater had begun to fill with more and more men, panic had overcome them. Body was pushed against body. They shoved and pulled; they lost their footing and fell to their knees as the loosened soil shifted beneath their feet. Men fell, one on top of the other, they pressed one another into the earth as, in a furore they fought and scrambled to free themselves. Hardly able to breathe… gasping desperately to fill their lungs… soon the crater became a living hell. Somehow Edmund managed to writhe over the top of the tumultuous human mass; he knew not how. All the time he kept his gaze fixed upon the sky and struggled with all his might not to lose sight of it. Then came the earth-shattering noise of the Confederate's artillery. They opened fire and men screamed in terror as bullets ripped through their flesh. The bodies of the killed and wounded lay everywhere, their life's blood draining away into the enemy's soil.

In a state of complete shock, his body shaking uncontrollably, Edmund continued to crawl upwards towards the top of the crater, up towards the sky, away from this horrific inferno. The sound of the enemy's fire grew louder and louder and suddenly there was a deafening explosion... a blinding flash of light, then momentary calm. Blood curdling screams... choking dust... another explosion, then another. Edmund found himself being elevated upwards by a tremendous blast.

"Oh God... is this my death?"

Eeerie darkness... sinking, sinking into oblivion... merciful oblivion. Awake again.

"Am I awake... what's that sound...?"

Pitiful cries... groans.

"Who is that begging for help? Please someone help!"

Then the searing pain... too much to bear! Edmund writhed in agony and slipped away.

The river looked cool and inviting, the small boy waded in knee deep. He stood looking intently into the clear, rippling water, watching the fish as they played. He plunged his hands in, trying to catch one, but they darted away quickly. He threw back his head and laughed happily. "Look Mama... look," he called.

"Be careful darling... don't go too far... stay near Minnie and Rosalind where the water is not too deep."

He could see his mother sitting beneath the shade of the trees with her sewing. How he loved her...

Oh the pain... his leg was burning... a fierce excruciating pain.

"Yes sir... Hetherington sir... New Jersey." How he wished his father had not made him join this army. He hated everything about it. He had no wish to fight... he could never kill anyone. The food made him sick... nothing but salt pork... salt beef... beans and hardtack or sheet iron crackers. He had grown so thin... his stomach churned at times when he saw the maggots

and worms in the hardtack, and the 'sow-belly' was so strong it could almost walk into the cooking pot.

"Is that you Joshua?" He looked into the kindly black face that floated in front of him. Yes, it had to be Joshua. He rested his head against the strong protective arm as he drank the warm soup, it tasted so good. If only the pain in his leg would go away. He drifted off to sleep again. Nature in its kindness and mercy bore him off into unconsciousness.

*

The coach suddenly lurched so violently that the passengers were awakened. Edmund fell forward awkwardly and Lilybee and Grace quickly reached out at one and the same time, to steady him.

"Oh my dear… are you alright?" asked his aunt concernedly.

"Yes… yes, I'm quite alright… thank you."

He smiled to himself at the kindness of these two women. They were forever attentive to his every need and he loved them for it. He thought of the unbelievable turn of events that had brought him to his aunt's home in North Carolina, and marvelled at the coincidence of meeting up with his uncle Percy. He was deeply saddened to think of how tragically that grand old gentleman had met his death, of how so many had met their deaths, and he knew that nothing could ever justify the colossal human sacrifice that had been made.

Three

Lilybee sighed as she looked across at Edmund. He had nodded off to sleep again. She too marvelled at the coincidence of his meeting up with his uncle; who would ever have believed it possible? She was convinced that had it not been for Mose bringing the boy back to 'White Lakes' then he would have perished, as thousands of others had perished, from the sheer want of adequate medical attention and proper food and nourishment. She relaxed now, and leant back, turning her eyes to look out at the passing landscape. Signs of the war's ravages were still evident all around; it would take many years to eradicate them. She thought of her beloved husband and wondered if she had passed near the place where Mose had lain him to rest. No matter that it was not meant to be in the good earth of his own plantation at 'White Lakes', for she would hold him dear within her heart until the day she died. A solitary tear escaped from the corner of her eye and rested on her cheek in fond remembrance of him. She would never get over his loss, never as long as she lived. She closed her eyes and gave free rein to her thoughts, allowing them to transport her back through the years to when she had first met Percy Mansfield- Brown... back to the year of 1831.

*

Lawrence Hetherington lifted the small pile of letters from the tray on the hall table and glanced through them casually; there appeared to be nothing of too much interest, until he came upon the last of them. It immediately captured his attention and he examined it carefully, a puzzled expression upon his face. He dropped the other letters on to the table and tore it open. As he read its contents his face paled; he hurried back to the breakfast room where his daughter was still lingering over the last of her tea and toast.

"What do you think? I have just received word from young Mansfield-Brown, informing me of his father's death." He shook his head sadly. "Poor Leonard... he died several months ago, out in India... he'd been ill for some time apparently." He fell unsteadily on to the chair that he had previously vacated at the head of the table. "What terrible news... I can hardly believe it. Such a shock you know."

Lilybee turned to the servant girl: "Would you pour the master another cup of tea Alice? Plenty of sugar, and not too strong."

She sat quietly watching her father whilst he sipped at the warm drink. He had taken the news badly, she could see he was deeply moved and she did not know what to say to console him.

"He was like a father to me when I first arrived in India... 1805... twenty-one I was... never forget it. He taught me all he knew about the East India Company... wonderful fella. Then, when I took your mother back with me after we were married, he and Imogen, his wife, couldn't have been kinder, the pair of them... just like parents to us." He sat deep in thought, his eyes unseeing. He went on: "Yes... your mother and Imogen hit it off straight away, great friends they were."

He took out his handkerchief and blew his nose loudly. "Terrible shock... terrible shock," he muttered over and over again.

Lilybee stood up and went to him. She placed a loving arm around his shoulders and bent over to kiss him gently on the cheek.

"I am so sorry Papa, it's terribly sad to lose such an old friend... but what of his son, was he out in India with his parents?"

"Oh, my darling of course, you won't remember young Percy, will you? He was sent back to England when he was old enough to go to school, and then when he grew up... in his twenties I believe he was, he joined his father in the Company... family tradition and all that. Your mother and I knew him as a young lad, of course, but once he was sent back to England to school, we never saw him again."

"Did he not have any brothers or sisters?"

"Oh, no... No, Imogen was never able to bear any more children after Percy, so your mother learned. Well, I suppose that was quite understandable... she wasn't a youngster you know, when she had him... not at all... of course, one was never indelicate enough to make reference to such a matter; a lady's age can be a somewhat 'ticklish' subject left well alone, don't you know, but I believe she would have been into her thirties when Percy was born." He sat in thought for a while, reminiscing over the past. "Yes, young Percy was quite a little fella, around three or four years old I should guess, when I first met his parents." He stopped again, then after several minutes went on: "Upon my word, that young man must be somewhere around twenty-nine years of age by now, if my memory serves me right. How the years do fly by. He will be all alone now that his father's gone, because his mother was taken with cholera, as was your own dear mother, some seven or eight years ago. I believe that was when young Percy went out to join his father in India, actually."

"Is he still out there Papa?"

"No, no… not according to this letter. It would appear that he has returned to England, to settle his father's estate. I think I should arrange to see him… I'll invite him to the club first, for a chat… men's talk, you know. Then perhaps he might appreciate an invitation to dinner, here with us, one evening. I'll see how he feels about it."

"That would be lovely Papa… he may be married, he could bring his wife. It would be so interesting to meet them, I should love to hear all about their life in India… and I know you would enjoy reliving old memories."

"Yes… yes, I would, very much."

Lilybee was pleased to see that she had cheered her father somewhat. He stood up and gave her a rueful smile. "Right then my dear, I'll pen a reply to young Mansfield-Brown straight away."

Less than one week later, Lilybee was carefully attending to her toilet and her dress, in readiness for their dinner guest. She felt unusually excited about meeting him, although, if asked, she could never have explained the reason why. Her father had discovered that he was still a bachelor; could this be the reason, she wondered? Her maid had brushed her honey-coloured hair until it shone like silk, and then pinned it tightly across the crown from the centre parting. Now she laboriously twisted each curl around her fingers, so that they fell in a cascade of ringlets down each side of her mistress's pretty face. Lilybee glanced down admiringly at her new rose-coloured brocade gown with its low waist and belled skirt. She had particularly chosen it to wear this evening, because she knew that it suited her so admirably. When she was absolutely satisfied with her appearance, Lilybee descended the stairs just in time to see Percy Mansfield-Brown entering the front door. He was a tall, fine looking man, fashionably attired, and she noticed how elegantly his dark blue coat, with its rolled lapels, complimented the immaculate white linen cloth that he wore at his neck. Lilybee was deeply impressed by the magnificence of him, and she felt her cheeks burning as her father proudly introduced her to their guest. The young man was just as overcome himself when he caught sight of the delightful Miss Hetherington. She appeared to him to be exceptionally beautiful, with her delicate complexion faintly blushing, and her perfect, petite figure.

They took to one another instantly, and chatted animatedly throughout the entire meal. To his host, the young guest talked at great length of all that was interesting and new out in India, and he listened patiently whenever the older man fondly reminisced about his own experiences there.

To Lilybee he spoke of his hopes and dreams for the future, of his plan to leave England again, but this time to make his fortune in the New World. He was negotiating the purchase of a cotton plantation in North Carolina, which he had been assured would prove to be a highly profitable venture.

Without doubt, the evening proved to be the most memorable that Lilybee had ever spent in her life and by the end of it, Percy Mansfield-Brown had won the admiration of both father and daughter alike. In fact, Lilybee had completely lost her heart to this gallant young man, so much so that when he asked if she and her father would care to accompany him on some sight-seeing tours of London, so that he might take a final look at its wonderful attractions, before he left the country again, they accepted wholeheartedly and without hesitation.

For the next week Lilybee and Percy spent as much time as it was possible to spend together, so that it soon became apparent to Lawrence Hetherington that the two youngsters had fallen deeply in love with one another. They had visited the theatre, had enjoyed the ballet and the opera, they had wined and dined in restaurants, both large and fashionably popular, or small and secluded, and every rendezvous had been enhanced by their deepening fondness for each other and the doting father knew that it would be but a matter of time before he lost his charming daughter to this most eligible of young men. He had not long to wait for the request he was happily anticipating, and it came as the highlight to a week of pleasurable activity.

Lilybee had specifically mentioned to Percy that he must pay a visit to the zoological gardens in Regents Park, which had been opened three years earlier in 1828, and of course he was delighted to agree with her suggestion. She would never ever forget that spectacular day... every minute detail of it would remain forever in her memory, treasured for all time.

It was a beautiful day in the late spring, the sun was shining, the birds singing, and there was a feeling of jubilation in the air. Lilybee and her father were ready and waiting when Percy came to call for them, and very soon they were on their way towards Regents Park. When they came to the entrance of the zoo, Percy was intrigued to see that the gentlemen were not allowed to take their whips with them; instead, they were requested to leave them for safe-keeping at the entrance. The ladies, on the other hand, were permitted to keep their parasols with them, but were politely requested not to poke them through the bars at the animals.

"Isn't this great fun?" laughed Lilybee, as they began their tour. "And hasn't the collection of animals grown since we last came here Papa?"

"Well... according to this pamphlet here, the collection of animals was augmented last year with the Royal Menagerie from Windsor Castle," said her father. He had taken Lilybee and her two brothers to the zoo shortly after its opening, as a special treat for her sixteenth birthday. People had flocked from far and wide at that time, to enjoy this novel form of amusement, and in the first seven months, it had attracted some thirty thousand visitors.

Percy was truly amazed by the impressive collection of exotic animals, among them, bears, monkeys, zebras, kangaroos, llamas, emus and turtles. He had never been so fascinated in his life, and remarked at the unbelievable changes that had taken place in his native country since he had been away. After they had been walking around for some time, Lawrence Hetherington begged to be excused, for he must sit down and rest awhile.

"You two take yourselves off, and come back for me a little later," he said, "I no longer have your youthful endurance," he chuckled quietly. The youngsters were acutely aware of his tactful ploy, specifically designed to allow them time to be alone together.

Lilybee bent down and kissed his cheek affectionately. "Very well Papa, if you feel that you simply cannot walk another step," she said teasingly.

From where he sat, Lawrence Hetherington could see his daughter and her handsome escort as they made their way along the path towards the monkey house again... what a perfect match they would make, he thought contentedly.

Lilybee noticed that Percy had, of a sudden, become strangely quiet. They were standing before a cage of monkeys who were playfully swinging back and forth and chasing one another between some thick tree branches that had been fixed in the cage for precisely that purpose. A couple with three small children were standing close by; the children were laughing loudly at the monkeys' antics. Suddenly their attention was drawn to another of the cages, where a monkey was screeching noisily and jumping around in an agitated manner. They ran off to investigate and their parents followed sedately. Although they were alone once more, Percy still remained silent. Lilybee glanced at him anxiously out of the corner of her eye, and saw that he was deep in thought, very sad looking. She was concerned and wondered what was bothering him, because it was strangely unlike him to remain so silent. She spoke to him quietly, almost afraid to disturb him. Perhaps she did not know him as well as she had imagined.

"Are you alright Percy... is something troubling you?"

He turned and looked directly at her and his heart missed a beat. Now he became afraid, afraid that she might reject his proposal.

"Er... yes... there is something troubling me... very seriously."

He heaved a sigh and turned his attention back to the monkeys momentarily. He could hardly bring himself to ask the question that had been formulating in his mind over the past week; the question that had kept him awake hour after hour, almost driving him to distraction every night. He had known since the occasion of their first meeting that he was in love with Elizabeth Hetherington, and the thought that she might refuse to marry him was more than he could bear. He gathered up his courage and turned to look at her again. Her eyes met his... beautiful clear eyes, now troubled and searching his face questioningly. He could stand no more of it; he must resolve the matter now. He wanted to make her his wife, but would she be willing to accept the conditions that her acceptance must impose?

He started haltingly: "As you know ... er... my visit to England is only meant to be a very brief one... it was never intended to be otherwise." He paused, swallowed hard, then continued "I did tell you so... when first we met. Do you remember?" He was looking at her intently.

Lilybee felt faint, her heart fluttered, he was going to tell her something unpleasant, something she did not wish to hear. It was that he would soon be leaving... she knew it... she knew it. She could not bear the thought of losing him, not when she loved him so very much.

"Yes... yes" she muttered breathlessly: "I remember that you said as much..."

He cleared his throat and went on: "I have some more business to attend to... affairs concerning my father's estate, but just as soon as that is done, I shall be leaving for America. I cannot delay the booking of my passage... I thought to do it this coming week, so that I can make the crossing in fair weather, during the summer months."

He felt embarrassed; the words he spoke were not at all what he would have her hear. "I do have a commitment... I need to finalize the purchase of the plantation before the winter sets in. You do understand that, don't you?"

He felt miserable... why could he not ask her what he so wanted to know?

Lilybee could not control her emotions for another moment, her eyes filled with tears, as she whispered: "Oh, Percy... we shall miss you... er, I shall miss you very very much. I don't know how I shall bear to see you go." She dropped her head, ashamed at having disclosed her feelings so.

Percy too was overcome how could he leave her? He blurted out: "Then come with me, oh, if only you would. I love you and I cannot bear the thought of never seeing you again." He took her hands and clasped them between his own. "Marry me Lilybee... I want you to be my wife. Will you marry me?"

Lilybee was taken aback, but only for a moment. Then, without a second thought she answered him: "Yes... oh, yes...

of course. I love you too." She was laughing and crying at the same time, and Percy felt sure that his heart would burst with joy; he could not believe what he had just heard, that the girl whom he loved with all his heart had agreed to become his wife... and moreover, had agreed to accompany him to America, to start a new life.

*

He took her in his arms and drew her close. "Oh, my love my love..." he murmured softly. Suddenly he heard voices, footsteps, a group of people were entering the monkey house. He released Lilybee immediately, lest their tender embrace be considered an impropriety.

His face reddened with embarrassment, but in the excitement of the moment Lilybee had cast aside her normal genteel reserve. "Perhaps we should leave now," she said quietly, hardly able to control her laughter at the very thought that any young man could conduct a caprice in such an unlikely location, but she loved him all the more for his unpredictability.

He could not disguise his embarrassment as they passed the strangers on their way out, and Lilybee immediately tried to put him at ease. She felt deliriously happy, and she would not have him otherwise.

"That must be the very first marriage proposal those monkeys have ever witnessed, don't you think?" she asked mischievously. She burst into laughter again, and Percy joined in, appreciating her humour; what a superb companion she would make, he mused.

He stopped in the middle of the path and turned to her. "I had thought of choosing a more romantic setting," he confided, "but if you had turned me down, then I simply would not have known what to do. In that event, I felt that at the very least the monkeys would provide a welcome diversion perhaps make me appear a little less foolish. You see, I was absolutely convinced that you would refuse me."

Lilybee nearly choked, as they both laughed uncontrollably. "Oh, you poor dear," she gasped: "But how could you ever think that I might refuse... surely a man capable of so much guile could easily win the heart of any poor unsuspecting female?"

They were still laughing as they approached Lawrence Hetherington, and Percy determined to make his intentions known just as soon as he could escort this fine old gentleman and his beautiful daughter home.

*

Lilybee quickly disappeared upstairs to her bedroom as soon as the front door had closed behind them, leaving Percy to speak to her father alone. She felt a twinge of sadness that she would soon have to leave him, and she wondered how he would receive the news. They had always been particularly fond of one another, and she knew that her presence had always been a source of comfort to him, a constant reminder of his love for her dear mother, whom she knew he had adored. His second wife, Evelyn, whom he had married on a whim, after a whirlwind romance, had never provided him with the companionship that he had been desperately seeking, and certainly the two sons that she had borne him had caused him more grief than Lilybee cared to recall. Now she waited anxiously to see what his reaction would be when he learned that Percy would very soon be taking her across the Atlantic, to his plantation in North Carolina, perhaps never to return.

Downstairs, her father and Percy were having their quiet tête-a-tête, one gentleman with another. Percy's request for the hand of his daughter in marriage, had certainly not come as a shock to Lawrence Hetherington, and he made no secret of the fact that he was truly delighted to grant his permission. He was, however, somewhat taken aback when Percy went on to explain that he wished to take Lilybee to America with him, and that they would need to leave very soon. The older man became thoughtful: "When I saw how fond of one another you two were becoming, I rather hoped that you might be persuaded to stay here, my boy" he said.

Percy could fully understand his reluctance to lose his only daughter, but somehow he could never envisage himself settling down to life in England. He could see the necessity of discussing the matter thoroughly with this kindly gentleman, to whom he was soon to be related, and he also felt it right and proper that Lilybee should be acquainted with everything that was discussed. "I do appreciate what you are suggesting, Sir, but I have never had the desire to remain in England... in fact, my decision to go to the New World was made long ago. Look, there is much that we need to talk about... I wish to alleviate any fears you might have for your daughter, but do you not think that she too would wish to join us in this conversation, for it concerns her future equally as much as my own?"

"Oh, yes... yes, of course, dear boy. I'll ask Lilybee to join us most thoughtful of you, yes indeed." He stood up and tugged on the bell pull.

His daughter heaved a sigh of relief when Alice told her that she was wanted in the study. She was longing to know what was happening between the two most important men in her life. As she reached the foot of the stairs she asked Alice if afternoon tea had yet been served to them.

"No Miss Elizabeth, not yet," came the reply.

"Then would you bring it to us right away... tea for three?"

The two men stood up as Lilybee entered the room, and she glanced from one to the other a little apprehensively. Percy was smiling, and her father opened his arms, beckoning her. She ran to him and he embraced her warmly, kissing her upon the forehead as he did so.

"You have my blessing my dear," he said, "And I am delighted to welcome this young man into the family... I could not have wished for a finer son in-law, and I feel sure that you will make one another very happy indeed."

"Oh, thank you Papa... I am so glad that you approve," said Lilybee ecstatically. She ran to Percy now and hugged him. "Oh, we shall be happy... we shall... I know it," she laughed.

There was a gentle knock on the door, and in came Alice with the tea trolley.

"Thank you Alice... I'll see to it," said Lilybee.

When the girl had left, the three settled themselves comfortably with their tea and cakes and Lawrence Hetherington began: "I understand that this young fella wants to steal you away very soon, my dear... much sooner than I had expected." He took a long drink from his teacup, then brought his bottom lip up slowly to gather the droplets that had collected on his moustache.

"I was telling your father that we cannot delay our departure for too long." Percy looked at Lilybee a little guiltily,

"He also tells me that he has never had the desire to remain in England," her father went on: "What do you say about that?"

"I would feel dreadfully sorry to leave you Papa... you know that don't you?" Lilybee pouted her lips: "But life in the Carolinas sounds so marvellously interesting."

"Are you sure that you would be happy to live there? To leave England for ever? You're such a youngster my dear I can't help wondering just how you'd take to it."

"I shall be perfectly alright. Percy will see to that, won't you my dearest?" She looked at him appealingly: "Besides Papa… I am no younger than my own mother was when you married her and took her off to India. She was but nineteen years old, isn't that so?"

Her father raised his eyes upwards thoughtfully. "Well upon my word, you're quite right, yes… yes, your mother was just nineteen." He nodded his head and smiled pensively. "Had you the following year… when she was twenty." He smiled again as he recalled happy memories. "I worried about your mother… about taking her on that long sea voyage. There were no steamships in those days you know. How we loved one another though she was just like you are now, full of enthusiasm, eager to see all that was fascinating and new across the sea." He paused and turned to Percy: "How is it on the steamships, m'boy?"

Percy answered him enthusiastically, trying to allay some of his fears for his daughter's safety. "They are remarkable Sir … I took less than four months to make the journey home to England. I can remember with what excitement we greeted the news six years ago, that the 'Enterprise' had arrived in Calcutta from England… she had rounded the Cape in one hundred and thirteen days, the very first attempt ever to reach India under steam."

"See Papa… how quickly we shall be able to reach America now," enthused Lilybee: "And it is so much nearer to England than is India."

"Oh, certainly Sir," broke in Percy, "It takes only a few weeks to cross the Atlantic under steam."

"Why, surely, if Mama could endure that gruelling trip to India all those years ago, then I could manage to survive a much shorter, speedier trip. So, you see, there is absolutely nothing for you to worry about."

Her father raised his hand to stem their bombardment. He chuckled and shook his head. "Alright you two... alright... I am more than convinced... but you can't blame a doting father for trying to prevent his daughter from leaving him, can you?"

He turned to Percy: "Certainly it would appear that you have considerable knowledge of the type of life to be lived in North Carolina, my boy, and obviously you have found it to be very desirable, otherwise I cannot see you so enthusiastically seeking to make it your home. I am also aware of your tremendous fondness for my daughter, and I firmly believe that you would never expose her to anything remotely unpleasant. Therefore, I shall raise no further objections whatsoever you have my word on it."

"Oh, Papa..." Lilybee hurried over to plant a kiss upon his forehead.

He took her hand and patted it lovingly. "I should be very interested to hear more of this plantation Percy... of how you came to decide upon its purchase. Would you care to come for dinner this evening... there is so much that we must talk about, not to mention your wedding arrangements?"

"I agree sir. I would love to have dinner with you both, so I had better be off now... and I'll return at... what shall we say... er, 7.00 pm?"

Percy stood up to leave. "Yes... 7.00 pm will be excellent. I shall look forward to a stimulating evening of discussion with you both and now you had better see this young man out Lilybee."

After they had left, Lawrence Hetherington seated himself comfortably in his chair and closed his eyes. He could hardly believe that his daughter was about to be married... he could see her still as a beautiful golden haired baby, taking her first tentative steps towards him, with her 'ayah' keeping careful watch just a few paces behind her, lest she should totter and fall. What was the name of her young nurse? It escaped him for a moment... yes, that was it, now he remembered... she was called Hadeel; a pretty young girl. Her mother had been their cook, and even now the very thought of her delicious meals could make his mouth water. He recalled the beautiful unleavened bread that she used to make, 'chapattis'... and the spicy curried dishes. Even in those days it had been possible to maintain adequate supplies of both native and European products; from England had come the hams and cheeses, beer and liquor, and from the Far East the spices, teas, silks and gems. Of course, that was no great wonder, for the East India Company had begun its trading two hundred years earlier, under the charter granted by Queen Elizabeth I, on the 31st December, 1599, and as its trade had developed, so its boundaries had expanded.

When Warren Hastings, the first Governor-General of India, left the country in 1785, the East India Company held control over Bengal province and a few coastal trading depots, like Bombay and Madras, but with the continual unrest and disputes between the ruling princes, it had gradually extended its domain until it controlled almost the whole of India, with the exception of the Punjab and Sind. To protect its trading ports Surat, Madras, Calcutta and Bombay, it had also established its own militia. Originally, it had been merely a monopolistic trading body, but had eventually become embroiled, albeit unwillingly, in politics, acting as agents of British imperialism in India. It was almost impossible to believe that it had been formed by English merchants, initially, for the exploitation of trade with the Far East and

India; merchants who wanted a share of the Indian spice trade, indigo, salt petre, and even opium from the Far East, but now the dominance of the British in this sub-continent was considered to be truly remarkable.

Every aspect of the East India Company's development came under discussion during dinner later that evening, and Lilybee listened with rapt attention as her father and Percy each related their own personal experiences of India itself. The older man came to understand Percy's decision not to return there again, when he spoke of the continual underlying tensions and growing disaffection of the natives.

"Is it really as frightful as you would have me believe Percy?"

"It is indeed Sir in fact, I would go so far as to say that at some time in the future we may well see rebellion throughout the entire country."

"Dreadful... dreadful... in that case, I am greatly relieved that my daughter will not be subjected to the possibility of such dangerous events. Why, when we left, my greatest concern for her well-being was the intense heat and the insufferable flies during the summer season. There was simply no escape... we used to cover the doors and windows with 'tattees', those grass screens you know, and the servants watered them continually, to keep the rooms fresh and cool; then the 'wallahs' would sit outside pulling the strings of the 'punkahs' that hung from the ceilings. Now I find it difficult to imagine how we tolerated such conditions... it was particularly harsh on the women and children, I recall."

"Things have improved to a certain extent now though, Sir, because it has become the custom to go up to the 'hills' during the worst of the heat; it started in 1819 when the first European house was built at Simla. Indeed, it is no longer considered a necessity to send one's children home to England for their education, now that they have such a retreat."

"What of the weather in North Carolina, is it more tolerable, would you say?"

Percy was pleased to be able to reassure Lawrence Hetherington, and he repeated every bit of information that he himself had been given. "Oh, yes definitely... most definitely, by all accounts. I have heard reports of the most spectacular mountain scenery over to the far west of the state; this in turn gives way to gently rolling hills, with dark loam and red clay soil. The land is lush and fertile, and lends itself admirably to the cultivation of the cotton and tobacco plantations. Can you imagine such a place Sir?" Percy warmed to his subject. "Then, of course, there is the Atlantic coastal plain, with its white sands, and healthful sea breezes... I cannot wait to see the beauty of it for myself, nor indeed to take Lilybee to such a paradise. You know, the first explorers were said to have described it as 'The explorers' goodliest land under the cope of heaven' and they established many pioneer settlements there. I have even been told that there is a Moravian settlement, which was founded in 1753, at Bethabara, and there is built a magnificent church, erected in 1788, which is supposed to be one of the finest examples of their architecture."

"If you go on in such a way, I shall be sorely tempted to uproot and go there myself," laughed his host, "Just to escape this cholera epidemic that is sweeping the country, would be enough of an inducement... don't you agree?"

"Indeed it would... I was most alarmed when I arrived here in England a few weeks ago, to hear that the pestilence is sweeping right across Europe now, with devastating loss of life."

"Oh, Papa... why do you not come with us?" implored Lilybee.

"No my dear, really I think not, for now I have sunk my roots far too deeply into British soil ever to contemplate tearing them up again at this time of my life. Besides, is it not enough that Darwin is making a round the world voyage with the crew of the 'Beagle'... do you not think that just a few. stalwarts should stay in the 'old'country, to try and maintain a little stability? And what of Earl Grey and his coalition cabinet... after the Whigs have been excluded from office for so many years, I am intrigued to know what kind of reforms these aristocrats might bring about. No one envies them their office at present, with the never ending disturbances and riots in our rural areas. There is increasing unemployment demands for better Poor Law payments, and who can blame starving destitute workers for destroying the threshing machines that are taking away their jobs?"

"This Reform Bill is causing riots too," put in Percy: "I hear that Grey put pressure on the King to accept it... his condition for forming the new administration, apparently."

"Yes... yes, that's quite correct. It is quite beyond me to fathom out what our 'Sailor William' is about... I do know that he is making himself devilish unpopular though. What times we are living in, to be sure."

Their meal now over, the three made their way to the drawing room, where they could continue their heartfelt discussions over coffee. As Lilybee tinkered with the cups, she decided to veer the conversation away from politics.

"Tell Papa how you first became interested in acquiring a cotton plantation Percy... I know he will enjoy the story."

"Indeed I would... I am curious to know how it came about."

"Not an awful lot to tell really Sir, but my heart has been set upon it from the first moment I heard tell of the fascinating life of the planters in the American South."

Lilybee gazed at him lovingly, and her father relaxed in his chair, engrossed in everything that his future son-in-law might relate.

"As you know, my father was devastated by the death of my dear mother almost eight years ago. Of course, I did not hesitate to make my way out to India... he had always assumed that I would take up a post with the Company, and I had never thought to disappoint him. However, as fate would have it, on my way out to Calcutta, I made the acquaintance of a most interesting young man, Adam Matthews; he was about my own age, so as you might imagine, during the long, arduous voyage, we became firm friends. We talked at length of our family history, although his proved to be far more illustrious than mine." Percy laughed quietly, and glanced at Lilybee mischeviously. "You may well have heard of his grandfather, Sir," he said to Lawrence Hetherington: Sir Wilfred Matthews; he was on the Committee of the Privy Council for Trade and Plantations, which became the board of Trade in 1696. It lost influence for a time, from 1730 until 1750, but when Lord Halifax revived it in 1750, Sir Wilfred was actively engaged in its running until 1782, when Edmund Burke abolished it. Apparently it was some kind of Colonial Office, specifically established to watch over Colonial affairs and protect England's commercial interests. Of course, when it was no longer considered a necessity, Sir Wilfred decided to take himself off to the West Indies, where he established a sugar plantation. Apparently, he made a colossal fortune, trading in sugar and molasses. His son Robert, Adam's father, went to sea when he grew up; he became the captain of a 'slaver', but finally settled in North Carolina, where he had met and fallen in love with Adam's mother. He too eventually became a planter, when he took over the cotton plantation that belonged to his wife's father."

Percy leant forward, looking concernedly at the older man: "I hope I'm not boring you unnecessarily with all this detail Sir."

"Not at all m'boy not at all; I find it most interesting. Do go on."

"Well, needless to say, Adam and I kept in touch with one another over the years... he bid me farewell when the ship left the Cape, said he was anxious to explore Africa somewhat, but we did exchange addresses before we parted. Then, almost two years later, he arrived in Calcutta quite unexpectedly. He spent several months in India... stayed with my father and me for a few weeks. We had a grand time together, and before he left, I had determined that the East India Company was not to be a lifetime career for me. Although he was on a prolonged exploration of the world, which I greatly envied, he was adamant that he would one day return to North Carolina and settle down. He never stopped talking of its splendour, and I told him that I was seriously considering the possibility of becoming a planter myself one day. When he left Calcutta, he promised to let me know when he finally arrived back in America, and that if ever he came to hear of a suitable plantation for sale, then he would notify me. Sure enough, some two years ago, I heard from him... apparently, some friends of his parents were contemplating the sale of their plantation... it is called 'White Lakes'... and he had told them of my interest in becoming a planter. Negotiations were begun immediately, and I had hoped to persuade my dear father to come to North Carolina with me. Unfortunately he fell ill, although I know that he would have preferred to stay in India, even if I had left. Of course, I could not consider it when his condition worsened, and I informed Adam to this effect. His friends were extremely understanding, and agreed to await developments concerning my father's health. Almost before I realized it, and as you are already aware from my letter to you, my father passed away. It was a tremendous shock, but I would not have wished him to linger in his sorry condition... his chest, you know."

Percy closed his eyes and swallowed hard: "I shall miss him terribly, but I know he would have wanted me to go ahead with my plans."

Lilybee went to him and placed her hand on his shoulder reassuringly; he took it in his own and pressed it to his cheek.

"I have you now though my dear, to share my life, and for that I am more than grateful... together we shall build our future in the New World. I wrote to Adam of my father's death, and confirmed that I should travel to North Carolina at the earliest opportunity to finalise the purchase of 'White Lakes'... from all the particulars he has furnished me with, I know it to be a goodly proposition at the price, and I also know that I am able to trust him implicitly with the negotiations."

"It does my heart good to hear that you have such a reliable friend, someone dependable with whom you are well acquainted. You will find his help invaluable when first you arrive in that strange land. I well remember the kindness of your dear father and mother when I first came to India, the way in which they helped me to settle there. Their generosity was unbelievable... I don't know what I should have done without them. They really were the best friends I ever had, and I shall never forget them... never." Lawrence Hetherington cleared his throat, "I know that they would have been overjoyed at your decision to wed my daughter... would have welcomed your alliance just as much as I."

"Thank you Sir... I very much appreciate the honour you do me in expressing such sentiments."

"No more than you deserve," said the older man, "Not at all... and what if we come around to discussing the formalities of this important event now then... have you any ideas to put forward Lilybee?"

He glanced at his daughter, who was sitting thoughtfully with her hands clasped together beneath her chin. "You haven't had much time to think about it, have you... and neither do you have much time to put it into effect, from what Percy tells me. Nevertheless, we shall do our very best to make it a memorable occasion, indeed we shall. Exactly how long do we have before you leave?"

"I imagine we could be off in about a month Sir," replied Percy.

"Right then... we had better not·lose any time, and my first duty is to place the announcement in the 'Times' er... proud to announce the betrothal of my only daughter to you m'boy; only son of the late... er... you know the kind of thing."

He rapped his fingers on the arm of his chair. "St. Luke's is it to be, Lilybee? Yes... that'll be it... St. Luke's Church, Chelsea; and what about the wedding breakfast? How many guests, etcetera, etcetera... where's it to be? Have to send out the invitations without delay, what?"

"I don't want a large affair Papa... the less fuss the better. Just a few close friends... and if you wouldn't mind, I'd like our wedding breakfast here, the garden is so delightful at this time of the year... what do you say Percy?"

"Yes yes... that would be perfect; whatever pleases you my darling... I am only sorry that it is all to be in such a hurry. I know what you ladies are for extravagant weddings."

"Oh, no... no, not I Percy; it is wonderful not to have to suffer months and months of agonizing over every little detail. I much prefer to have the whole business over and done as quickly as possible."

Percy laughed quietly: "What an amazing young woman you are, to be sure. I'll make you a promise though my dear... we shall have the most wonderful honeymoon ever, once I have settled the purchase of the plantation. How about that?"

"I shall keep you to your promise young man," laughed Lilybee.

*

Small and unpretentious though the wedding was to be, Lawrence Hetherington's generosity knew no bounds; everything possible was done to make it absolutely perfect, not only for the bride and groom, but also for the guests who were invited. Neither was anything spared in the expense of his daughter's trousseau; it was to be the very finest that money could buy, and to this end, Lilybee enlisted the assistance of her closest friend, one Henrietta Whitmore, who jumped at the opportunity to tour around town, day after day, in her friend's coach, chaperoned by Alice her maid, helping to choose all manner of beautiful clothes and accessories, not to mention the most luxurious household linens to take to America with her. Henrietta was completely enraptured by the romance and excitement of Lilybee's whirlwind courtship, and more especially by her imminent departure for a life in the 'New World'.

The three young women were driven from place to place by the Hetherington's head coachman, Alfred Blake, much to Alice's delight, for the two were very fond of one another, in fact they had had an arrangement for quite some time. Alfred knew London as well as anybody, "Much better than most," boasted Alice, as they made their way through the city, all along Bond Street and Oxford Street, up Hosier Lane and Cloth Fair, coming into Smithfield, to visit the fur traders and milliners, the ostrich feather merchants, and even the fringe and button makers

Just as soon as Lilybee had selected all the materials and trimmings she required, it was off to the seamstress to have the profusion of silks and satins, velvets and furs, made up into the most elegant designs. Lilybee found herself having to return time and time again to be measured and fitted for the various garments, but the tedium of the hours thus spent was more than recompensed when the finished wardrobe was finally presented to her. The tiny bespectacled seamstress and her young assistants had laboured day and night to have everything ready for their extremely affluent client, and Lilybee stood aghast at what the nimble fingers of these industrious women had managed to accomplish in the short time allotted for the task. She was absolutely beside: herself with delight as she scrutinized their exceptional handiwork, and she praised them for its excellence, but never more so than when she saw the exquisite wedding dress that had been designed for her. It was a breath-taking creation made from the very finest cream brocade, laboriously worked with the tiniest crystal and seed pearl beads. As she slipped it on and espied herself in the cheval glass, quite a recent innovation, of which this select establishment was extremely proud, her eyes filled with tears. She touched it gently, her hands caressing the folds of the skirt lovingly: "It is beautiful... really beautiful," she whispered. "I have never seen anything more lovely... thank you very much." She stood unmoving as the seamstress raised her forefinger, urging her to stay exactly where she was. The small spritely woman disappeared into an adjoining room, and returned a few moments later, wafting a gossamer-fine length of the most exquisite lace that Lilybee had ever seen in her life. Realising that expense was of no consequence, the astute seamstress had had this unique handmade tambour lace sent especially from Coggeshall in Essex, where it was said to have been introduced by a Frenchman who had settled in the village in 1810. It had been delicately attached to a silk flowered headdress, and now the tiny woman climbed upon a footstool and proceeded to arrange the neat coronet in an attractive manner on her client's golden hair; the veil tumbled in a vaporous cascade about Lilybee's shoulders, and she was completely spellbound.

*

All the while Lilybee was busily engaged in her preparations, Percy too found much to keep him gainfully employed. There were the intricacies of his father's estate to be attended to, and then the all-important booking of the passage across the Atlantic for his future wife and himself. He still found it difficult to believe that his life was to be blessed with such a delightful partner. He made frequent visits to her home in Chelsea, and in the evenings they would keep one another amused by exchanging details of how they had each spent their days.

Halfway through their month of frenzied activity, Percy insisted that Lilybee spare just a few hours to accompany him on a trip to town. "What is it... where would you have me go?" pleaded Lilybee.

"Just wait patiently and you shall see," teased Percy.

It was not long before they came to Piccadilly, and Percy called the coach to a halt at Burlington Arcade. Lilybee's heart raced as she was led into a fashionably expensive jewellery shop, where the assistant hurriedly produced a most beautiful ring for her inspection. It had obviously been selected by Percy on a previous visit, and now he turned to Lilybee and asked, "What do you think of it my dearest?" He was gazing at her questioningly. "If it is not exactly to your liking, then you shall have another." He took hold of the exquisite emerald and diamond cluster, and slipped it on to her finger.

"Oh, Percy... I like it very well... I could not like it better," Lilybee said happily. She held her hand at arm's length and turned it first one way and then the other, delighted at the way in which the expertly cut stones glinted as they caught the light.

"It is my wedding gift to you... a token of my undying love," whispered Percy softly.

"And now you shall have a special gift from me; what should it be?" Lilybee wandered around for some time, looking carefully at all that was on display in the smart glass-fronted cabinets, and finally she decided upon a gold 'Godemar Freres' Swiss quarter repeating watch.

She called to Percy: "I would like you to have this as a token of my love... I think it is quite the thing, don't you agree?"

Percy accepted her gift graciously, more than content with anything that she herself had chosen for him. He particularly admired the ornate decoration of its case. "I shall treasure it always," he said, "And whenever I look at it to know the hour, it will remind me of you; so you see, it is a perfect gift."

*

Percy had occasion to use his new timepiece a number of times on the day of his wedding, as he sat waiting in the church for the arrival of his bride. As the minutes ticked away, a small shadow of doubt arose in his mind... supposing his love decided, after all, that she could not face the prospect of starting a new life in a strange and foreign land... supposing the thought of leaving her father and her friends, never to see them again, was too formidable? She was so young and beautiful, would she change her mind, he wondered? But he had no need to fear any of these things, for but a few miles away Lilybee and her father were just preparing to leave for the church.

It was a glorious day, with the sun blazing from a clear blue sky. Nothing was to mar his daughter's wedding day, Lawrence Hetherington had seen to that, so he was not in the least surprised that the weather too was at its very best.

"Oh, Papa, aren't I lucky to have such ideal weather... today of all days?"

"Luck has nothing to do with it my dear I arranged that everything should be exactly right for you today, and that includes the weather," beamed her father.

Even her two young brothers, thirteen year old Gilbert and twelve year old Douglas, had been given a stern warning that if they dared to misbehave, then they would be returned to their school immediately. Now Lawrence Hetherington glanced at his watch: "I think we should leave for the church, don't you my dear? You mustn't leave young Percy waiting nervously for too long."

Lilybee smiled and nodded. "Could he be as nervous as I?"

"Of course, of course... I well remember how I felt when I was waiting for your dear mother" His eyes filled with tears as he gazed admiringly at his beautiful daughter. "You look radiant, just as she did on the day we were wed. You make me extremely proud."

The wedding ceremony and the reception were over all too quickly, in fact, Lilybee found herself scarcely able to recall in detail precisely what had taken place. Several times throughout the day she had wondered whether she was dreaming, for it all felt so unreal. Was she now a married woman, about to embark upon a strange new adventure? She found it difficult to believe that her life had changed so dramatically in such a short time, that she was now on her way to where her new life would soon begin.

Percy took her hand as she stepped from the carriage: "Take care... mind your foot does not slip," he said concernedly. They were newly arrived at the 'Bull and Mouth' in St. Martin's-le-Grand, one of the very finest coaching inns in London, with its impressive courtyard and galleries. It thrived on the passenger and mail coaches that left St. Martin's each day for all parts of the country.

Lilybee could hardly contain her excitement; she inhaled deeply and clung to Percy's arm. "I do believe that I shall faint, I feel so sick with excitement," she whispered confidentially. "I cannot remember ever being so happy in my life, isn't it all so wonderful?"

She gazed around her, fascinated by the hive of activity that surrounded them, the hustle and bustle as the porters carefully stowed all the luggage of the passengers aboard the coach. She could see her hand-stitched leather cases, recently purchased in St. John's Street, piled upon the stout trunks belonging to Percy, and she flushed with pride. She knew that she was the envy of her friends at having captured such an eligible gentleman. The horses were stamping their hooves and champing on their bits, anxious to be off on their familiar journey up to Liverpool, for that was where this particular coach was bound. Everyone climbed aboard, the driver cracked his whip, and the horses responded with a noisy jingle of their harness as the wheels of the coach were set in motion. They were passing in front of the magnificent General Post Office building that Sir Robert Smirke had finished constructing two years earlier. Lilybee peeped at it from the coach window; its grand Greek- style portico was very similar to the facade of the British Museum that he had also built in 1823. Her heart lurched at the sudden realization that she was leaving London, never to return again. She thought fondly of her father, who had not been able to bring himself to accompany them as far as the coaching inn, for fear that he would be overcome with emotion at her final departure. He would find it far less embarrassing to give vent to his grief in the privacy of his home, where none could witness it.

Percy sensed her sudden sadness, what she must be thinking, and he sympathized deeply. She looked absolutely beautiful in her pretty new bonnet and fine silk cape, her eyes grown enormous with sorrow. "You are perfectly lovely," he whispered, "I cannot believe my good fortune in finding you. We shall have a good life together my darling, I know it."

She smiled at his thoughtful reassurances. "I am aware of my own good fortune too, Percy, for surely there cannot be a kinder man than you in the whole world."

*

During the next four days, along the road that they travelled, Lilybee found much more to gaze at in fascination, but nothing so awe inspiring as the town of Liverpool. She recalled reading Daniel Defoe's 'Tour thro' the Whole Island of Great Britain', wherein he had extolled Liverpool as '… one of the wonders of Britain… large and handsome'. On his third visit there, he had gone on to say that 'There was no town in England, London alone excepted, that could equal Liverpool for the fineness of the streets and the beauty of the buildings', and then: 'What it may grow to in time, I know not'. All this he had observed more than a century earlier, and if he had been so impressed then, what might he make of its prosperity at the present day, wondered Lilybee?

Now, once again, she stood watching the activity on the wharf with undisguised interest, as the cargo and the passengers with their luggage were taken aboard the ship. Nothing could have prepared her for the magnificence of this sea-going vessel, and she could not wait for it to set sail on the evening tide, to carry her off to a life that she had hitherto never even dreamed of.

The enormity of the ship had greatly impressed Lilybee, upon her first sighting of it at the dockside, but after a week at sea in its abnormal confinements, it seemed pitifully reduced in dimension. Nevertheless, despite the many occasions when it seemed certain that the vessel would sink beneath the mighty Atlantic Ocean, borne down into its depths by the gigantic waves that rose in towering blue-green walls, which in an instant would crash and thunder relentlessly upon its decks, sending the passengers scurrying below to cower in their cabins; and despite the violent bouts of seasickness to which she was so prone, when the enormous swell sent every moving object sliding in turbulent motion throughout the ship, despite these unknown terrors and the restrictions that they imposed, Lilybee still found much to stimulate her interest during that long and perilous voyage.

On the evenings when their passage was calm, when she was not feeling sickly, she and Percy dined with the Captain, and enjoyed hours of stimulating conversation with him. The many and varied tales of this much travelled gentleman delighted and amused them, and they were particularly interested to hear of his visits to the Carolinas many years before. When he heard that they were bound for North Carolina, he assured them that they would never regret the decision to make it their home, for it was a wondrous place that he himself had set his heart upon when the time came for him to give up his seafaring life, and his envy was undisguised when they finally bid him farewell.

Having heard nothing but praise for the place that was about to become their new domicile, Percy and Lilybee were naturally most anxious to see it for themselves, without delay. However, after so many weeks at sea, they both decided that a short stay in New York would give them time to recover a little; besides which, they would enjoy some sightseeing and possibly some shopping. Lilybee was particularly interested in the exotic and new goods which might be available in this foreign land.

So they found themselves a highly reputable and comfortable hotel, and stayed there for a few days; long enough to take a tour around the fast-growing city, which had been founded by the Dutch in 1625. Peter Minuit had bought the island of Manhattan from the local Indians with miscellaneous goods worth just sixty guilders, and nobody doubted that the natives had been most pitiably cheated. There the Dutch had established the first colony and named it New Amsterdam. In 1664, however, the English took New Amsterdam and the New Netherlands from the Dutch, and henceforth it had become the city and colony of New York.

The young newlyweds were greatly interested in everything they saw during their excursions, and despite the fact that it was just in its infancy, comparatively speaking, they were remarkably impressed with the way in which this fascinating city was developing. All manner of entertainments were available, and on their last evening they visited one of the many new theatres, and afterwards dined at 'Delmonico's Restaurant', which provided the perfect ending to a most memorable stay.

Early the next morning they set off in the stagecoach to travel through New Jersey and over the Delaware River into Pennsylvania; from there through Delaware into Virginia, and finally down to North Carolina. At times Lilybee seriously doubted that they were ever going to reach their journey's end. She had lost count of the number of weeks since she had left her father's house, but at the same time she never once failed to marvel at her great good fortune, how privileged she was to be able to see for herself this brave new world that most only heard tell of. She could hardly wait to send her first letter home to her father, to describe to him in detail the wonders that she was seeing each and every day. She knew that she would never be able to describe with accuracy the grand untamed beauty of this vast continent, what little she had yet seen of it. How could she possibly put into words the unspoilt magnificence of this fertile country, its rolling hills and dense forests; how could she begin to describe to him its lush vegetation, its deep lakes and fast-coursing rivers? As tired as she was of the endless travel, she knew that for as long as she lived, she would never regret for one single moment that she had undertaken this momentous journey; would never forget the beauty and grandeur it presented day after day. It would remain with her, a treasured memory forever and ever.

At long last their journeying was at an end; they had finally reached North Carolina. It took very little time to locate the Matthews' plantation, not too far distant from Raleigh; indeed, the family appeared to be extremely well known and highly respected, and the reason became clearly evident when Percy and Lilybee arrived at their grandly impressive home, 'Hope Manor', for it stood amid acre upon acre of sturdily growing cotton, tended by scores of dutifully toiling negro slaves. Lilybee caught her breath as their carriage turned into the wide dusty path that led through the cotton fields and on up to the mansion. It came into sight atop a gently rising knoll, its elegant tall windows commanding a view across the plantation to the winding river below.

"Oh, Percy... have you ever seen such a sight?" breathed Lilybee ecstatically, "And can you imagine what it would be like to have a home such as this?"

Percy took her hand confidently, nodding his head in approval at all that he was surveying. "I can imagine it... and what is more, I am sure that 'White Lakes' will prove to be equally delightful to you, if what Adam has told me of it is true... and I have no reason to doubt him, none whatsoever."

Their carriage pulled up in front of the magnificent doorway, sheltered by a wide flower-bedecked verandah that was built across the front of the house. Their arrival had been noticed well in advance, and now two immaculately dressed manservants were hurrying down the wide steps to carry in their luggage. The door was flung wide and a loud greeting resounded joyfully across the verandah, as Percy carefully helped Lilybee from the carriage.

"Welcome to the New World and to North Carolina my friend; lovely to see you." Adam Matthews bounded down the steps and thrust his hand into Percy's, shaking it vigorously up and down, almost as though he would shake it off. "I have been expecting you this last month or more... concerned about how you were faring on the long journey and all that... but no matter, now you are here. It is lovely to see you," he repeated again, smiling broadly.

His newly arrived guests appreciated his magnanimous welcome, and found it most heart-warming after the rigours of their travels. Percy beamed back at his friend and turned to Lilybee as he introduced her: "I am very pleased and proud to present my wife Lilybee… we were married shortly before we left England."

Lilybee held forth her hand; Adam took it, raised it to his lips, and brushed it gently with a kiss. "It is an honour to meet you madam," he said politely: "I had no notion that dear Percy was thinking of marriage, but it would seem that he is indeed a most fortunate fellow."

Lilybee inclined her head slightly in deference to his compliment, she was very much taken with her husband's amiable friend. She smiled sweetly into the jovial sun-tanned face before her. Adam Matthews was several inches shorter than Percy, very stockily built, and his charm of manner completely allayed any fears she might be experiencing at their unceremonious arrival upon his family's threshold. In fact, his welcome could not have been more friendly and sincere.

"Now, please do come in, my parents are waiting to receive you." He led them into the luxuriant interior of that great house, and Lilybee was truly astounded by the beauty of its furnishing and decorations.

They followed Matthew through the magnificent hall, with its wide polished-wood staircase rising to an overhead gallery; then into a very large drawing room, which was tastefully furnished with the most elegantly upholstered chairs, chaise longues, and occasional tables; there were the finest paintings adorning the walls, and priceless ornaments and rugs in evidence everywhere.

When the introductions were over, and Matthew's parents had welcomed them most hospitably, the young guests were shown to their rooms in order that they might rest and refresh themselves for an hour or two, before joining the family at dinner later in the evening. They were grateful to be excused, and sank exhausted onto the comfortable bed which had been made ready for them. Lilybee drifted off to sleep happily in the peaceful atmosphere of that delightful bedroom, to dream contentedly of what her life was to be as a wealthy planter's wife.

A few hours later they were awakened solicitously by the servants who had been sent to wait upon them. Lilybee particularly appreciated their attentive assistance, as she had sorely missed Alice since leaving England. She had entreated her maid to come with them to America, but as fond as she was of her mistress, she could not be persuaded to leave London, nor her Alfred, because as she had resignedly pointed out, "They had an arrangement."

Once they were bathed and dressed, Percy and Lilybee joined the family for their evening meal. It was as they were seated around the enormous dining table, with the candlelight flickering on the exquisite glassware and cutlery that adorned it, that Lilybee marvelled anew at the very grandeur of what she was witnessing. Again she was astounded by the opulence of the Southern planter's lifestyle, and it was not that she herself was in any way unaccustomed to affluence or luxury, but simply that she had never anticipated it to such a degree in this far distant, predominantly uncivilized country. To her delight she was discovering, hour by hour, that her life in North Carolina could indeed be very much to her liking.

Throughout the meal, Adam's father answered the questions that Percy eagerly put to him, and he patiently explained the essentials of successful plantation management. He pointed out that in purchasing 'White Lakes', Percy was fortunate indeed, for it had been long established and, therefore, he would not be beset by the problems of clearing the land, cutting roads, erecting landing places on the river, or building houses for the slaves. The present owner, one Alexander Mott, whom it would seem was a very close friend of Adam's father, had many years ago taken it upon himself to surmount all these problems, he had built his plantation from nothing, as had Adam's grandfather, Frederick Hope. These two had been friends long before Robert Matthews had come to 'Hope Manor', stalwart men with perseverance and the will to succeed against all odds. They had been two of the first of the pioneers, settling in the area some fifty-odd years before, but now into his seventies, old Alex had decided to take a well-earned rest. "Of course; his overseer, Ralph Clayton, runs the place, and has done for the past nine years, there is nothing that he doesn't know about running plantations. You will keep him on, I take it?" queried Robert Matthews.

"Certainly… certainly I shall, for there is so much I need to learn, and who better to teach me than the man who knows everything about it. Do you suppose he will be willing to stay on and work for me when Mr Mott sells the place?"

"Of course, of course dear boy, why not? He has settled there now, no reason to up and leave is there?"

By the end of the evening, Percy had learnt that cotton required careful cultivation, but that it was much easier to grow it on a large plantation such as 'White Lakes' or 'Hope Manor', where crop rotation and heavy manuring could restore the poorer land and make it profitable. He also learnt that crops varied greatly; that normally an acre of land would yield one to one and a half bales of cotton, maybe five hundred to seven hundred and fifty pounds; and that the prices varied from year to year. "A well run plantation will provide all the wealth you could possibly want Percy, and always remember that 'Hope Manor' is near, should you ever run into problems; only too pleased to give you any help you might need," said his host.

*

It was when they were driven to view 'White Lakes' two days later, that Percy and Lilybee understood what Robert Matthews meant when he had said that 'Hope Manor' was near. It was the nearest plantation to 'White Lakes', but even so the journey took an hour and a half, and they passed no other dwellings on the way. Lilybee was somewhat taken aback at the thought of being so far from their nearest neighbours, but Helena Matthews quickly restored her sagging spirits by telling her of the active social life that the planters enjoyed. It was customary for them to visit one another frequently, to throw large parties, and to entertain their friends lavishly.

Robert Matthews suddenly called the carriage to a halt: "I would like you to step out here for a moment or two, with your wife young man," he said to Percy. "From this point you may survey your future home to the best advantage... and I feel sure that you will not be disappointed." All five occupants stepped from the coach; Adam had decided to join his mother and father in accompanying Percy and Lilybee to see the Motts. Now they walked just a few paces so that they were on the brow of the clearing, and there before them, in all its glory, lay 'White Lakes'. The young couple were completely speechless at what now met their gaze, for it was a sight far beyond their wildest imagination. The plantation could not have been more aptly named, because from where they stood it did indeed resemble white lakes; they stretched for as far as the eye could see, acre upon acre of soft white cotton, reflecting brilliantly in the morning sun. In the distance stood the magnificent house with its fine landscaped gardens, approached from the road by a wide driveway; then the river beyond, curving and twisting along its course. Percy and Lilybee surveyed the scene with utter disbelief, for it greatly exceeded their expectations.

"Well, my dear... what do you say to that?" asked Percy.

Lilybee took a deep breath and shook her head slowly from side to side. "I simply cannot believe it Percy... it is absolutely wonderful. I feel that I must be dreaming, I really do."

Robert Matthews chuckled heartily. "You like what you see then, do you?" He too stood surveying the breath-taking panorama for several seconds. "I knew you would... it's a grand sight, isn't it?"

"Oh, yes... yes," said Percy and Lilybee in unison.

"Adam's description of it was certainly not an exaggeration," said Percy "I am truly delighted... indeed I am."

Lilybee could have added that she liked it even better than 'Hope Manor', but it was not in her nature to be so ungracious.

"Let us be on our way then... mustn't keep Alex and Emily waiting. I sent them a note by messenger yesterday, so they are expecting us. You'll like them, I'm sure... a lovely couple."

Lilybee was wondering how they could bring themselves to sell such a delightful place; what would induce them to part with it. She asked: "Do they not have children who might wish to take over the running of 'White Lakes'?"

"No... no... tragic really," replied Robert Matthews. He cleared his throat and went on, "Had two boys... twins they were... Terence and Timothy." He thought for a few moments. "Drowned in the river when they were young... seven or eight years old, I believe. Terrible loss... particularly as there were never any more children."

Lilybee shuddered; she could not begin to imagine how she would cope with such a tragedy. "How dreadfully sad," she whispered.

*

Emily and Alexander Mott were sitting on their verandah waiting for their guests when they arrived, and they were exactly as Robert Matthews had described them, a lovely couple. They welcomed the party most courteously, and after a cooling drink, Percy and Lilybee were shown all over the house from top to bottom. They found it admirable in every respect; in fact, Lilybee's enthusiasm was such that she could hardly wait to take up residence, so that she might set about arranging her home exactly to her liking. They discussed with the Motts what would and would not remain of the present furnishings, and it was all agreed upon very amicably.

After their noonday meal, they were taken on a leisurely drive of inspection around the whole extent of the plantation, covering every inch of its length and breadth. There was much of enormous interest to them both, and Lilybee was particularly fascinated by the slaves' quarters, never having seen anything quite like them before. At various stages of their tour, old Alex would introduce several of the slaves, who in turn should tell all the other slaves at 'White Lakes' that the new owners would soon be taking over.

Lilybee was completely enamoured by these dark-skinned people, and especially by the children with their friendly smiling faces and their beautiful dark eyes, gazing upwards in wonderment as they clustered around her. They were awestruck by this beautiful fair- skinned lady in her fine silk gown, with her golden curls bobbing as she talked animatedly. Her appearance completely mesmerized them, but they could not know that she found them equally fascinating, for this was the first time in her life that she had come upon a community of negroes and she was curiously drawn to them, enraptured by all that she saw. She also felt a twinge of pity at the thought that they were to be bought by her husband, along with the property and the livestock, as part and parcel of all the goods and chattels at 'White Lakes'.

Finally they made their way back to the mansion, where they were taken on a walk through the luxuriant gardens, abundantly over-filled with roses and jasmine, blossoming vines and shrubs. Altogether it was agreed that 'White Lakes" was a most desirable property, and before they left the Motts, Percy had sealed the bargain, he had undertaken to buy it, lock, stock and barrel.

"Now that the business is out of the way, would you not care to come and stay here with us until we leave; no sense in waiting, is there? We shall soon finalize our arrangements to move, should be ready to go in little more than a week. What do you say? You are more than welcome; it might even be of benefit... you could familiarize yourselves with the place before you take over."

Percy glanced at Lilybee, whose eyes were shining brightly in anticipation. She smiled and nodded enthusiastically.

"We shall be delighted Mr Mott... extremely generous of you, to be sure," replied Percy.

"Good... then we shall expect you as soon as you like to fetch your belongings from Robert's place, eh? And do call me Alex, the pair of you."

*

The next afternoon, Percy and Lilybee watched as their luggage was stowed for the very last time upon their conveyance, to be carried with them to their new home. They bid a fond and tearful farewell to their very dear friends, and nearest neighbours, with a solemn promise to come and visit them soon.

"Don't ever feel that you must wait for a formal invitation," Helena said to Lilybee as the carriage started to move away.

"Nor you, nor you," replied Lilybee, "You will always be welcome at our door, for we could never repay you for all that you have done for us… thank you once more."

*

It was not long before they found themselves at 'White Lakes', about to embark upon a life that promised to be filled with interest and pleasure, and blessed with love. Percy took Lilybee's hand and spoke softly from his heart, "Remember my promise to you as we set off on our journey from London, my dearest?"

Lilybee nodded happily. "You told me that we should have a good life together… and I can see that you mean to keep your promise, for how could life be anything but good in such a wondrous place? In truth I can find nothing that displeases me about it, and I love you the more for bringing me here."

She could recall just one unpleasantry that irked her, and that was her meeting with the Mott's overseer, Ralph Clayton. She remembered her meeting with him as distinctly unpleasant, she knew not why, but she brushed aside her doubts concerning him, for she would permit nothing to overshadow their happiness on this most important of days.

Percy took her in his arms and kissed her with a passion hitherto unknown to her, and she responded just as eagerly. Indeed they would have a good life together, of that she had not the slightest doubt.

They were still clinging to one another as the carriage came to an abrupt halt, and they laughed aloud as they were thrown awkwardly and toppled. Percy took fast hold of his wife's upper arms to steady her, afraid that she might suffer some hurt. "Are you alright Lilybee? We are here, we are here."

"Yes... yes..." she answered.

*

She felt the pressure of hands upon her upper arms... she opened her eyes to find Edmund sitting beside her now, looking intently into her startled face. "We are here Aunt." he said softly, "You have been in a deep sleep for quite a while. Are you alright?"

Lilybee stirred, and turned to look out of the window. The coach had stopped and their luggage was being lifted down. "Oh, Edmund... I was having the most lovely dream. Yes, I'm perfectly alright my dear; I'm awake now. Grace, will you help Master Edmund down first? I can manage by myself. We'll hire someone to take us the rest of the way... we should be in Asbury before night fall."

Their journey had taken several days, with many a stop along the way, but now their coach had reached its final stage. It did not take long to find a local hire, and they were soon driving the last short distance to the small town of Asbury.

*

Strangely for Grace, it was not until they were on this final part of their journey that she began to experience the strongest doubts. From the moment she had learnt that her mistress was to take her to the North, she had been in a state of complete elation, but now the moment was upon her, that she had believed would never come, that precious moment she had dreamed of for the past seventeen years, she was filled with apprehension.

Throughout the journey, she had passed the tedious hours with bitter- sweet memories of the child she had loved more than life itself; relived those happy days from her birth until she was cruelly stolen away; but suddenly, in this moment before their reunion, had come the realization that her darling child, her baby, would now be a full-grown woman. She suddenly realized, and it caused her infinite pain, that if she passed her in the street, she would have no way of knowing her. It was now that she came to comprehend how great had been her loss; now the cruelty came into stark focus. Grace realized, for the first time, that the years of separation had stealthily removed the child she loved, and replaced her with a woman she did not know. She felt very afraid... would her daughter, no longer a child, remember her mother; would she remember how much she had been loved; could she believe that she had lived in her mother's heart for all those years, that she had never been forgotten?

When the coach drew to a halt, Grace's seventeen years' wait was over. The three weary travellers had come to the end of their arduous journey, all the way from North Carolina to New Jersey, and they could not have been more relieved, but the loud ecstatic welcome they received as they entered 'Fortune's Hand' made every gruelling mile of it worthwhile. Tears and laughter intermingled as emotional greetings were exchanged, sisters with brother, aunt with nieces, sister-in-law with sister-in-law, but none so deep, so heartfelt, as those between Celia and her son, or between Grace and her long lost daughter Minnie.

Minnie 1866

One

When news was received that Edmund and Lilybee would soon be leaving North Carolina to attend Rosalind's wedding, the Hertherington household was thrown into a furore of activity. The servants were put to work in making rooms ready for the new arrivals and excitement mounted daily. Rosalind and her mother kept up the pretence that they were engaged in wedding preparations; they spent much time chatting confidentially, seemingly planning for the forthcoming event, but although outward appearances would indicate this, in actual fact they were solely concerned with how best to effect Rosalind's escape. Her mother was confident that they could rely on her Aunt Lilybee's understanding and help, but in the meantime, to allay any suspicions, they were forced to make regular visits to Mrs Day's dressmaking establishment and to Amy Perkins the milliner, to choose the materials and patterns and to have fittings for the dresses and hats that they needed for the special occasion. Rosalind was sick with apprehension, wondering if her mother's plan would succeed. Her father seemed to be ever-present at home, something to which the family were unaccustomed and completely out of character for him, but he was most anxious that his daughter had not the slightest opportunity to thwart his plans. Her marriage to Henry Youngman was of dire necessity to him. On no account must that particular deal be allowed to fall through.

*

Rosalind did not take at all kindly to being fettered by her present circumstances, and knowing that the young mistress had never been blessed with a goodly share of patience, Minnie was fully aware of just how difficult she was finding it to exercise self-restraint. "I shall lose my mind before very long Minnie, I know I shall," she complained petulantly. "I simply cannot tolerate this waiting day after day."

She was pacing back and forth across her bedroom. "How I wish Edmund and Aunt Lilybee would come, for Mama cannot arrange for me to get away with Benjamin without their help."

Minnie always did her best to placate her rebellious charge, to keep her from antagonising her father, if at all possible. Now she went and stood looking out at the bleak landscape; the winter had been particularly long and hard this year, and the branches of the trees stood naked, showing no sign of life. She did notice however, that the snow and ice were melting away rapidly; proof that spring would not be long in coming. As the weather was so much improved, she thought it a good idea to suggest they take a breath of air, go for a walk down by the river. Rosalind too thought it a marvellous idea, glad of any excuse to escape from her father's menacing presence.

In no time the girls had put on their cloaks and slipped quietly from the house. It was good to be alone for a while, free to talk as young girls would, with no fear of being overheard. They breathed in the cool, fresh air, the found it exhilarating to be out of doors again after the long confinement of winter. With the temperature gradually rising and the days lengthening into spring, the frozen depths of the snow were at last responding to the gentle warmth of the sun's weak rays, first dissolving into a wet mush and then transforming into huge lakes that the hard ground could not absorb; these in turn poured river-like down the sides of the mountains, the rapid torrents carrying with them earth and loosened stones, which spilled into the Muscanetcong and caused it to swell at an alarming rate. As its icy, glass-like surface melted and the muddy silt poured into it unchecked, its normally gentle, clear flow became an angry swirling cauldron of brown, murky water, cascading over the rocks and fallen trees which littered its bed.

"Ugh," exclaimed Rosalind with a shudder, "The river looks so wild, doesn't it? It is hardly recognisable, not a bit like it is in summer, when we wade in its cool, clear shallows."

Minnie ignored her; something unusual had caught her eye and she was staring intently at it. She took a few steps down the slight incline, holding fast to a low hanging branch of a tree; for fear that she might lose her footing and slip.

"Minnie, be careful, what are you doing?" Rosalind called anxiously, "What are you looking at?"

"Look... look Miss Rosalind... aint that a boat caught up down there? I's sho' I can see sump'n at the bottom of the bank."

"Where... I can't see anything... oh, do come back before you fall."

Minnie joined her mistress again. "Come along here, where there ain't so many trees... I's sho' there's sump'n'."

The two girls hitched up their skirts and trod warily along the bank to a small clearing, where their view was unobscured. Minnie stepped down towards the water again, across the lower incline and peered back towards the tangle of dross caught in the exposed tree roots. "Look, see there," she called excitedly, "It a boat or sump'n'... no it ain't... it's a canoe."

She suddenly clamped her hand over her mouth to stifle her loud gasp. "Oh no... there someone in it." Her eyes grew big and round as she looked up at her mistress.

"Rosalind was curious now; she joined her maid at the water's edge to see for herself what she found so intriguing, paying no heed to the mud that sucked at the soles of her boots. Sure enough, just a few feet away, she espied a canoe; it had become entangled in a collection of broken twigs and branches that had been swept along by the fast flowing river, but the current had somehow swung it into the bank, under some low lying trees, where it had become trapped between their roots. She too could see something, or someone, lying in the bottom of it. She too gasped aloud as she recognised what she saw. "It's an Indian, Minnie... an Indian," she breathed fearfully. "What shall we do?"

Minnie answered, solemn-faced, "He a man, Miss Rosalind... that what important. He ain't jus' a Indian, he a man and he look like he need help."

Rosalind became alarmed, "But we can't help him... there's nothing we can do. Anyway he isn't moving... supposing he's dead?"

"Well we gotta do sump'n, cos there ain't nobody else... and supposing he ain't dead? We best take a look."

Both girls were afraid but their curiosity surmounted their apprehension.

"I'll jus' git sump'n so we can pull the canoe away from the bank. You stay here and keep watch."

Minnie went to find a stout branch and returned a few minutes later. She crouched down and made her way through the trees that clustered low over the river bank, until she was directly above the canoe. She pushed and poked at it with as much strength as she could muster, until it gradually freed itself and was once again borne along in the fast flow of the river. It swung precariously from side to side as it was propelled along towards Rosalind. Minnie hurried along with it and once again lunged at it with the stout branch. She almost lost it several times but finally managed to manoeuvre it towards them and hold it steady. It was then that they could see quite clearly that the occupant was indeed an Indian and he lay, seemingly unconscious in the bottom of the craft. "We gotta git him out," said Minnie authoritatively. She stepped into the icy water and, grabbing the canoe with both hands, heaved it up on to the clearing.

Rosalind stood rooted to the spot, terrified that the Indian might suddenly leap up and attack them.

"Come on... help me to lift him... he too heavy for me by myself," urged Minnie.

As if in a dream, Rosalind followed her maid's instructions and between them they managed to lift the prostrate form from the canoe and carry it awkwardly away from the water's edge. They found a small, clear space between the undergrowth where they could lay down their weighty burden. Minnie knelt down beside the injured man to check whether or not he was alive. She could feel a slight pulse in his neck but he was losing blood from an injury in his left shoulder.

Both girls found it puzzling that he was wearing a Union Army jacket over his buckskins and they had noticed an army cap in the canoe. Minnie peeped apprehensively beneath his jacket and she gasped yet again. "He bin shot... look Miss Rosalind... and he bleeding real bad. We gotta stop the bleedin' or he gonna die." She lifted her skirt and deftly tore a wide strip from her cotton petticoat, which she promptly folded into a thick pad and pressed it to the wound to stem the flow of blood. "We has to find somewhere to hide him, to keep him safe, while I goes back to the house to git some things to clean and dress this wound."

Rosalind was shaking her head slowly, from side to side, completely aghast. She spoke in a whisper, "But Minnie... where should we hide him? No... no we can't... we can't."

Minnie cast her eyes around in desperation, there must be a place. Suddenly she remembered. "I know... I know, what about that old cabin back there towards the house? The place down by the river. It ain't never used no more... we could try to hide him in there. Just until we see if there anythin' we can do. Poor man... he near enough dead... we can't just leave him here, no sir, 'cos he gonna die for sho' if we does."

She laid her hand on her mistress's arm and looked at her imploringly, "Please Miss Rosalind... don't let him die," she pleaded urgently.

"Alright... alright... but we must be quick, before anyone sees us."

Again they lifted the unconscious form between them and struggled awkwardly until, little by little they managed to reach the old store cabin that stood unused on the bank of the river, not too far from the house. Inside they found an assorted jumble of objects, long since of any use; large wooden toys from when Rosalind, Edmund and Esther were children. Various old boxes and baskets, piled one upon the other; Joshua's gardening implements and heavy tools for cutting back the undergrowth and trees, but the most useful of all were some old fur robes for carriage and sleigh use in the bitter cold of winter; too good to have been thrown away when they had been replaced by newer ones. Besides these were a few horse blankets, which the children had spread upon the ground when playing out of doors. Minnie quickly cleared a space on the floor and threw down some of the old bearskins, then after they had lain their Indian to rest upon them, they covered him with the horse blankets.

"We must get back now Minnie... we have been gone so long, we are bound to be missed. Come now, before someone comes looking for us." Rosalind was peering nervously out of the door, to ensure they had not been observed.

"Alright Miss Rosalind... I'm comin'... but I must come back straight away to clean that wound and maybe fetch him some food and drink. He'll need sump'n if he ever comes back to life again, cos he gonna be weak after losin' all that blood."

They left the cabin stealthily and hurried back to the house.

"Where's you two bin all this time... is you tryin' to catch your death or sump'n?" chided Delilah as the girls came through the kitchen door. "Here now... you jus' come and have sump'n warm to drink."

She went to the stove and lifted a large coffee pot that always stood atop it to keep warm.

"I'll have mine in my room Delilah... Minnie can bring it for me," said Rosalind, "And perhaps you'll find me something nice to eat with it, the cold has made me quite hungry."

She glanced slyly at Minnie, who immediately understood her clever mistress's intentions, and whilst Minnie waited for the tray to be prepared, Rosalind slipped away to her father's study, careful to avoid being seen. She listened intently at the door and when she was quite certain her father was not there, she stepped inside and went straight to the drinks cabinet. She chose a bottle of whisky from the large array of spirits and slid it beneath the short, thick jacket that she had put on beneath her cape before going out earlier. She pressed the bottle close against her, concealing it with her arm as she left the study and hurried upstairs to her room.

Minnie joined her just a few minutes later and they talked surreptitiously of how she could return to the cabin with the food and drinks and then to tend to her wounded Indian.

There were dainty sandwiches and small sponge cakes on the tray, with a pot of hot coffee to which Delilah had thoughtfully added a tipple of rum to warm the girls. Minnie packed them most carefully into a small basket provided by Rosalind, together with the bottle of whisky and some clean cloths and salve with which to cleanse and dress the injured shoulder.

"Wait here Minnie... I'll just make sure that there's nobody about," said Rosalind. She strolled from her room and checked that the hallway and stairs were clear, then urgently beckoned to Minnie, who was anxiously peeping through the door, waiting for the signal to leave. "Do take care and don't be away too long. Perhaps you can go to the cabin again after dinner. I'll try to get some warm soup for you to take then... it's much better for a sick patient than sandwiches and cake. Your absence won't be noticed so easily in the evening either."

Minnie nodded in agreement, "Thank you Miss Rosalind... you'se the kindest mistress ever born... yo' sho is." So saying she slipped from the house quickly and made her way precariously down to the cabin, holding the basket steady lest its contents be spilled.

*

The Indian was still lying unconscious where she had left him, so without a moment's hesitation she carefully removed the blood-stained jacket and set about bathing and cleaning the wound with neat whisky. Upon closer inspection she was relieved to find that the bullet had passed straight through the shoulder and although there had been considerable loss of blood, at least there was no danger of lead poisoning. When she had made him as comfortable as possible, Minnie raised him gently into a sitting position, supporting him against her as she tried to pour a little of the whisky, droplet by tiny droplet, between his lips. He began to choke and splutter and his eyes fluttered open momentarily, to close again almost immediately. Minnie felt elated, her pulse raced; when she had almost given him up for dead, he had of a sudden shown her the slightest flicker of life and it was all she needed. Now she became enthused with hope... she had something to work on... she would keep him alive. She lowered him onto the bearskins once again, noticing as she did so, how handsome he looked. She studied him closely for several seconds, admiring his finely chiselled features, the long, thick, black hair, his strong muscular physique. She felt strangely moved by him, strongly protective... he lay completely helpless and she would care for him, provide for his every need. She covered him with the blankets to keep him warm whilst she was gone, then she pulled the boxes and baskets around him so that he was well hidden from view before she left. She knew she must not stay away from the house for too long, but she would return again to her Indian after nightfall, when it was more safe.

*

When the time came for her to go down to dinner, Rosalind sent Minnie to the kitchen with a message that she was not feeling too well and that she would like some soup sent up to her room.

"There... I knowed it... that 'cos you two was out in the cold this afternoon," scolded Delilah, "Now for sho' she done got herself a chill… why you let Miss Rosalind stay out so long Minnie?"

"It didn't seem so long Delilah… and Miss Rosalind jus' wanted to git out for a bit. You know she don't like being shut up too long." Minnie felt guilty, but she consoled herself with the thought that her mistress was not really feeling unwell.

"You take her some o' Delilah's good chicken broth, that put her right in no time. Shouldn't gone out in the cold… no sir… I knowed this'd happen."

Delilah was muttering all the while she was ladling out the nutritious broth into a deep serving bowl. She placed it on a tray with two soup plates and spoons and handed it to Minnie.

"Here you is… enough for the two of youse, 'cos I 'spects she'll want yo' to stay up there with her now."

Minnie nodded, "Thank you Delilah… yes, I'll stay with Miss Rosalind… keep her company."

*

When all was quiet and peaceful, Minnie once again stole down to the cabin, taking the chicken broth with her. She tried to revive the Indian with a few more drops of the whisky, but still he did not awaken. She knew he was weak from loss of blood and suffering from exposure to the cold. He was in desperate need of warmth, so Minnie gently lifted the blankets and slid beneath them, lying as close as she could to the still form, hugging the cold body against her own.

In the quiet of the cabin, with the light fast fading, Minnie quickly dropped off to sleep, but she awoke some hours later with a start. By now darkness had fallen and for an instant she wondered where she was. As she tried to move her numbed arm, she felt it drag across the still form of the Indian and she immediately recalled what had happened. They had lain unmoving, for how long she did not know, but now she was very hot, sweating beneath the thick wool blankets. She could feel that the body beside her was no longer icy cold. She moved away very gradually, wondering for how long she had been asleep, she had no way of knowing, but it seemed to her like hours. She suddenly became afraid and knew she must get back to the house before she was missed. She rearranged the warm blankets carefully around her Indian and reluctantly left him once again. "I'll come back as soon as I can... please don' die Indian," she whispered as she crept away.

*

She could see a small light flickering in the kitchen as she came towards the house, she approached quietly, anxious to see who might be there before she went in. She pressed her face to the window and peered in; she could see her mistress by the table, she appeared to be preparing some food. Minnie gave the lightest tap on the window with her fingernails and her mistress turned around immediately. She rushed to open the kitchen door and pulled her maid inside, pressing her forefinger to her lips. "Sshh... sshh... don't make a sound," she said. She returned to what she was doing at the table, she had piled a small plate with food and was filling a mug with milk. She beckoned Minnie to help her replace several things in the larder, then she handed the plate to her maid and took the small lamp with them as they left the kitchen to return to her room.

They could hear voices as they passed the study; it was obvious that the master was entertaining a guest. The rest of the house was quite peaceful.

Once back in her room, Rosalind burst out, "Oh, Minnie... why were you away so long... I was scared that something dreadful had happened to you?" She took Minnie's arm and pulled her towards the bed, saying, "Sit here beside me and tell me what you have been doing."

She lifted a piece of pie from the plate and took a bite of it, at the same time offering the plate to Minnie, who shook her head and proceeded to give an account of exactly what had happened. Rosalind's eyes grew wide with alarm when she heard her maid had fallen asleep hugging an Indian. "Weren't you afraid of him?" she said incredulously. "Oh Minnie, you should be careful."

Minnie smiled, a dreamy look on her face. "There ain't nothin' to be afraid of. Anyways, I jus' trying' to keep him alive; yo' don't s'pose he gonna kill me for that does yo'?"

Rosalind munched hungrily at the pie and took a long drink of her milk. "Don't you feel hungry?" she asked. "I miss not having my dinner... I had to wait until all the servants had cleared the kitchen before I could steal something to eat. It's a good job I was there to let you in when you returned. Here... take something... I don't suppose you've eaten either."

Minnie shook her head, "No thank you... I ain't hungry... I too worried 'bout my Indian to bother with eatin'."

Rosalind smiled at her knowingly, "Well, don't you get too interested in him, because if he doesn't die, then he'll probably run off just as soon as he regains consciousness."

They talked together for a while, as Minnie prepared her mistress for bed, but as soon as she was dismissed, her maidservant went to her own room that adjoined her mistress's closet. There she lay waiting for what seemed like an eternity, longing to return to the cabin down by the river. She dared not leave her room just yet however, for she did not know whether her master would be paying her a visit. She closed her mind to the formidable prospect, as she had learned to do for so many years. The time passed slowly, much too slowly, and eventually Minnie could no longer stand the interminable waiting. She decided to find out for herself if her master had left his study and gone to his room. She crept quietly along the passageway past the many bedrooms. The whole household seemed at rest. When she came to her master's room, she pressed her ear to the door and listened, almost afraid to breathe... then, through the stillness came the unmistakeable sound of his snoring. Immediately the tight constriction in her chest evaporated away in an enormous sigh of relief. He had probably consumed far more brandy than normal, whilst he was entertaining his guest, with the consequence that it had sent him into a deep slumber as soon as he retired to his room. Minnie lost no time in returning to her room to put on her clothing, then she stole out into the night, unable to wait until she could once again take the still cold body into her arms, hold it close, coax it back to life with the warmth of her own body. She needed to know that she, and she alone, had saved this man, had helped this one human being to survive. Despite the bitter, cold night air, she felt afire as she sped through the tangle of trees towards the cabin. Her pulse raced anew as she slipped beneath the thick blankets and drew him against her. She felt him stir slightly and she smiled contentedly, she knew that he was still alive.

As dawn was breaking, Minnie awoke slowly, she felt warm and comfortable, in fact she had never felt more warm and comfortable in her life. She glanced toward the small window of the cabin and knew that it would soon be daylight. She did not want to move but she knew that she must. She slipped her arm gently away from the warm, recumbent body beside her and as she did so the Indian too awoke. She raised herself onto her elbow and looked steadily into the puzzled eyes that were gazing up into her own. She smile broadly and with a deep intake of breath she whispered confidentially, "Hello... I'se Minnie... I found you yesterday down at the river. I thought you was dead."

The Indian winced with pain and his right hand moved to his injured shoulder. He could feel the dressing and his eyes glanced towards them. "You do this for me?" he asked quietly, disbelievingly.

Minnie nodded enthusiastically, smiling even more broadly. "Yes... you was bleedin' real bad. I cleaned you up some with the massa's whisky... here drink a little... it make you feel better."

She reached for the bottle and the Indian took a few sips. He spluttered and shook his head, then fell onto his back again.

"I brought you some food too, but you wasn't in any fit state to eat last night." She eased herself from beneath the blankets and knelt beside him. "I gotta git back to the house now but I'll bring you a warm drink and something to eat later. You jus' rest here and don't move... ain't nobody gonna know you'se here jus' long as you stay hid."

The Indian was feeling very weak; he just lay on his back and closed his eyes. "I'll come back as soon as I can," Minnie called from the door as she left.

*

She floated through her morning chores, fetching her mistress's coffee tray from the kitchen, awakening her and preparing her toilet, helping her to dress, then brushing and combing her hair. It was as she curled and pinned the golden tresses that she confessed to having gone to the cabin again in the dead of night. When Rosalind heard that the Indian had regained consciousness early that morning, she became keenly interested.

"Did he say anything to you Minnie... do tell me what happened?"

Minnie told her mistress precisely what had taken place and asked if she might take a warm drink and a little food to her Indian soon, as he was weak from hunger by now.

"Of course, yes, you wait here and I will fetch something for him from the breakfast table... it will take but a moment."

Rosalind went downstairs straight away, knowing that her mother and Esther would not be down for breakfast so early. She took some warm rolls and ran with them back to her bedroom. "Now you go to the kitchen and tell Delilah that I have asked for some more coffee before I go down to breakfast this morning."

Eventually, Minnie found herself again hurrying towards the cabin, the rolls and coffee wrapped together in a cloth to keep them warm. She opened the door of the cabin very slowly and called, "It all right, Indian, it only me, Minnie." She moved aside the boxes and baskets that were keeping him concealed and sat on the floor beside him. She watched in fascination as he drank the warm coffee and ate one of the fresh rolls hungrily.

"Good," he said, nodding his head in appreciation. Minnie was enchanted by him. "Where this place?" he asked, slowly enunciating every word.

"This is 'Fortune's Hand' in Asbury," Minnie replied.

"'Fortune's Hand'? What place is that?"

"It my massa's house... Massa Hetherington."

"Your massa... Heth...rin...ton....?" The Indian looked puzzled. "I belong to massa Hetherington... I his daughter's maid. I fetched here when I was a small girl, to take care of Miss Rosalind. She jus' a baby then, but now she a grown woman. She helped me to hide you here after I find you. But what you doin' here all alone… how did you git shot?"

"Long story," said the Indian. He felt tired, all this talking exhausted him.

Minnie was longing to know everything about him, but she knew that he needed to rest. "You sleep now," she whispered kindly. "I come back later and clean your wound… we talk a little more then."

His eyes closed and Minnie left him to rest.

As Minnie returned to the house, all kinds of questions began to formulate in her mind, questions that she would ask her Indian later.

*

Fortunately for Minnie, her mistress was busily engaged during the next few days with trips into town, accompanied by her mother. Firstly they attended a formal lunch with the Youngman family, in order to discuss the wedding preparations, followed by visits to Mrs Day who required continual fitting sessions for the many dresses that had been ordered. Then came frequent appointments with Amy Perkins who was in sole charge of producing all the new bonnets and headdresses for each of the young girls and ladies.

The town of Asbury was agog at the elaborate preparations and the Hetherington girl's wedding was a constant topic of conversation. In actual fact, Rosalind was beginning to enjoy playing this particular charade with her mother and the Youngman girls, for as her mother had so rightly pointed out, she would eventually need a wedding dress and trousseau if she planned to marry Benjamin Richmond.

With her young mistress so conveniently occupied, Minnie found little problem in stealing away to the cabin down by the river, and with Rosalind's help, she managed to provide her Indian with warm soup and drinks, and an adequate supply of food to sustain and nourish him. Her fascination with this handsome stranger grew deeper and as he began to recover, he too found himself captivated by the courageous young woman who had saved his life and put her own at risk by hiding him. Her undisguised admiration and kindly concern for him gradually removed his fear and suspicion and in response to her innocent questioning, he revealed the moving story of how he had come to be drifting along the Muscanetcong river injured and alone.

"What your name, Indian... what you doin' in these parts?" Minnie asked kindly.

"My name Run Swiftly," he replied proudly, thrusting his right hand forward with a jerk, in a straight line from his face to indicate that he was fleet of foot, "Name soldiers give when I scout for them in war."

Minnie's eyes opened wide, "Soldiers... was you in the war?" she asked incredulously.

Run Swiftly gave one firm nod of his head. "Soldiers come my village one day... small troop... say want scout, show way to big camp... take many days. Give my father, Chief Running Deer, fine horse, fine gun... he say good I go with soldiers... help them in war. Learn how white man talk... how white man think. My father old and wise... say man most clever when he fight enemy... most cunning. He say I learn white cunning, help my people if soldiers come to fight us."

Minnie nodded her head in solemn approval, for although she realised how greatly everyone feared the Indians, believing them to be ferocious savages, she was also fully aware of the way in which they were blatantly mistreated by the whites. Of course she could sympathise with this dark-skinned native, for was not her own race equally maltreated by the whites. Many were the stories of how the military attacked and destroyed the Indian villages in order to drive them away from the land the white settlers would claim for themselves.

She gazed at Run Swiftly in rapt attention as he sat cross-legged upon the pile of bearskins, a thick horse blanket wrapped around him for warmth. He appeared magnificent to her and she became mesmerised by this son of an Indian Chief as in his broken English he haltingly related to her strange and fascinating details of life in the land of his people.

"I Lenape Indian... my people Lenape," he said.

Minnie moved her mouth slowly, trying to copy his pronunciation, "Len-ar-pay," she whispered softly.

He nodded. "White man... name Sir Thomas West, he say we Delaware Indian... but we Lenape. He Lord Delaware so he gave us same name, but my people here long before white man come... my people here from beginning of time."

Run Swiftly took a long, deep breath, his eyes gazed into the semi-darkness of the cabin as he went on, "Lenape one of the first tribes living in this land... our name mean 'ordinary people'... before white man come, life good. We hunt, we fish, our women plant corn, maize, beans. Earth our mother, this land good to my people... give everything we need. Give us buffalo, dear, bear to hunt; rabbits, beavers, ducks and turkeys. Skins of animals make our clothes, bones of animals make our tools and weapons."

Minnie listened in awe to everything her Indian had to tell about himself; about his people and their way of life. In her mind's eye she could see the beautiful pictures that he painted with his words, and gradually she began to realise that they were not the most ferocious savages that many people believed them to be. Instead, she learned that the Lenape was a peaceful tribe; they had never been hostile or war-like. Their ancient culture and customs, their skilled crafts had been handed down for generation upon generation and this man, whose life she had saved, was rightly proud of his heritage.

In painstaking detail, Run Swiftly explained how the women of his tribe would utilise the skins and pelts of every animal in the making of clothes, how the skin of the deer was scraped and dried before being sewn into clothing. He told Minnie that in the summer, the men wore a strip of buckskin passed between their legs and held up by a belt around the waist. Over this, they wore a short kilt and on their feet soft, comfortable moccasins. The women wore just a skirt with their moccasins but in winter they would wear a full dress and ponchos made from beaver or bearskins, whilst the men would add a buckskin shirt and leggings tied around their legs for warmth.

Minnie was surprised at how important was the role played by the Lenape women; they provided the clan mothers who sat on their councils and it was they who decided which men should be their elders. It was only the women who tended the growing of crops, cleverly planting squash between their beans and corn in the same field, so that they would be well protected until they were ready to be picked. Then, when the menfolk returned from hunting with the animal hides and furs, it was the women who cleaned and tanned them. In fact, whole families would wear the pelts of the beaver, to season them for the trade. When enough pelts and skins had been collected and made ready for trading, the women would take them along the Delaware river, for it was there they could barter with the Indian agents and exchange them for a wide variety of other goods, particularly rum, to take back to the men in their villages.

It was on one such trading expedition that the tragedy occurred, which had eventually brought Run Swiftly to 'Fortune's Hand'. Earlier that winter the hunting had been good and the men had returned to their village with many pelts of fattened beaver and moose. There was great rejoicing in the long houses in which the families lived, for theirs was a communal existence and everyone joined in the celebrations when the hunters returned. Then, after long months of work, when the women cleaned and tanned the skins, when they decided that they had enough ready to trade, they piled them into their canoes and prepared for their journey along the Delaware river. They talked and laughed excitedly, they could not wait to see what brightly coloured cloths, beads and jewellery the Indian agents would have to barter with them.

Just as they were about to leave, Chief Running Deer called them before him and spoke solemnly, "Remember, women of my tribe, your men have worked long and hard for the fine skins that you take with you... you must make good trade... make sure you receive a fair exchange. Do not allow the white man to cheat you, as he cheated our people long ago... you know how the grandfather of my father was cheated."

Chief Running Deer was referring to the fraudulent 'Walking Purchase' of 1737 in Pennsylvania, when the Delaware Indians were dispossessed of all their land, he was reminding them of the tragic story that each generation had told to their children, of how Thomas Penn, proprietor of Pennsylvania, had wanted the land at the Forks of the Delaware river so that he could sell it to pay off the debts of his family. At that time the Forks were inhabited by Pennsylvania Delawares and refugee Delawares from New Jersey. These tribes were persuaded by Penn that an old and unsigned deed dating from 1686 was a legally binding bill of sale for the land around the Forks. The Indians did not understand just how much land was conveyed by this original deed and they accepted what Penn told them. They thought that the adjustment to the boundaries of which he spoke would be a relatively small one, as it would only add as much land as could be covered in a walk lasting a day and a half from a specified point. However, it did not state in which direction the walker should proceed. In 1737, Penn hired men with axes to clear a path for three strong walkers, two of whom soon gave up from exhaustion, but the third man covered sixty-four miles in the day and a half. He reached far beyond the Forks of the Delaware. In actual fact he reached twenty miles beyond the Kittatinny mountains, which extended the area of the claim to approximately one thousand, two hundred square miles. Not only did this fraudulent exploitation rob the Delawares of Pennsylvania and New Jersey, but it also dispossessed the Minisink Delawares.

The women paid careful attention to Running Deer's words of warning, nodding in unison as they acknowledged that they would make sure they received a fair exchange of goods for their valuable furs. Then they quickly made their way to their canoes, accompanied by a laughing group of women and children from the village, who would impatiently await their return with whatever fascinating baubles their trading might produce on this particular trip. The small children shouted and waved to the five women as they set off in two canoes, each of which pulled behind it another craft piled high with all manner of lush animal pelts and skins.

They laughed and talked as they deftly paddled along the river, proud of what their fine hunters had provided. In the first canoe sat Laughing Eyes, the sister of Run Swiftly and the daughter of Chief Running Deer; she had recently been married to a young brave named Storm Cloud. With her was her cousin, Bead Jacket, and alongside them in a second canoe, were two older women, Morning Breeze and No Talk, who had also brought along her daughter Little Owl, in order that she too might learn how to trade.

They made their way steadily towards the place where they were sure of meeting up with Indian agents. In fact, a number of white settlements were now to be found along the banks of the Delaware, so if the women were not successful in the first of them, then they would continue their journey until they came to a place where they could barter for goods. Suddenly Laughing Eyes noticed a coil of smoke drifting upwards between the trees on the bank of the river. She called to the other women and pointed to where she thought they might find an agent or two. They drew their canoes alongside the bank and listened intently; sure enough, they could hear voices coming from a short distance away, and noises to indicate that there was some kind of camp there. Laughing eyes and Bead Jacket went to investigate whilst the others stayed in the canoes. The two young women approached apprehensively, careful not to be seen until they were sure there was no danger. As they came upon the camp fire, Laughing Eyes looked at Bead Jacket and smiled broadly, nodding in approval, for she immediately recognised the men who were sitting around it, drinking and smoking. She had traded with them many times in the past and she was pleased to see familiar faces, men with whom she was acquainted. She beckoned to Bead Jacket and the two young women stepped from the cover of the trees and slowly approached the small group of men.

"Well... jus' look who's here... it's good to see you ladies," called one of the group. He stood up as they came closer. He was a giant of a man with a fiery red beard, which almost concealed his face. Laughing Eyes knew that he was known as

Dutch. Again he spoke, "Have ye come to trade? What d'ye have for us this time?"

Laughing Eyes nodded, "We bring fine furs... fine skins... make good trade."

"Good... good," said Dutch, "Let's see what you have then."

With another nod of her head, Laughing Eyes turned away, once again beckoning to Bead Jacket to follow her.

As they disappeared out of sight, Dutch shook his head and chuckled "That's what I like about these Indian squaws, they don't have too much to say for themselves."

The other men guffawed loudly. "Don't you forget what the boss said; we gotta cut down on what we gives them natives, Dutch. Musn't be too generous with 'em."

"I don't need no remindin' from you Willy," growled the Dutchman. There was a menacing hiss from the fire as he spat into its glowing embers. "You jus' leave the dealin' to me and everything'll be fine."

It did not take Laughing Eyes and Bead Jacket long to run back to the other women, and breathlessly they gave them the good news that they had found some interested traders. Each of them then took as many skins as they could carry, piled high one upon the other, and made their way precariously, following Laughing Eyes to where the traders were waiting. When the men saw the fine quality of what the women had brought, they glanced knowingly at one another, fully realising that their boss would be very well pleased if they could return to his storehouse with such an array of luxuriant skins. They must obtain them for as little as possible though, that was his instruction, and they knew they must abide by it.

He had never been an easy man to deal with, but of late they had found Gilbert Hetherington becoming more and more objectionable in his business dealings, his demands almost impossible to meet, but here they could see the quality of the merchandise that would more than meet with his approval.

The women felt proud of their beautiful skins and pelts as they spread them carefully on the ground. They stood in silence as they watched the men examine each one, stroking the furs and feeling its thickness, testing how soft and pliable were the skins. Finally, Dutch gave a grunt and shook his head disconsolately, glancing at the other men. They withdrew a short distance and spoke quietly to one another, seemingly discussing what they thought of the goods on offer. The Indian women knew this was all part of the game that had to be played, so they remained silently watching. Dutch returned to them and spreading his arms as though embracing the whole array of skins, he frowned and nodded several times before saying, "I'll take everything you have then ladies."

It was obvious to the women that he was trying to give the impression that he was doing them a great favour. Laughing Eyes was not to be so easily fooled. "What you give for them?" she asked, narrowing her eyes, for she was confident that he very much coveted what they had brought.

He turned and strode over to a covered wagon that stood a short distance away. He lifted down a large box and selected a few items from it, together with a brightly coloured blanket and some bottles of rum. When he had placed them on the ground for the women to examine, No Talk became animated, making small grunting sounds as she tapped Laughing Eyes urgently on the arm. She shook her head vigorously and indicated with her own particular signs that their furs and skins were worth far more than this cheating trader was trying to give for them.

Laughing Eyes placed her hand on No Talk's arm and soothingly signed back to her that she too realised what the trader was up to and that she had no intention of accepting such a poor exchange for their goods. She turned to Dutch, "You not give enough... this not good trade." She waved her hands over the mound of furs and pelts strewn on the ground before her, "We give many skins... fine furs... you not give fair exchange."

Dutch laughed unconvincingly. "Aw... come on now ladies... you ain't getting more than that. Look at this fine woollen blanket... and how 'bout this?" He picked up a small mirror set in a pretty gilt frame.

Laughing Eyes was intrigued by it, she wanted it but she knew they were being cheated badly. She looked down at the various furs and turned to the other women. They spoke softly together for several moments, then she returned to the bargaining. "We take what you give," she said nodding at Dutch, for she knew the hunters would be waiting for the precious rum back in her village. She looked towards the other women and motioned that they should pick up the items they had been offered. They gathered them up hurriedly and started back to the canoes. At the same time Laughing Eyes quickly retrieved a magnificent buffalo hide and several of the beaver furs they had brought to trade. "Now we go," she said haughtily, looking Dutch straight in the eyes.

"Hey... what you doin'?" Dutch asked angrily. He stepped towards Laughing Eyes, making a grab at the buffalo hide. He could see its magnificent quality and knew that it was of great value. He fully realised that such a robe could easily fetch one hundred dollars in the markets of Europe, for that was the going rate for a buffalo hide that had been processed by an Indian squaw, whereas the green hides only fetched a dollar and twenty-five cents.

"You give more for this," demanded Laughing Eyes ... "or we take to other traders."

She clutched the hide and the beaver pelts tightly and pulled away from Dutch with all her might. She was angry that he should try to cheat them so, and she remembered for how long the women and children had to wear the beaver pelts next to their bodies in order to make them pliable and downy... for one and a half years they would endure wearing them, so that they could produce a fine plush underhair, about an inch thick. Then and only then would they be suitable for the making of the felt hats which were so fashionable among the white man.

"You ain't getting nothin', the tradin's been done, they're mine."

As he was shouting at her, Laughing Eyes turned and fled. The Dutchman chased after her, "Come back here... you damn squaw... come back."

Laughing Eyes could hear him shouting abuse, threatening her as he followed close behind. The weight of the hide and furs slowed her pace, but she was determined to hold on to them... determined that this cheating trader would not have them. Suddenly she felt his enormous hands upon her shoulders... he grabbed her tightly and pulled her against him. She could feel his hot breath on her neck as he gasped and choked after the exertion of the chase. She struggled free of him and gathered the furs against her again... they had fallen as he caught her to him. She leapt forward and tried to run, but he was too close. His enormous hands snatched at the buffalo hide, and with a tug he wrenched it from her. She lost her footing and was thrown violently to the ground. As she fell her head struck a boulder with a resounding crack. The last sound she heard before she sank into a black void was her assailant's voice hissing, "You little... "

Dutch picked up the hide and the furs and made his way back to his friends, who had left the camp fire and were standing peering towards him, watching what was happening. They slapped the Dutchman on the back and laughed loudly. "We best git on our way... don't want them Indians comin' back stirring up trouble... we'll git back to Asbury with this lot soon as we can," he said.

When Laughing Eyes failed to return, No Talk and Bead Jacket went back to look for her. Bead Jacket gasped in horror as No Talk fell to her knees beside the still form, gently raising the young girl's head and cradling it in her arms. As she did do, she saw the blood oozing from her ear; saw how it had stained the ground where she lay. No Talk's long melancholy wail rent the air as she began to sway back and forth rhythmically. Her cry carried down to the river where her daughter and Morning Breeze were waiting. Little Owl stiffened in terror, then sped through the woods in search of her mother, fearful of what she might find. Seeing her mother's distress, she placed her arms lovingly around her shoulders and coaxed her to her feet, then together, the three women managed to carry Laughing Eyes to the canoes, where they made her as comfortable as possible for the journey back to their village.

By the time they arrived, the young girl's life had ebbed away. No loss could have been more devastating and a great sadness descended over the tribe as they mourned the tragic death of their chief's daughter. They began their ritual, melancholy chanting, accompanied by the slow beat of their drums, which spoke their heartfelt grief. This was all the more intensified, for a few moons ago they had been rejoicing at the marriage ceremony of Laughing Eyes and Storm Cloud.

*

Very soon it became necessary for Chief Running Deer to call a council of the Elders, to determine what action should be taken to avenge his daughter's death. After much grave deliberation, it was decided to send just a few of their braves to deal with the culprits. They would not launch a full scale attack, for there was animosity enough against the native Indians. Far better, they agreed, to exact their revenge discreetly, thus avoiding the possible wrath of the military authorities, who would welcome yet another excuse to invade their village. So the decision was made that the chief's son, Run Swiftly, should accompany the grief stricken Storm Cloud on his avenging mission, together with Dancing Bear and Grey Hawk. They would glean all the information they could from Bead Jacket, Morning Breeze, No Talk and Little Owl and then they would track down the cheating Indian agents who were responsible for the death of Laughing Eyes.

It was early in the morning when the four braves set off in sombre silence, their first intention being to find the Indian agents who their women had described in such vivid detail. Bead Jacket had also provided valuable information concerning the big man with the beard of red fire, who was known as Dutch. He, it seemed, was their leader and it was he who had given so few goods in exchange for all the skins and furs offered by the women. Bead Jacket told of how Laughing Eyes was determined not to be cheated by him; how she planned to take back the most valuable of the pelts with the fine buffalo hide. It soon became apparent why Laughing Eyes had been so callously attacked.

*

By nightfall, the braves had located the place where Laughing Eyes had lain. It was difficult for his companions to pacify

Storm Cloud, for at the sight of his wife's blood he lost all control and casting caution aside was intent on journeying on alone to find her murderer. Run Swiftly stood before him and gripped the distraught young man firmly by the upper arms. He gazed into his sad eyes and spoke quietly, comfortingly to him, "My brother... try to stay calm. I more than anyone know the pain that is in your heart, for was not Laughing Eyes my own sister? Still I cannot believe that she is gone from us. Think carefully before you act... however difficult you may find it. If we are to trace the men responsible for her death, then we must take our time. We must first seek them out, no matter where they are... then we must watch and wait; plan how they should be punished. Only in this way will your bride's, my sister's, death be properly avenged. I know the way of the white man, for did not my father send me among then to learn their ways... how they think, how they act. Now we can put to use what I have learned... trust me and you shall have retribution. I promise."

Storm Cloud's head fell to his chest and he nodded dejectedly in agreement. "Let it be so," he muttered softly.

*

Early the next day, they studied the tracks left by the Indian agents, determined the direction in which they had gone, then returned to their canoes. They knew they could make better progress on the networks of rivers and streams in their canoes than they could by trekking through the woodlands on foot. Eventually they came upon a cluster of wooden cabins set back a short distance from the river. This appeared more promising than several of the places they had previously passed, so they hid their canoes carefully and made their way stealthily towards the settlement, making sure they were not observed.

They watched and listened for some time in the hope that they might learn something of the men they were seeking. They saw several women and a number of children around the settlement, together with a goodly number of men, but none resembled the Indian agents described by their women. They kept watch until late into the evening, and just as Run Swiftly was about to signal to the others that they should retire for the night, they heard the sound of men approaching on horseback. Suddenly, through the darkness, came the sound of a rifle being cocked and a man's voice called gruffly, "Who's there... who is it?"

Then a woman appeared in the light of an open doorway, calling, "Is that you Willy... Dutch?"

There was no answer; the men just dismounted and tethered their horses before going in through the open cabin door. As the light fell upon the tallest of them, highlighting his fiery, red beard, Storm Cloud began to tremble, unable to contain his rage; his emotions once again threatened to run out of control. Run Swiftly laid a hand heavily on his shoulder to restrain him, at the same time pressing his forefinger to his lips, warning Storm Cloud that they must not make a sound before they formulated their plans. He beckoned to Dancing Bear and Grey Wolf to follow him and they left as silently as they had come. Now they knew the whereabouts of their quarry.

They stayed close by through the night, but very well hidden, so that they would be aware of any activity in and around the cabins. Their vigilance was rewarded at dawn the following morning when they saw Dutch and his men preparing to leave. Amid loud exchanges, the men finally mounted their horses and set off slowly through the woods, completely unaware that they were being followed. Run

Swiftly could hear the words they spoke to one another quite clearly.

"Is that right you gonna go over to Hetherington's place first thing Dutch. If'n that's so, what you say we wait some place for you. He's sure gittin' more like a bear with a sore head every time we see him. Seems like their ain't no pleasing him no more. I don't know why we has to put up with it."

The big man turned and looked back over his shoulder, "You ain't got no more sense than Willy, have you Gabe... you think I'm gonna load that wagon myself... and where you think you gonna git all that rum you're so fond of drinkin' if it ain't from Mr Hetherington, eh? You just tell me that." He spat vehemently on the ground and barked, "Now jus' keep your mouth shut... and mind what you're saying about him, 'cos he ain't the kind to be messin' with... you hear? Not if you intends to stay outa trouble he ain't."

The group continued through the woods in silence and Run Swiftly signalled to Dancing Bear and Grey Wolf to run up ahead of them to prepare for an ambush when they came to a place that was well secluded, for if at all possible the Indians would ensure that they left no trace of ever having been there after they vindicated the death of Laughing Eyes. Dancing Bear and Grey Wolf moved quickly and quietly on either side of their unsuspecting foe, waiting for the signal to attack.

It came suddenly, violently, before Dutch and his men knew what was happening. At just a glance from Run Swiftly, Storm Cloud hurled himself at the last of the men in the slow moving group. He leapt up behind him on to his horse, emitting a blood curdling scream, then as his arm closed tightly around the terrified man's neck, he plunged the knife hard and deep into his flesh. The man's lifeless body fell heavily to the ground as Storm Cloud jumped away, ready to eliminate another of the group.

Whilst he was thus engaged, both Dancing Bear and Grey Wolf had each taken on one of the other men, dragging them roughly from their horses onto the ground, rolling over and over as their victims tried desperately to fight off their attackers. Run Swiftly had chosen the big man for himself, and he flung himself wildly against his horse. Filled with hatred, he pulled the Dutchman to the ground as his beast reared up on its hind legs, petrified by the frenzied assault. The two men struggled back and forth, fighting ferociously, punching at one another as each endeavoured to overcome the other. Several times they broke apart and when they did, Dutch reached out, frantically clawing at the ground in an effort to retrieve the gun that had fallen from his grasp when Run Swiftly had first attacked. Both men were nearing exhaustion, their breath coming in painful gasps. Run Swiftly glared into the eyes of his despicable opponent… "You killed my sister," he breathed, "Now you pay… I kill you."

Dutch spat on the ground, his lips curled back in a menacing grin, he was strong, very strong, in fact Run Swiftly had never before encountered a more resilient opponent, but his anger, his determination to make this man pay for the dastardly crime he had committed, rose up within him, creating an upsurge of strength that was hitherto unknown to him. He leapt savagely towards the formidable hulk but Dutch threw him aside and scrambled yet again for his gun. This time he managed to grab it, as Run Swiftly found his knife lying nearby on the ground. He lunged with all the force he could muster and managed to thrust the blade deep into the enormous chest. Dutch roared in pain and swayed unsteadily to and fro, then just as his gun was about to slip from his hands, he pulled the trigger and sent a bullet clean through Run

Swiftly's left shoulder. Both men sank to the ground, their energy spent, their bloody injuries now the focus of their attention. Storm Cloud was beside Run Swiftly immediately, deeply concerned at his gunshot wound. He glanced at the big man but he was already dead. As he tried to raise Run Swiftly to his feet, there was a scuffling sound. Grey Wolf's opponent had mounted his horse and was affecting his escape through the woods. Run Swiftly urged Storm Cloud to make chase, he must prevent that lone survivor from reporting what had happened. Storm Cloud lost no time in jumping upon another horse and following fast on the heels of the escapee, determined to catch him and kill him.

Run Swiftly was in extreme pain, his wound pouring with blood. He knew that he must get away as quickly as possible. Dancing Bear and Grey Wolf were lying motionless, he could see they had been killed in the fighting. He checked all the other men, they too were dead. He must get back to the river, but his strength was fast failing from loss of blood, so with agonising effort he managed to pull himself up on to one of the abandoned horses. The exertion made him feel faint and he fell forward onto its neck as it carried him slowly through the woods, back to where the canoes were hidden. Sheer willpower kept him going just long enough to reach his canoe. He slid it from its hiding place, down into the water and crawled into it. He took the paddle in his right hand and pushed it against the bank to set himself afloat in the fast running stream that he knew would bear him back along its course towards the Delaware River.

His greatest concern was for Storm Cloud, as he collapsed tired and bleeding on the bottom of the small craft; concern for his friend's safety and wellbeing, but of that he needed to have no fear, for Storm Cloud encountered no difficulty whatsoever in catching up with the last of Dutch's men. He galloped alongside the runaway and skilfully unseated him from his horse. The man screamed in terror as the Indian pinned him to the ground and sat astraddle his body, his knife held high ready to strike.

"Don't kill me... please... don't kill me," he begged.

Storm Cloud paused for a moment. "You kill my wife... you cheat her, then you kill her."

"No... no... it wasn't me... I swear it wasn't me." The man's eyes were wide with fright. "It... it was Hetherington... he made us cheat you... he told us not to give so much to you Indians... It was Hetherington... it was... it was," he blubbered.

Storm Cloud could only see the beautiful face of Laughing Eyes as he thrust the knife deep into the last of her murderers. He savoured his moment of revenge, now his task was accomplished.

He threw the dead man face down across his horse, then took him to where Dutch and the others were lying. Remembering the warnings of Chief Running Deer and the Elders, that any action should be discreet to avoid military reprisals, he carefully removed the bodies of Dancing Bear and Grey Wolf and secured them onto two of the horses. Then he meticulously erased every sign that might indicate the presence of Indians. All this completed, he disappeared stealthily into the woods where he would remain safely hidden until nightfall.

As soon as it grew dark, Storm Cloud made his way slowly in the direction of the river, and when he came to where the canoes were hidden there was no sign of Run Swiftly. Only one canoe remained, and he could see where the other had been slid into the water. He hoped with all his heart that his wife's brother had managed to escape safely. Now he placed the bodies of Dancing Bear and Grey Wolf in the remaining canoe and began the sad, lonely journey back to his village.

*

"So you ain't seen Storm Cloud since he went achasin' after the last of them Indian agents then?" queried Minnie. Run Swiftly shook his head sadly. "D'you 'spose he catched him? 'Sposin' he didn't." Her eyes widened in wonderment.

Run Swiftly remained thoughtful for a few moments, then he turned his head and looked solemnly at her. He spoke convincingly, "Storm Cloud brave warrior... good warrior. He know he must kill the men who kill his wife. He catch coward who run away... sure... because spirits go with him, help him."

A smile of relief spread across Minnie's face, "Oh good," she said. She had every confidence in her Indian, it never entered her head for one moment that what he said might not be so. "I best git back to the house now," she said reluctantly, suddenly realising how long she had been away. "We is mighty busy 'cos we is expectin' guests. They be comin' from North Carolina. They be here almost any time now, but I'll bring you some food tonight, soon as everybody's gone to bed."

Run Swiftly watched her go and settled down to rest again. He needed to regain his strength, for he knew that he would soon have to leave.

Two

Tobias burst into the kitchen crying excitedly, "They is here… the guests is here… I seen the carriage come up the drive… they is here."

"Well jus' you git out and open the door to them," said his mother, flapping a kitchen towel at him.

Delilah then turned to Bella, "And you run up and tell the mistress… quick, you hear."

As the young girl started to climb the stairs, she met her mistress already on the way down. Celia could hear the excitement in the young girl's voice as she blurted out, "The guests is here ma'am… the guests is here."

"I know Bella, I know," came the kindly reply. "I heard the horses in the drive."

As Tobias pulled open the huge front door, it seemed suddenly as though the whole house had sprung to life. Celia looked anxiously towards the door as the new arrivals were escorted in. Her heart missed a beat as she caught sight of her son, closely watched by Grace, making his way towards her on his crutches. "Edmund… oh, Edmund," she breathed inaudibly.

"Mama," he replied hoarsely.

Their arms were about one another and their tears mingled as they clung together, sobbing with joy.

"Oh son, how I have missed you. I can't believe you're home at last. It is so good to see you."

"It's good to see you too Mama... I'm sorry I couldn't come sooner... "

His mother broke in, "I know my dear... I know... I understand." She pulled away and placed her hands on either side of his face. "Let me look at you... how you have changed." She looked into her son's eyes. She could see the sorrow in them, what he had suffered had changed him. "Everything will be alright now, I promise," she said reassuringly.

She turned to her sister-in-law, "My dear, dear Lilybee, it is good to see you. How are you?"

The two women hugged one another warmly for several seconds. "I'm very weary from all the travelling, but apart from that I am well, thank you," said Lilybee laughingly. "I had quite forgotten how far it was from 'White Lakes' to 'Fortune's Hand'."

Edmund was embracing Rosalind and Esther in turn. They had come running down the stairs, fast on their mother's heels, eager to greet the new arrivals.

"Where is Minnie?" asked Edmund, looking from one to the other of the servants who had congregated to witness the jubilations. Jassy hurried towards the kitchen, wondering whether Minnie might be there by now. She knew she had gone out into the grounds some time ago. Indeed she had noticed that Minnie seemed to be continually disappearing into the grounds of late. She could not understand it at all. She pushed open the kitchen door just as Minnie entered from the garden.

"Where's you bin gal... the guests is here," scolded Jassy, "... and Massa Edmund he askin' where you is."

Minnie's face lit up, "Massa Edmund... is he here... is he here at last?" she gasped as she sped across the kitchen and out into the hallway to meet him.

"So is your mammy... she come too," whispered Jassy kindly as Minnie brushed past her.

Minnie's footsteps faltered, her legs seemed suddenly to weaken. "My mammy?" she breathed incredulously.

As he caught sight of her, Edmund called excitedly, "Minnie... dear Minnie... come here." He held out his arms as she walked shyly towards him, then he pulled her close sighing happily.

She hugged him for several seconds, her warm tears dropping gently on his neck. "Welcome home Massa Edmund... welcome home," she said softly.

He half turned from her, looking for Grace as he did so. "Look who's here Minnie... see who has come with me." He beckoned the older woman towards them. "Come and meet your daughter Grace," he urged.

Grace had been mesmerised, watching the daughter she not seen for seventeen long years. She had been staring intently at her, sadly overwhelmed by the realisation that she would never have recognised her if the boy had not called her by name. The two women approached one another as though in a dream. They looked at one another in silence for several seconds, not knowing what to say. As Minnie gazed at the beautiful face before her, as she looked into the large sorrowful eyes, a smile of faint recognition slowly spread over her face, for although the woman before her looked more careworn than she remembered, and her hair was now turning to grey, she could not fail to remember those enormous, beautiful eyes. Now the faded memories of her childhood, so long submerged, gradually began to awaken in Minnie's mind. "Mammy?" she queried softly.

They were standing close, almost transfixed, then with a heartfelt sob Grace drew her daughter into her arms. "Oh my child... my child," she moaned softly.

Minnie too was overcome, she sobbed bitterly, unable to utter a word.

The greetings exchanged were both prolonged and heartfelt and the tears of joy flowed unchecked, but when they subsided, Celia called upon the servants to show Edmund and Lilybee to the rooms that had lovingly been prepared for them, so that they might refresh themselves before dinner. Grace and Minnie accompanied their mistresses upstairs to help them bathe and dress for the evening, happy in the knowledge that they would be able to spend precious time together later, whilst the family was dining. There was so much that they would talk about, so many questions to ask.

When they did finally return to the kitchen, it was to find the other servants frantically engaged in the last minute preparations for the special dinner that night. Even Massa Hetherington was to eat in the dining room with the family on the occasion of his son's homecoming, but they all knew this was purely for appearances' sake, because his sister was visiting. He had not been in when the guests arrived earlier but most certainly his presence had not been missed.

Once the family had gathered together to partake of their meal, Grace and Minnie joined the servants who were seated round the long kitchen table eating their food. As they ate, mother and daughter recounted details of their lives since their tragic parting, and bitter tears of regret were shed anew for the years spent so far removed; lost years that could never be regained. Minnie asked after Mose, and Grace told of how she had eventually come to marry him, and of their son Sunny Blue. Jassy and Joshua were just as fascinated as Minnie to hear all that had been happening during the years since they had left 'White Lakes'. Many were the questions they asked of family and friends whom they had left on the North Carolina plantation. Their voices became hushed when they learned of how Mose had been set free by the Lady Lilybee and of the circumstances in which he and Sunny Blue had been forced to run away to the North, away from their hated overseer, Ralph Clayton. They needed no reminding of the evil nature of that man.

So the evening was spent by both servants and family, all glad of the opportunity for pleasurable conversation and reminiscing; all that is with the exception of Gilbert Hetherington, who could not wait to take his leave. He rose from the table muttering that he had business problems requiring his attention in the study, but in actual fact he had received some irksome news that very afternoon, that his men had been found dead in the woods further up river. It would seem that they had been fighting among themselves, or so it was said by those who found the bodies, and it had certainly come as no surprise to the local inhabitants, who knew that Hetherington's roguish crew were notorious for their drunken brawling.

As soon as he could, the dissipated man slumped in his chair beside the fire, imbibing his favourite brandy. Behind the closed door of his study there was no longer a need for pretence. He was distraught at the loss of Dutch and his motley crew and wondered how he would manage without them. His affairs had certainly been going from bad to worse for longer than he cared to remember, but no matter, with his daughter on the brink of marriage to Henry Youngman, his fortune must change, of that he had no doubt. He drained down the last of his drink and made his way slowly upstairs.

*

The whole household appeared to be asleep. The lamps in the hallway had been turned down to a low flicker for the night, their dim glow barely penetrating the gloom, so when one of the bedroom doors suddenly opened to the side of him, it quite startled Gilbert Hetherington. He gasped and stumbled backwards as he caught sight of his sister's maid. She too was visibly shaken as she stepped quietly from the lighted room and almost collided with him. Recognition was instantaneous, and with a deep shudder she pressed herself against the wall and slid past him as quickly as she could. As the odour of his breath enveloped her, she felt a tight constriction in her throat; it was the same smell of drink that would always remind her of her vicious attackers. She fled along the hallway in terror. Despite the time that had elapsed since he was at 'White Lakes', Gilbert Hetherington did not fail to recognise who she was. In those few seconds before she closed the door behind her, as she stood silhouetted against the light, he saw her and recognised her immediately. Age had not yet robbed her of her exquisite beauty, and he was greatly affected by it. Before he had time to compose himself, she had disappeared into the shadows of the hallway and he heard a door closing at the other end of it, where the female servants slept.

He went to his room, his mind filled with the memories of her. He undressed and slipped on his robe. The shock of his encounter with her had aroused him, driven his sleepiness away. His lips parted in a lascivious smile; if he could not take his pleasure from her mother, then her daughter was his for the taking.

He crept along to Minnie's room and groped his way to her bed; she was not there. He was stunned... where could she be? Suddenly he became angry, determined to find her. He left the room and was about to make his way stealthily towards the stairs, when Minnie emerged from the top of them. He could barely see who it was, but as she came closer he recognised her form. "What are you doing... where have you been?" he growled menacingly.

Minnie almost jumped out of her skin with fright, her hand flew across her mouth to stifle the scream that was about to escape. She felt the powerful grip of her master's hand on her upper arm as he pulled her roughly into her bedroom and flung her towards the bed. She could not stop shaking and her teeth chattered uncontrollably. Suddenly he held her in his vice-like grip again, his hands squeezing her shoulders spitefully. He shook her vigorously and demanded again, "Where have you been eh... tell me... tell me?"

Minnie's mind was in a turmoil as she tried desperately to find some excuse to give him. "I ain't been nowhere massa," she sobbed. She could not tell him that less than an hour ago, Miss Rosalind had given her leave to slip out and take food to her Indian. Knowing of her concern for him, Rosalind had urged her maid to go down to the cabin just as soon as everyone had retired for the night. She had even unlocked the door and told Minnie that she would leave it on the latch for when she returned.

"Don't lie to me girl... now where have you been?"

Minnie could not speak, she was so overcome with fear. Suddenly a resounding slap to her face sent her reeling backwards. She fell against the bed and toppled onto it. Gilbert Hetherington hurled himself at her like a man possessed. "You will tell me... I'll know the truth, damn you."

He was no fool, he knew that she must have been out of doors or she would never have become so cold. He could still feel the chill of the night air on her clothing. He was suddenly filled with suspicion as he recalled several times of late, when he had come to her, he had noticed she was icy cold. The coldness of her firm young flesh had cooled him pleasantly after his excessive drinking had charged his blood; it had thrilled him even more than normal, he had found it strangely exhilarating. Now the explanation became crystal clear; of course she had been out of doors. He struck her again and again, his temper flaring out of control. She held her hands on either side of her head and raised her elbows to ward off his blows. She tried to curl herself up, but he tore at her clothing and forced her into submission. He was her master and she his unresisting victim, subdued by his continual abuse and completely oppressed by his tyranny.

*

When she went down to fetch her mistress's coffee first thing in the morning, Minnie was thankful that Jassy and Delilah were alone in the kitchen, for she felt deeply ashamed of her appearance. Jassy tut-tutted quietly and shook her head sadly. Minnie kept her head lowered as she prepared the exquisite silver tray and Jassy placed a sympathetic hand on her shoulder. She spoke not a word as the poor girl winced with pain, for she had witnesses the massa's cruel treatment of her so many times over the years. Minnie too remained silent. She finished preparing the tray and carried it up to her mistress's room.

Rosalind propped herself up on her pillows and reached for her coffee. She yawned sleepily, she still felt tired after all the excitement of the previous evening, but she had so enjoyed her brother's homecoming. She cast her eyes around the room to see what Minnie was doing. Her maid had fastened back the curtains and was now busily tidying the dressing table; anything to delay turning her face to her mistress. "Oh do come and sit by me Minnie," she pleaded. "I want to talk to you about Edmund. Leave that... come now... what do you think of him. Isn't it wonderful to have him home again?"

Minnie turned reluctantly and walked slowly towards the bed.

"Sit here... sit here," said Rosalind cheerfully. She patted the coverlet with her hand. Then she caught sight of Minnie's swollen face and her smile evaporated. "Oh no... no," she cried. She replaced her coffee on the tray with a clatter and threw back the bedclothes. She was on her feet in an instant, enfolding Minnie in her arms. "Why has he done this to you... why... what is it this time?" she moaned.

Minnie gave a deep shuddering sob and blurted out, "He waiting for me when I come back from the cabin last night... he knowed I bin out somewhere."

"Oh no, you didn't tell him anything, did you?"

Minnie shook her head resolutely, "I didn't say nothin'... I ain't gonna get my Indian killed."

"Oh, you poor thing... it must have been terrible for you. He is so cruel, so cruel." Rosalind's voice caught in her throat. She remembered her own suffering at her father's hands just a short time ago. "You must be careful Minnie... he mustn't catch you again."

"I knows Miss Rosalind, I knows."

Minnie performed her duties mechanically for the next hour or so, first dressing her mistress and then putting her room in order whilst she went down to breakfast. All the while she was preoccupied with thoughts of Run Swiftly, deeply concerned for his safety. It was becoming more and more difficult to keep his presence concealed; every day he remained put him in more danger. She could hardly bear the thought of his leaving 'Fortune's Hand' but she knew he must and very soon. How she wished that she might escape with him, for she knew now that she loved him and it would break her heart to see him go.

Eventually she realised that as much as she dreaded it, she could no longer delay her return to the kitchen; she could no longer hide what had happened from her mother. She wondered how many times she must endure the painful humiliation of her massa's attack. She swallowed hard and pushed open the kitchen door. Her mother was there, sitting at one end of the table, drinking coffee and talking confidentially with Jassy. Delilah was busy at the far end, preparing vegetables and noisily chopping them for use later in the day. She could not look at her mother, but she was overcome with emotion as she heard her cry out in anguish, then suddenly, she felt arms tenderly enfolding her, the loving, comforting arms of her mother, the arms she had longed for so many times over the past years. Grace held her close, stroking her head and speaking soothingly to her. She knew instinctively who had beaten her daughter; there was no need for her to ask.

"I knows who done this to you child," she whispered. As mother and daughter clung to one another, rocking to and fro, Jassy motioned Delilah to leave them alone together. She crept quietly from the kitchen with Delilah close behind her.

Grace urged Minnie to sit at the table while she fetched her daughter coffee, she was burdened down with grief at the thought that her daughter had been beaten by Gilbert Hetherington, but she was completely unaware of the full extent of his abuse. She refilled her own cup and sat opposite her daughter, gazing at her concernedly. "Why did he beat you Minnie?" she asked simply. She was loth to distress her daughter with her questioning, but she must know why, how he could do such a thing.

"He always beat me... he just like beating me." Minnie gulped at her coffee.

Grace was aghast, her worst fears beginning to materialize. She leant forward, "You tellin' me he beat you before... when?" She could not bear to hear the confirmation of her fears.

Minnie's face contorted in loathing. "He beat me when he come to my room in the night, after everybody goes to sleep."

Grace found it difficult to comprehend the vileness of what Minnie was telling her, she felt nauseated. Surely she had misunderstood, but no, deep within her she knew he was capable of anything. "He come to your room at night?" she whispered disbelievingly.

"Whenever he in the house... after everyone gone to bed... ever since I was small girl."

Grace could sense Minnie's shame. She banged her clenched fists on the table and stood up. She paced back and forth along the kitchen, holding her head between her hands. She wanted to scream her vengeance, she could hardly control herself. For almost all her life she had hated and despised Gilbert Hetherington for what he had done to her, for his violation of her when she was a young girl and then for his inhumanity in stealing Minnie from her at such a tender age, but to learn that her daughter had been subjected to his vileness continually, was completely intolerable. She wanted to kill him; she wanted to rid the world of his evil. Her eyes fell upon the hard steel blade of the knife that lay where Delilah had been preparing vegetables; she noticed its razor-sharp edge, its vicious point. In that instant she knew what she had to do. "How could he... how could he," she was muttering uncontrollably, "Knowing you his own daughter?"

Now it was Minnie's turn to believe that she had misunderstood her mother's words. Her stomach churned. "What you say Mammy... What you say?" Her eyes were wide with horror.

Grace returned to the table and stood facing Minnie across it. "You his daughter child... I wish you wasn't, but you is." She collapsed heavily onto the chair.

Minnie was dumbstruck for several seconds, trying to come to terms with what she had been told, then she began to shake her head disbelievingly from side to side, again and again without stopping. "No... no... he ain't my pappy, he ain't. Mose is my pappy, not him... not him."

Suddenly there was a noise at the kitchen door. The two women turned abruptly to see Edmund standing there. It was obvious from his expression that he had heard every word they had said.

"The door was open as I was passing by," he mumbled apologetically. Unbeknown to Grace and Minnie, Delilah had accidentally left it ajar in her hurry to leave the kitchen. Edmund's crutches clattered against it as he hobbled awkwardly into the room, and he closed it firmly behind him. "I didn't mean to pry... I couldn't help overhearing... please forgive me." He joined Minnie at the table.

"Let me git you a cup of coffee Master Edmund," Grace said quietly, glad of something to do to alleviate her embarrassment. She moved quickly to the stove to fetch the coffee pot.

Minnie felt she wanted to die; she sat completely motionless, her head bowed, her hands covering her face. She could sense Edmund sitting beside her, but she could not look at him. How would she ever be able to look him in the face again? Of a sudden she had realised they were half-brother and sister and she was unable to cope with the thought of how that knowledge would affect him. A deep, shuddering sob welled up within her and she wept pitifully.

Edmund laid his hand gently on her arm. "Don't Minnie... please don't," he whispered kindly. "I know what you must be feeling, believe me. I would give anything not to have that despicable man for my father. He is the most loathsome, vile creature. I have always hated him for the way in which he treated my mother and my sisters... but now this." He shook his head in disbelief. "He is beneath contempt."

Grace placed the cup of steaming coffee on the table before him and looked at her daughter helplessly. "Ain't no one can choose their own father... we all has to learn to live with that. Now, bad as it is, you jus' try not to think about it... don't let him do you no more harm than he already done."

Her daughter continued to weep. "Minnie... you hear me child... please... please?"

Minnie simply could not bring herself to accept that the man she had feared and hated so vehemently, for so many years, was indeed her father. She could not, and would not accept it. She raised her head slowly and gathered up her apron to wipe her tear-stained face. With sorrowful eyes she looked at her mother, "I always knowed that Mose my pappy, 'cos you told me I named for his mammy." She felt confused as she went on, "I knowed he must be my pappy because of that."

Grace shook her head sadly, "No honey-chile, he ain't... I wish he was, but he ain't."

"Why you name me for his mammy then?"

"'Cos he take care of me ever since I come to 'White Lakes'... he like a pappy to me from the first day I come there... I was just a child and he so good and kind to me. Then, when I had you, I wanted to do somethin' special for him, show him how much I loved him for takin' care of me... for bein' so good to me... that was the only thing I could think of doin' for him." She paused thoughtfully, "But then, when I growed up some, I could see what kinda man he was... ain't too many men like him, no sir, there ain't... and I jus' loved him in a different way then, loved him way a woman should love a man like Mose."

Edmund was nodding his head in agreement. "You're right Grace, there aren't many men like Mose. He is a fine man, very fine indeed. I owe my life to him... but for his courage and loyalty I should have perished along with the thousands of others in that dreadful war. I think of him often... wonder how he is... where he is now. May God keep him safe and well."

"Amen," said Grace softly.

Edmund reached for his crutches and stood up to go. He was murmuring, almost as if talking to himself. "Mose and my father... what a comparison... good versus evil. It cannot go on... it mustn't be allowed to go on."

Just as he reached the door it was opened by Jassy, closely followed by Delilah and his sister. "Oh there you are Edmund... I have been looking everywhere for you," she said cheerfully, "Come with me now, come and talk with me."

As he joined her, she leaned towards him and whispered conspiratorially, "I have so much to tell you."

She led him slowly towards the library, where she knew they would not be disturbed, for she had seen her father leave the house just a short time before. She closed the door behind them and helped Edmund into one of the comfortable chairs beside the fire. She seated herself opposite him and sighed deeply, clasping her hands together against her chest. Her voice full of woe, she gasped, "Oh, Edmund, I have such a lot to tell you... there is so much, I hardly know where to begin...
"

"Before you do Roz, there is something I must tell you." His sister raised her eyebrows in surprise. "It is something I think you should know... it cannot wait."

His face was grave and Rosalind could see that he was deeply troubled. Her curiosity was aroused. "What is it... tell me... tell me?"

Edmund's eyes were cast down, he could not look at his sister as he spoke. "I overheard something dreadful Roz, really dreadful. I didn't mean to overhear it but I was just passing the kitchen and the door was open." He paused and swallowed hard.

"Yes... what was it... what did you hear?" His sister was becoming more and more intrigued.

"It was Grace and Minnie talking... in the kitchen." He bit his lip and shook his head disbelievingly. "I didn't mean to overhear." He was finding it far more difficult to repeat what he had heard than he could have imagined.

"Yes... go on, what were they saying?"

"Well, Grace was telling Minnie that her father," he paused again, "Er... umm... well... our father is Minnie's father Roz... can you believe that?"

Rosalind was dumbstruck for several seconds, trying to make sense of what her brother was saying. The silence seemed interminable to Edmund. He glanced up at his sister, wondering what her reaction would be.

"How can he be her father?" she asked incredulously.

Edmund shrugged his shoulders, "Maybe he went to 'White Lakes' when he was a young man... I don't know. Grace has never been to the North before... she told me so when we were preparing for our visit here. Papa must have gone down to North Carolina... that is the only explanation, isn't it?"

Rosalind's hands flew to her face, "Oh, how dreadful," she moaned. "I can't believe it, really I can't... he is a monster."

"And did you know how he treats Minnie?" Edmund stopped short, too ashamed to say another word.

Rosalind simply nodded her head; her eyes were full of tears. Never a word had been spoken of her father's maltreatment of her servant, but she had been aware of it for many, many years. "What are we to do Edmund... things seem to be going from bad to worse?" She became quiet, wondering how one man could cause so much misery.

"He seems intent upon ruining all our lives... first you..." The words made her choke, she jumped up from her chair and fell to her knees before Edmund. With a sob in her voice she went on, "How could he send you into that terrible, terrible war? You were no more than a child... it broke Mama's heart. Now look at you... he has ruined your life. She took hold of her brother's hands and looked at him intently, "... and now he wants to ruin mine by forcing me to marry that horrid old man, whom I despise. He is wicked... everyone hates him, dear Mama, the servants, even Aunt Lilybee. Mama has told me that even his own sister cannot tolerate him. That is why Mama thinks that Aunt Lilybee will help me to escape with Benjamin."

Rosalind was breathless with anxiety as she spoke. "Mama thinks that Aunt Lilybee will allow us to go down to North Carolina with her."

Edmund was completely taken aback. "You escape... what do you mean... and who is Benjamin?"

"That is what I was about to tell you, Edmund; you have no idea what has been happening here since you went away."

Rosalind began to relate everything that had taken place. "This is the whole story dear brother," she said, "I shall leave aside no detail. As you know, Papa would have me marry Henry Youngman. For some obscure reason he has made an agreement that I should marry that vile old man. He has spoken of it for a very long time, but I never believed that he would force me into it. Since I was a child, I always detested

Mr Youngman… he is lecherous… unbearable… I could never marry him, never." She shuddered in disgust. Then her expression changed as she went on to tell of how she had first met Benjamin Richmond, who he was and how they had come to love one another. She told of her father's rage when he had discovered them together, and of how he had insisted upon preparations being made for her marriage to Henry Youngman. "Now do you understand why I must run away? Mama has tried to reason with Papa, pleaded with him to change his mind, but he will have none of it. You know how violent he can be if anyone dares to oppose him. Aunt Lilybee is our only hope… there is no alternative, is there?"

Her brother did not reply, his mind was in a turmoil. Rosalind was right; he did know how violent his father could be, for he too had suffered miserably at his hands. He sat brooding, his mother's face swimming before his eyes, as it had done so many times over the last few years. He could hear her voice once again, pent with emotion, pleading with his father not to send their only son to war. Suddenly he clamped his hands over his ears to close out the sounds that haunted him, he closed his eyes tightly against the sounds that constantly tormented him, that would probably torment him for the rest of his life. "No, No," he screamed in anguish. His limbs began to tremble and his body shook uncontrollably.

Rosalind was terrified, she gasped as she leapt to her feet, not knowing what was ailing her brother. She stumbled away from him, afraid, "Oh Edmund… Edmund… what is it," she moaned. She was clutching nervously at her skirt, too frightened to touch the strangely contorted figure before her. "Oh dear… oh dear… I'll fetch Mama."

She fled from the room, calling hysterically, "Mama… Mama… come quickly, it's Edmund. Oh, Mama, quickly."

Before she knew it her mother was there with Aunt Lilybee and several of the servants, who had responded immediately to her frantic call. Grace and Lilybee took charge instantly, being fully experienced with Edmund's attacks. They remained completely calm and Lilybee pressed her forefinger to her lips as she glanced around at those who had gathered, urging them to stay composed. She raised her hand reassuringly to his mother, whom she could see was greatly distressed. Then, while Grace enfolded Edmund in her arms to still his tremors, Lilybee spoke quietly, soothing and comforting him. Once the shaking began to subside, she beckoned to Kingston and Harvest and together the two manservants lifted him gently and carried him upstairs to his room.

As soon as he was comfortably settled in his bed, with Grace keeping a watchful eye on him, Lilybee drew his mother from the room. She closed the door quietly behind them and turned to Celia. "I know how alarmed you must feel my dear, but this is exactly what I was trying to warn you of. Edmund suffers from these attacks from time to time, especially if he becomes agitated or upset. I very much feared that something like this could happen... he has to be treated with utmost care. I hope and pray that his father will do nothing to upset him, poor boy. He really needs constant support and a great deal of patience and love if he is to make any kind of recovery."

Celia gazed at her sister-in-law disconsolately. She shook her head and said sadly, "As you are fully aware, Lilybee, there is no chance of him ever receiving any love or support from his father... none whatsoever, but of one thing I am determined, I shall no longer stand by and watch that evil man destroy their lives. They have suffered enough; we all have, and now the time has come to put an end to his tyranny... and that is what I shall do... may Gold help me... that is what I shall do."

Lilybee placed her arm around Celia comfortingly, "You know, my dear, I would do anything within my power to help you… anything at all." She could see how badly her sister-in-law had been affected by her husband's cruelty to their children; how the years of suffering and torment had taken their toll. "It is not difficult to imagine what all of you must have suffered over the years, for I am sure that he has changed not one little bit. He was intolerable as a child and he became even more so as he grew into manhood. I fear that he will never be any different… never… never. Now do try not to fret too much… we shall talk more of this later. You just leave Edmund to me for the time being, for I have grown accustomed to his attacks."

"Are you sure there is nothing I can do to help?" asked Celia concernedly.

"Not a thing my dear… Grace will do what is necessary, she is extremely capable and we shall have Edmund much improved in no time at all."

Celia left reluctantly and made her way downstairs once again.

*

The mood throughout the household that day was one of gloom. The sight of her son in such a pitiful state was the final straw for Celia. She could endure no more. Even though she had had a long discussion with Lilybee earlier in the day, and despite the fact that her dear sister-in-law had agreed to take Rosalind and Benjamin Richmond down to 'White Lakes' with her, where they would be safe, she realised with utter despair that Edmund and Esther would still be at their father's mercy. For their sakes alone she must act, and act now… she had pondered the problem long enough, so now she must solve it once and for all.

Three

As darkness fell, Celia became aware that her husband had returned home; he had been away all day. She could hear him downstairs shouting to one of the manservants. It would seem that he was calling for the brandy in his study to be replenished. She was relaxing in her bedroom working on her embroidery. She suddenly leant back wearily in her chair and closed her eyes, drawing her breath in through her teeth; the mere sound of his voice jarred her nerves. Her hand dropped on to her lap, still holding the fine muslin cloth on which she was working. She felt the scissors resting in the folds of her skirt and her back stiffened. She sat bolt upright and leaned towards her workbox at the side of her chair. It was a large ornate, polished wood box on four legs and it was filled with everything a lady might need for her handiwork. Celia rummaged in its depths and found a large pair of shears, the ones she used for the cutting of cloth. They were of strong steel with very long, sharp blades. She held them dagger-like and studied them for several seconds, then she took up the small pair of scissors that were lying in her lap, replaced them, together with her embroidery, in the box and closed its lid very slowly.

Downstairs, Gilbert Hetherington was becoming impatient as he waited in his study for Amos to bring his bottles of brandy from the cellar. He paced to and fro, wondering what on earth was keeping him so long. He was already irritated because he had had to remind the man that there was no more brandy in his cabinet. He strode over to the door and opened it, meaning to chide his servant for taking so long, but as he did so he heard his daughter's voice quite distinctly coming from further along the hallway.

"Oh, Amos… have you seen Minnie? I'll need to dress for dinner soon."

"She jus' gone out, Miss Rosalind," came the reply. "I seen her jus' a minute ago… she gone out in the grounds."

"Well, when she returns, will you send her up to my room Amos?"

"I sho will Miss Rosalind… I sho will."

That was enough for Gilbert Hetherington, he could not imagine what would induce Minnie to go out into the grounds so late in the day. He must satisfy his curiosity; he desperately needed to know what she was up to. His daughter was now on her way upstairs, so he wasted no time in setting off after the young servant girl. She must not get too far away, or he would lose sight of her. In his haste he almost collided with Amos and the brandy bottles. "Out of my way," he said angrily, as he pushed him aside.

Once out of doors, he stood for a few seconds, allowing his eyes to become adjusted to the darkness. He shivered a little in the chill night air. He thought he heard something… a sharp sound, not too far distant. Yes, there it was again… twigs breaking underfoot. He peered in the direction of the sound; then he caught sight of her darkened shape between the trees, hurrying down towards the river. He too began to hurry, following at a distance, taking care not to be seen. He was deeply intrigued, wondering where she might be going and for what purpose.

As Minnie came to the cabin, she was surprised to see that the door was slightly ajar. She approached cautiously and pushed it open, calling softly, "Run Swiftly… is you there…

Run Swiftly?" She stepped inside and found to her dismay he had gone. A deep sadness welled up inside her and she moaned pitifully, "Oh no... no... " She stepped from the cabin and closed the door, wondering if she should venture along the bank of the river to where the canoe had been concealed. Suddenly she heard a sound. She leaned forward, straining her eyes to see through the shadow of the trees. Her heart began to pound at the thought that Run Swiftly might not have left yet. Then again, through the stillness, she heard it; crack, crack. She could sense someone behind her.

She spun around as Gilbert Hetherington caught her arm in a vice-like grip. He pulled her close and growled, "So this is it... this is your guilty secret, eh?"

Minnie cried out as his fingers dug into her bruised flesh, still painfully tender from his previous beating. He twisted her arm spitefully, demanding, "Who is it you are so anxious to see... tell me... who is it?"

Before the terrified girl had a chance to speak, another figure stepped silently from the shadows. Her eyes grew wide with alarm as she saw the raised arm brandishing a weapon; watched in horror as it plunged, with lightning speed, into the back of her attacker. He screamed in agony as he staggered unsteadily back and forth, his hand clawing desperately at his back in a futile attempt to withdraw the cold steel that was buried deep between his shoulder blades. Minnie was paralysed with fear, unable to move. She could not bring herself to assist her hateful master as he writhed in pain and stumbled blindly through the undergrowth, finally falling headlong down the bank. She heard the loud splash as his body hit the water, heard him spluttering and gasping for breath in his brief struggle... then silence... a chilling eerie silence.

Minnie stood alone in the darkness, she wanted to run but she could not move, neither could she believe what she had just witnessed. Her body started to shake, her teeth chattered uncontrollably, Then, without warning, she felt a body pressed close to her own and she heard the familiar voice of Run Swiftly whispering in her ear. He was beside her, his arm pulling her close to reassure and comfort her. She turned to him and flung her arms around him, sobbing; "I thought you gone... without saying goodbye... I thought you gone." She buried her face in his neck and he waited until she had stopped shaking.

"Run Swiftly not go... wait here for you... say thank you for saving life. Now I go, not safe here... "

Minnie broke in, "I knows... I knows... I jus' comin' to tell you it not safe anymore. Massa follow me here... now... now he... " She could not finish what she was about to say. Instead she took a deep, shuddering breath and went on, "I don' want you to go but I knows you must." She felt her heart would surely break. "Will I ever see you again, Indian?" she asked quietly.

Run Swiftly nodded his head twice. "When this good," he touched his injured arm, "I come... take you my people. They see woman who save my life... brave woman... my woman." Minnie was touched by the sincerity of his words. "You want be woman of Run Swiftly?" he asked solemnly.

"Yes... oh yes. I'll be here when you come. I'll wait for you... I promise."

Run Swiftly took her hand and pressed it to his chest, then he turned and disappeared towards the river as silently as he had come.

Minnie called after him, "Be careful... be careful Indian." Then she bowed her head and prayed that God would keep him safe.

For how long she stood there, she did not know, but a voice in the distance caught her attention. She felt vague, in somewhat of a dream-like state, in fact she almost felt that she was dreaming. Certainly the events that day seemed completely unreal to Minnie. When the voice called again, she turned and made her way slowly towards it. As she came nearer, she could see small lights flickering, moving to and fro, she could hear voices... several voices... people talking to one another urgently. Then loudly though the darkness, the call came again, long and drawn out. "ED... mun... d... Ed... mun... d where a... re you... Ed... mun... d?"

Suddenly there was a slight movement to her right, accompanied by a muffled sound. She stopped and looked more closely. She could make out a darkened shape moving along the ground; an awkward shape, dragging itself slowly through the undergrowth. Minnie threw her head back and screamed in terror... the scream went on and on, it came in wave after wave, she could not stop it. She had suffered far too many shocks for one day, now she simply lost all control. She was still screaming when her mother gathered her into her arms, holding her tightly, urging her to stop. She cajoled and soothed her as she led her back to the house.

*

Kingston and Harvest were carrying Edmund, whilst his mother and aunt talked earnestly to each other, trying to piece together what had happened. "I can't understand it... Grace left him only briefly, for just the shortest time," Lilybee said apologetically. "He was sleeping peacefully, so she was sure that it was perfectly safe to leave him... Oh dear, oh dear... it is so dreadful. Then when she returned to his room, she found he was gone."

"Well, we have found him now, thank God, so don't fret yourself," said Celia, "But I wish I knew how he found his way out here in the dark. Whatever possessed him to come out here alone?" She was deeply concerned.

"You know, my dear, he has such terrible nightmares during these attacks… he seems to believe he is back on the battlefield, poor boy. He is not at all aware of his surroundings, it is most distressing to hear him. He relives all the horrors of the war, over and over again. There is no knowing what was going through his mind when he left the house… I doubt if we will ever know; and even more surprising is that he managed to get out without anyone seeing him. It is almost beyond belief."

Celia remained thoughtful for quite a while, then she murmured, "I wish we knew what caused his attack in the first place… something or someone must have upset him."

*

Everything was in utter chaos that night at 'Fortune's Hand' and Delilah could be heard complaining bitterly, "Ain't nobody wants to eat after all this upset… what I gonna do with all the food we cooked Clarissa?" She tut-tutted, "And the massa… he ain't back yet. Amos said he went rushing off not long after he come home."

Amos nodded in confirmation. "Yessir… the massa he in a mighty hurry to git some place. I almost dropped the brandy bottles I was acarryin'… one minute he shoutin' for his drink… next he goin' off some place like the devil was after him."

It was difficult for the servants to make sense of what had been happening throughout the evening, and while they were talking, Grace came into the kitchen. She sat down at the table, sighing wearily, "I jus' put Minnie to bed."

"How is she Grace… is she any better?"

Grace looked at Jassy sadly, "I don' know, she ain't said nothin'."

"Aw, she jus' need to git some rest... she feel better in the mornin'... I guess we all will. This sho bin a bad night, I be glad when it over."

*

Despite Jassy's optimism, the following day saw no improvement as far as Minnie was concerned. She remained completely withdrawn, saying not a word to anyone. Grace was distraught and tried several times to coax her daughter into some kind of response. She felt that she was wholly to blame for so thoughtlessly disclosing her father's identity. How she wished that she had kept the sordid truth concealed.

As for Rosalind, she too attributed Minnie's strange quiet to embarrassment at discovering who her father was. In fact, she was experiencing considerable difficultly herself and had no wish to discuss the matter with her maid. She found the knowledge deeply offensive and as much as she loved Minnie, as much as she had adored her for as long as she could remember, she had no desire for it to become known that they were half-sisters.

Four

It was a further two days before Gilbert Hetherington's body was discovered. Two young boys found it floating in the river between Asbury and Bloomsbury. News of the gruesome discovery spread like wildfire throughout the area. Rumours abounded as to how he had met his demise, but his loss to the community was certainly not a cause for concern. The inhabitants of Asbury were questioned at great length to determine whether anyone had seen anything suspicious, or again, whether they had heard anything that might arouse suspicion, but to no avail. An examination of the body revealed that he had been attacked, stabbed in the back presumably, then his body carried along the river by the rapid current. It might well have been washed out into the Delaware had it not become entangled in the dross that was cluttering the riverbank.

Apart from the continual gossip among the townsfolk, urgent discussions took place in the kitchen at 'Fortune's Hand'. All the servants had frightening suspicions, but could not voice them. They carefully avoided mentioning what they dreaded may have happened. Finally Maybelle's daughter, Bella, blurted out, "S'posin' it was Master Edmund done it... he was out in the grounds all alone, with blood all over him... and Delilah said her knife was gone missin'."

Delilah almost dropped the coffee pot she was about to replace on the stove. Jassy broke the shocked silence, "Now you jus' hush child... there ain't no sense in you spreadin' them kind of rumours," she said sharply. "Besides… Delilah got her knife back agin' now… jus' as likely it wasn't missing in the first place."

"It sho was… I knows if my knife is missin' or not."

At the mention of the knife, Grace slipped quickly from the kitchen, before anyone noticed the guilty look on her face, although she was certain that no one had seen her replace it early that morning. She had wanted Gilbert Hetherington dead for so long that her sense of relief was overwhelming. Strange, she thought, how nobody had expressed one word of sorrow over his death and the only sorrow she felt was that she had been robbed of the opportunity herself, of putting to death the man who had caused so much pain and anguish, not only to her, but to her beloved daughter. She tried to fathom out who could have killed him. She knew that suspicion had fallen not only on Master Edmund but also on Minnie. Why, she wondered, would she not say what she had been doing out of the house that night. Amos had seen her leave, then the master not long afterwards. Grace's mind was racing, she could not, she simply would not believe that her daughter was capable of killing anyone… not even a man like Gilbert Hetherington. Beside there had been no blood on her clothing… not like Master Edmund's. She had had to remove his things and cleanse him when he had been carried into the house. Surely it was not Edmund… the blood could have come from the cuts he had to his hands and arms. He had been found crawling through the undergrowth, so his injuries might have been caused in that way. Grace found it difficult to believe he could have killed his own father… it was just not possible. She knew what the servants were whispering, but she also knew that they would never condemn her daughter… not after all the years of abuse she had suffered. Neither would they point an accusing finger at Master Edmund, for they loved and respected him too much. Of one thing she was certain, Minnie had witnessed something horrifying that night... she must have seen what happened. Why else would she have been in such a state of shock? Who had she seen? If it wasn't Master Edmund, then who was it? Maybe she would never tell a living soul, but no matter, as far as Grace was concerned, justice had been done and she would always be deeply grateful to whoever the murderer might be.

*

Upstairs in her room, Celia sat pondering over her husband's death, but she knew without a shadow of doubt that her son could not possibly have killed his father. She sat staring into her workbox, which stood with its lid open beside her chair. She was still staring into it, deep in thought, when Rosalind came in to see her. "I have just received this note from Yoonie, Mama," she said, "They have their notification of Papa's funeral... they will all be there, but she is calling on us this afternoon... with her father."

Her mother made no response. She lifted her hand to her forehead and ran her fingers back and forth across it, completely preoccupied with her own thoughts.

"Mama, what is it... what is the matter?" Her daughter suddenly became concerned. She placed her arm around her shoulders and shook her gently. "What is it Mama?" she asked again.

Her mother took a long breath, "Your father... I... I... am responsible for his death." She covered her face with her hand.

"Oh no... no... oh, Mama... how... what happened?"

"I... don't know... I wanted him dead. More than anything I wanted him dead." She paused, going over in her mind what she had done on that dreadful night. She was having difficulty in recalling the exact sequence of events.

Rosalind was dumbfounded, she had fallen to her knees beside her mother and now she remained completely silent, listening intently.

Her mother went on haltingly, murmuring to herself, "My shears... I took my shears... I went downstairs... down to his study, but he had gone. I heard him shouting at the servants, so I knew he had come home... but when I went to his study he was not there."

She stopped again and sat clasping and unclasping her hands nervously, desperately trying to remember what had happened after that. Her daughter asked gently "What then Mama... did you go to find him?"

"I can't remember... " She began to sob, "I wanted him dead."

Rosalind was deeply moved by her mother's distress. She did not know how to alleviate it. "You stay here Mama. I'll fetch Aunt Lilybee."

The girl fled from the room and went in search of her aunt. She found her resting in her room and blurted out what her mother had just told her.

Lilybee was as shocked as her niece had been at the startling news. She sat and thought for several seconds, then her brow creased in puzzlement. "But your mother was in the study alone when Grace was running around searching for Edmund, and according to her, Amos had just seen your father leaving the house a few minutes earlier. In fact, Amos appears to have been the last person who saw him alive. All the servants have been questioned... your mother could not possibly have left the house until she came with me to look for Edmund outside."

Lilybee rose and beckoned Rosalind to accompany her back to her mother's room. Celia had not moved, she was still sitting in her chair, just as her daughter had left her. "My dear, my dear... what is this you have been saying?" Lilybee asked kindly. "What makes you think you are responsible for Gilbert's death?"

Celia raised sorrowful eyes to her sister-in-law, "I wanted to kill him... I went to find him. I wanted him dead."

"Ha," scoffed Lilybee, "Just because you wanted him dead, as I imagine, did a good many more, it does not mean that you are responsible for his death, does it?"

"But, don't you see... I wished him dead and now he is dead... don't you see? Oh, I am so confused." Celia covered her face with her hands and shook her head slowly from side to side.

"Now listen to me Celia... Gilbert had more enemies than anyone I have ever known... you must realise that and you were certainly not the only one who wished him dead. You cannot blame yourself, it is utter nonsense and I shall hear no more of it. Besides he was killed somewhere near the river, so it seems, therefore you could not possibly be responsible... you had not left the house when I came to fetch you from the study."

Celia stared at her sister-in-law disbelievingly. Lilybee took hold of her hands, "Don't you remember how concerned you were when I told you Edmund was missing? Can't you remember how frantically we searched the grounds for him? Come, come... what on earth has possessed you to blame yourself? Don't you see that you could not possibly have killed Gilbert? Now, please... pull yourself together."

She drew Celia to her feet, and placing an arm around her shoulders, led her towards the door. "It has all been too much for you my dear... let us go down to the drawing room. It does you no good at all to sit here brooding by yourself. Perhaps Rosalind will ask one of the servants to fetch us some coffee will you dear?" She smiled sweetly at her niece.

"Of course Aunt... of course." The young girl skipped down the stairs, greatly relieved that, thanks to her aunt, the suspicion surrounding her mother had been removed.

*

Later that day, Mr Henry Youngman and his daughter, Eunice, were dutifully shown into the drawing room by Tobias, where Celia, Lilybee and Rosalind were the very picture of decorum, attired in mourning dresses and waiting to receive their callers. It was Lilybee's first encounter with this gentleman, and it took her no time at all to establish why her sister-in-law had been so vehement in her objection to him as a suitor for Rosalind, for she too found him utterly loathsome. For a start it was obvious that God had not seen fit to bless him with a very modicum of good looks, but what Lilybee found even more distasteful, was the sight of his ill-fitting artificial teeth, which seemed to be persistently on the move, entirely of their own volition.

After an initial introduction, it fell to Lilybee to converse with him for the most part, because, as she politely pointed out, her sister-in-law was still somewhat in a state of shock at the nature of her husband's death. "Perfectly understandable, to be sure," murmured Mr Youngman, "It has come as a shock to us all, indeed it has."

When Lilybee rang for tea, Rosalind begged that she and her friend, Eunice, be allowed to leave the room, so that they might talk particularly to one another. Her aunt excused them immediately, "Certainly you may go... I know how much you young girls enjoy an intimate chat," she said.

Once tea had been served, Henry Youngman could not resist the urge to lead the conversation around to his forthcoming marriage. "Of course, I expect the arrangements will have to be delayed for a short while... er... due to the funeral... is that not so?" he queried, "But as you will appreciate, I am anxious for it to take place at the very earliest that you feel would be fitting."

Lilybee did not answer immediately; instead she lifted her cup to her lips and sipped its contents demurely, at the same time casting a critical eye in Henry Youngman's direction. He shifted in his chair uncomfortably. She looked at him steadily as she replaced her cup in the saucer and daintily dabbed at the corners of her mouth with her serviette. Finally she spoke. "Mr Youngman, I hardly think this is an appropriate time or place to be discussing plans for a wedding, but as you have broached the subject yourself, then I feel duty bound to advise you that you should put any such thoughts from your mind. In fact I feel that you would be well advised never to mention the matter again."

Henry Youngman was visibly taken aback, his mouth dropped open, causing his teeth to dislodge yet again. His face suffused with colour as he stammered, "I... I... er... don't understand... "

"To put it bluntly sir, my niece will not be marrying you... she has no desire to marry you... not now, not ever."

"But... we had an understanding... your brother and I. We struck a bargain. I have made preparations... Rosalind has been promised to me... "

"No... no... never," shrieked Celia.

Lilybee was beside her in an instant, consolingly she placed a hand on her sister-in-law's shoulder. "Mr Youngman," she said emphatically, "There can be no further discussion on this matter. What my brother arranged with you, I neither know nor care… it is of no consequence whatsoever. Do you understand? You have been told that there will be no marriage between my niece and yourself, so let there be an end to it."

She could not resist adding, "I cannot possibly imagine how you could conceive of it in the first place, for she is but the same age as your own daughter. Now… if you will excuse us, we have funeral arrangements to attend to."

Henry Youngman had already risen to his feet before Lilybee summoned Tobias to show him out. He bowed his head deferentially and left hurriedly, not bothering to wait for his daughter, for he was completely overcome with embarrassment and felt an urgent need to escape as quickly as possible. In fact, he was not a little shocked that a lady, of her obvious refinement, was capable of delivering such a stinging rebuff.

As for Lilybee, she pressed her hands to her burning cheeks and took an enormous breath once the door had closed behind their departing guest. She too was finding it difficult to believe that she had been so outspoken to a comparative stranger… but she regretted not one word of what she had said, for she found him the most repellent of men. She smile jubilantly, "There, my dear," she said to Celia, "At least you no longer have need to fear for Rosalind's future happiness. She is now free to make a marriage of her own choosing. Is that not what you have always wished for her?"

Celia's gratitude was evident as she looked at her sister-in-law, "Yes, oh yes. That is all I ever wanted for her. I could not bear the thought of her suffering the same miserable fate that I have. Thank God all our months of despair are now over."

*

145

The mystery surrounding the death of Gilbert Hetherington still remained unsolved a week after the discovery of his body. It was that fact alone which prompted so many of the Asbury townsfolk to turn out and watch his funeral procession as it made its way slowly from 'Fortunes Hand' across the bridge and along Main Street, to the Methodist church. Only one person held the answer to the innumerable questions that were still being asked, but although she knew exactly where and how he had been killed, she had no intention of divulging the truth. Since Run Swiftly had left, Minnie had scarcely spoken. For that matter, most of what had been said at 'Fortune's hand' had been in subdued tones, both among the servants as well as the family. Now it was hoped that as soon as the master of the house had been laid to rest, then life would again take on some semblance of normality.

*

The service and burial were not unduly elaborate and those who attended did so more from sympathy and respect for his widow than for the deceased. Beside the immediate family, with the exception of Grace and Minnie, who had volunteered to watch over Edmund and Esther, all the Youngmans were present. Only their father had stayed away on the pretext that he was not at all well that day, much to the relief of Lilybee, Celia and Rosalind, but to Rosalind's great delight his nephew, Benjamin Richmond, had decided to attend in his stead. He had been one of the first to send his condolences, in addition to his other more personal messages, via Eunice. Now there would be no longer any need for surreptitious communication; he would be welcome to visit 'Fortune's Hand' as often as he wished.

*

After the funeral, everyone returned to the house to partake of the luncheon that had been prepared early that morning by Delilah and Maybelle, but as soon as the meal was over, as so often happened on such occasions, the younger ones began to drift away, leaving their elders to their sombre discussions. Eunice and Benjamin tactfully ushered the Youngman children from the dining room, to afford the adults some peace and quiet. Rosalind joined them, eager to spend some time with Benjamin after their long enforced separation. Just as soon as they had all entered the library and closed the door, Benjamin clasped Rosalind's hands and whispered, "Oh, how I have missed you Roz... you will never know how much. It has been so difficult to stay away these past weeks."

"I have missed you too, Ben, but now it is over, you are free to come and go as often as you please... isn't that wonderful?"

They gazed at one another rapturously. Eunice, who had overheard Rosalind's remark, came towards them and asked mischievously, "So, am I to understand that my services as your messenger are no longer required?"

"That must surely be a great relief to you cousin," laughed Benjamin, "... and we are very much indebted to you for all that you have done. We could never repay your kindness and loyalty."

"No, indeed we could not," agreed Rosalind, "It must have been very difficult for you to deceive your father on our account. You are, and always have been, a true and trusted friend, Yoonie." She flung her arms around Eunice and hugged her tightly.

"What are your plans now?" asked Eunice concernedly. "My father has become most sullen and withdrawn since we visited you last. I can only assume that he learned something that greatly displeased him whilst he was here, but he has said nothing of it to me."

Rosalind flushed slightly with embarrassment. "My aunt told me that whilst he was here he mentioned the marriage agreement he had made with my father, but she told him that I had no wish to marry him." To spare her friend's feelings, she did not elaborate any further.

"Oh now I understand why my father has been so ill-humoured. That explains it."

"I am sorry Yoonie, but you know that I had no intention of marrying him. Only my father and he knew why they struck such a bargain in the first place... certainly I was never in agreement with it. You do know that, don't you?"

"Of course I do Roz... of course, but there is bound to be trouble when he discovers that Benjamin is calling on you." She looked at her cousin and asked kindly, "What will you do Ben?"

"Well... I know that my situation will now become impossible, so I have been considering moving into one of the hotels along Main Street. One thing is for sure, Uncle Henry will not tolerate my presence from now on... either in the house or at the yard. I shall have no choice but to leave."

Rosalind's concern was immediate. "It need only be a temporary arrangement Ben, for just as soon as Mama has settled Papa's affairs, then I am sure we shall be able to consider making plans for our marriage. Of course, there has to be some delay... that is only proper, isn't it, but it shouldn't be for very long."

"Whatever you say my dear Roz... I am just happy that we shall be able to marry sometime soon and that there is no longer any need for us to hide."

*

As Benjamin had predicted, his situation did become impossible when his uncle vented his spite upon him. Not only did he lose his job, but he was promptly turned out of the Youngman home. However, before he had the chance to install himself in a hotel, one of the employees at the yard offered him a room in his own home. Benjamin was well liked and he had acquired many friends since joining his uncle's business, friends who greatly sympathised with him in his unfortunate situation and who wanted to help him as much as possible. At the same time, and unbeknown to him, Rosalind had begged her mother to permit Ben to stay at 'Fortune's Hand', but both her mother and her aunt had quashed her request immediately, pointing out that proper etiquette should be observed during their period of mourning. The townsfolk already had enough to set their tongues wagging, as far as Celia was concerned, without inviting guests to stay; it simply would not do. So Rosalind had to content herself with seeing her husband-to-be whenever he could manage to visit, which he ensured was as often as possible.

Five

The days that followed were idyllic for Rosalind, nothing could mar her joy, for Benjamin Richmond's frequent visits did much to lighten the atmosphere throughout the entire household, and as they came to know him, his company was much enjoyed by Celia and Lilybee. They were particularly moved at the way in which he befriended Edmund and slowly coaxed him to participate in the family's activities. Than gradually, as the apprehension and subdued whispering ceased, the daily routine at 'Fortune's Hand' began to return to normal. So much so that nobody would have believed their lives were about to undergo yet another dramatic change.

It was as the family sat at breakfast one morning that the letter arrived, requesting Celia to come, post haste, to her husband's bank in New York. Nothing more was contained therein, but it did cause Celia considerable consternation. She sat staring at the letter for some time; the very fact that it appeared to be so innocuous was what disturbed her most. She bit her lip as she handed it to her sister-in-law. "What do you make of it, Lilybee?" she asked, "and why would the bank wish to see me most urgently. Could it be that Gilbert's affairs are causing undue problems, do you think?" She placed her hand to her forehead and shook her head disconsolately.

Lilybee could see she was deeply troubled, and she sympathised. "Now don't start worrying before you know what this is all about," she said.

"I wish I could feel more optimistic, but for some reason I am filled with foreboding. Would you come with me to New York? I don't think I could go alone."

"Of course my dear, you know I could never allow you to face such a proposition on your own. We shall make ready to go at once, no sense in delaying it. What do you say we take the train from Ludlow. It will make the journey so much quicker, don't you think?"

"Oh yes, yes, Kingston can drive us to the station and we could be in New York by late afternoon. We shall need to find a hotel for the night, then we can go to the bank first thing tomorrow morning. As much as I dread it, I want it over as quickly as possible." She turned to her daughter, "Rosalind, you will be alright here with Edmund, won't you darling... and Benjamin will help you take care of everything?"

"Of course Mama... we shall be perfectly alright. There is no need for you to worry about us."

"That young man will be an asset to the family," enthused Lilybee, "You are a most fortunate girl Rosalind."

Her niece beamed with delight, "I know Aunt... and I still can't believe my good luck in finding him. I hope we shan't have long to wait before we can wed. Ben is as anxious as I am to settle down. He hopes to find himself another job quite soon. He is considering a few promising proposals at this very moment, and when he has decided which to accept, then we shall be able to choose where we make our home."

"All in good time... all in good time," laughed Lilybee, "but I do believe a joyful occasion is something that would benefit us all after what we have lived through of late. Yes indeed a wedding in early summer would be just the thing."

Celia leaned over and patted her daughter's hand lovingly, "You will not have to wait too long my dear... I promise." Then, turning to Lilybee, she urged, "Now we really must hurry, there is no time to lose if we are to get to New York today."

They packed and left in record time and after an uneventful journey, the two women arrived at their destination. As they stepped into the carriage that was to take them to their hotel, Lilybee had suggested returning to the 'Irving' where they had spent such an enjoyable time on their last visit to New York. Celia was only too happy to comply because it held nothing but pleasant memories for them both. As they entered the restaurant, later that evening, she wistfully recalled the magic of their chance meeting with Ian Forbes, some seventeen years before, and dreamed of how wonderful it would be if he should, by chance, happen to appear again. He filled her thoughts as she wondered where he was at that very moment, how he was and whether he still travelled to and from New York on business. It hardly seemed possible after so many years, with all the changes that had taken place since the war. Her thoughts drifted, uninterrupted. By now, he may even have married and settled in England with a wife and family. She tried to imagine what he would look like as a mature man, and her heart missed a beat at his image materialising before her. She jumped as she was brought out of her reverie by Lilybee demanding, "Celia... stop daydreaming... tell the waiter what you would like to drink while we decide which of these delicious dishes to order."

The waiter smiled, and she realised that he was nothing like Ian Forbes, nothing like him at all.

"Have you ever seen such a menu?" asked Lilybee, thrusting the grand looking object into her hand.

She concentrated her thoughts on what she wanted to eat and drink for the next hour or so, but she could not resist an occasional glance around the restaurant in the hope that the man she so wanted to see might, miraculously appear. Eventually she realised how futile her hope had been and how unlikely it was that she would ever again meet Ian Forbes.

Their meal had been leisurely and they lingered for far too long over their coffee and liqueurs, but both agreed that it had been most enjoyable. "Should we not retire now sister-in-law. I feel so relaxed after all that good wine that I shall drop off to sleep in a trice. How about you?" asked Lilybee.

"I feel tired too… yes I suppose we ought to get to bed if we are to make an early start in the morning. I am filled with dread at what our visit to the bank might bring forth." Celia was filled with despondency as she rose from the table and cast just one more furtive glance around the elegant room. Then with a disappointed sigh, she made her reluctant departure.

*

"Yes, do come in ladies… do come in," said the bank manager, as the clerk opened the door of his office to admit Celia and Lilybee.

"Mrs Hetherington and her sister-in-law, Mrs Mansfield-Brown sir," muttered the clerk, almost inaudibly. He left abruptly, closing the door behind him.

"Good morning to you both. Please take a seat." He flung his arms wide indicating the two chairs that stood in front of his overly impressive desk, one to either side.

Lilybee was quick to notice his immaculate appearance; his spotless linen and his silk cravat; his beautifully tailored black frock coat and waistcoat. She also noticed, with great concern, his inaccessible manner. He lost no time at all in outlining the reasons why he had summoned Celia to see him so urgently, and despite her prior misgivings, she was still deeply shocked at the gravity of his disclosures. She had no conception of just how much money her husband had squandered over the years.

"You see, Mrs Hetherington," intoned the bank manager, "Your husband's debts are of such magnitude, and have gone on mounting steadily for such a considerable length of time that the bank has no alternative but to foreclose. It is highly regrettable, but his creditors are demanding settlement without delay. In short they are no longer willing to wait for their money. To this end, madam, I have the unenviable task of requesting that you either settle your husband's debts forthwith or remove yourself from the property in Asbury, New Jersey, within twenty-eight days." He paused momentarily to clear his throat, then went on, "Of course, furniture and fittings must remain intact... they will belong solely to the bank... we have the legal power to seize everything, lock, stock and barrel."

He leaned back in his comfortable chair, his elbows resting on its arms. His fingers were outspread, tips pressed together. He brought them under his chin and sat gazing at Celia, completely detached, allowing her time to assimilate everything he had said.

She remained silent for several seconds, hardly able to believe what she had heard. She was completely stunned, but finally she managed to ask quietly, "Twenty-eight days... I am to leave 'Fortune's Hand' in twenty-eight days... but how... what about my children?" She knew there was absolutely no possibility of her ever being in a position to settle any kind of debt. She took a deep, shuddering breath and looked at her sister-in-law, "What will we do?" she asked helplessly.

Lilybee felt as distraught as Celia, and deeply ashamed that her brother had brought his family to such a pitiable state. She looked at the bank manager and asked earnestly, "Sir, would you not consider your request a trifle harsh? As you know, my dear sister-in-law has been recently widowed in the most traumatic circumstances. Indeed, she is still suffering from the emotional stress brought about by her husband's untimely death, and yet you suppose she is able to withstand the unimaginable pressure that you are bringing to bear?"

The bank manager interrupted. "Madam, if you will excuse me… as I have already pointed out, this is not a recent problem. Mr Hetherington's debts have been of great concern to the bank for some considerable time. He was warned on a number of occasions that he was in serious default and he was made fully aware of the consequences. In fact, it was only when he notified us of his intended merger with Youngman's haulage, that our present action was held in abeyance, but again it was made perfectly clear to him that this was to be for a very limited time, and only dependant on his forthcoming merger with such a reputable company. He gave every assurance that all his financial debts would be met once the partnership took place, but of course, when the news of his death began to circulate… and bad news travels fast, it became evident that there was no longer the likelihood of any merger taking place and, therefore, no settlement of his debts."

He added as an afterthought, and most unconvincingly, "Of course I regret what has to be done, but unfortunately Mr Hetherington was not a well-liked man and… "

Now it was Lilybee's turn to interrupt, "Of that we are painfully aware. You have no idea of the suffering he has caused this family for all of his life, and it would seem that even after his death, he is still capable of destroying our lives."

Lilybee's eyes met those that were looking at her so dispassionately from the other side of the desk and it was apparent that a gentleman of such sobriety and respectability had not one iota of sympathy for a roué the likes of her brother. She placed her hands upon the edge of the desk and leant over it conspiratorially, "Sir I beg you to reconsider... would it not be possible to grant an extension, at least allow a little more time for arrangements to be made... please?"

"It is not in the bank's interests... as much as I would like to help... er... " Suddenly he wanted to be rid of the two women. He wanted to bring the unpleasantries to an end. "Oh, very well, six weeks then... but that is the most I can offer. There cannot be a day longer, do you understand?"

As they stood up to leave, he cast an appraising eye over the young widow, and the thought occurred to him that it would surely not be very long before she was married again, for rare beauty such as hers could capture the heart of any man. In fact, now he had met her, he found it difficult to believe that her husband could ever have been so unfaithful, but it was common knowledge. His reputation was notorious.

*

The two women had decided to return home as soon as their business with the bank was completed, and it was as they sat alone in the carriage on the last part of the journey between Ludlow and Asbury that Lilybee put forward a suggestion to Celia. They had spoken very little to one another on the train, but Lilybee had been busy formulating a plan to which she hoped Celia might readily agree.

"Celia, my dear," she said hesitantly, "I have a suggestion to make that I hope you might find acceptable. I have been giving it careful thought the whole time we have been travelling from New York... now I would like you to give it equally careful thought. Will you do that?"

Celia looked at Lilybee and said half-heartedly, "I would be grateful for any suggestion... any suggestion at all, if you think it might help to improve my situation."

"Well see what you think. The bank have given you six weeks in which to make ready to leave 'Fortune's Hand', but that does not allow you much time to find another home, does it? Now, what would you say to bringing your family down to 'White Lakes' and making your home there with me?"

Celia drew in a shocked breath.

"Don't say anything... not yet... just think about it; but I would point out that it may not be a bad thing for you to get away from Asbury... get right away, I mean, after what happened to Gilbert. And now... to be losing 'Fortune's Hand' on top of everything else. You need to make a new start Celia, try to forget all the tragedy. Please... think about it, and think carefully, my dear." She was looking at her sister-in-law intently and her heart almost broke as Celia's chin fell on to her chest and she began to sob. "Oh, my dear girl... " Lilybee was beside her in a second, placing a comforting arm about her shoulders. "My dear girl... " she whispered again. Both women wept together.

"Oh, Lilybee, what would I do without you?" said Celia.

"Well, you need someone to care, indeed you do, for you have received precious little love from that despicable brother of mine... and I know you will agree with what I am about to say, although you might never bring yourself to say it, and that is I am truly glad he is gone... the world will be a better place without him."

*

They were greatly relieved to be home at last, after an arduous two days, and as Celia handed her cloak to Tobias, she entreated him to have some tea sent into the drawing room, as she and Lilybee felt in desperate need of some refreshments. "Where are the family Tobias?" she asked.

"Miss Rosalind and Massa Benjamin is in the study with Master Edmund, and... er... Miss Esther, she in the kitchen with Jassy Ma'am."

"Oh, thank you... I'll fetch Rosalind and the gentlemen from the study, they can join us in the drawing room, so perhaps you will ask Delilah to send in enough tea for us all."

"Yes'm, I sho' will."

As they made their way slowly along the hall, Celia said quietly, "I had better break the news to everyone as soon as possible, don't you think... no sense in delaying it, is there?"

"No, not really my dear," agreed Lilybee, "But don't be too despondent. Things will work out quite well... you'll see."

Rosalind could tell there was something seriously wrong immediately her mother's face appeared around the door of the study. She ran over and hugged her. "It is good to see you home safely Mama. Did your journey go well?"

"Yes, thank you, the travelling was quite uneventful... extremely tiring though. Your aunt and I are just about to take tea in the drawing room... it is hours since we had anything to eat or drink. Would you care to join us, there is something I must tell you."

Almost before they had seated themselves, the tea trolley was brought in by Clarissa; it was laden with tasty sandwiches and fancy cakes. "That looks lovely Clarissa, thank you. We'll manage ourselves." Celia waited for her servant to go; and she bobbed a curtsey and left.

As she closed the door, Rosalind pleaded, "What is it you have to tell us Mama... you look so worried. What is it?"

Her mother related all that had taken place at the bank, leaving out not one detail, and when she heard that they must leave their home in just six weeks, Rosalind cried, "No... no... what will happen to us Mama; where shall we go?" She turned to Benjamin, who was sitting beside her and clasped his hand urgently, "And what of our wedding... we have been so looking forward to it. We shan't have to postpone it for a very long time shall we? I couldn't bear it."

"Well, we are not completely destitute, thanks to your Aunt Lilybee. She has invited us to go to 'White Lakes' and make our home there with her. It is wonderfully kind of her, I think you will agree, and I for one can think of no better place to go... and I know that Edmund has grown to love it too, after all the time he spent there whilst he was convalescing. As for your wedding, my dear, instead of postponing it, I think we should do the exact opposite." She smiled lovingly at her daughter and Benjamin, then went on, "How would you like to be married here in our own family church... it will not take too much arranging, and you can wed before we leave?"

The young couple gasped in surprise and turned to one another expectantly. They nodded in unison and laughed as they said breathlessly, "Yes, oh yes."

It was as though Celia could take no more sadness; she wanted to lift the veil of misery that had hung over everyone at 'Fortune's Hand' for so long. If their lives were to change so dramatically, then they were to change for the better and she would do everything in her power to make sure that their future would be a happy one.

Suddenly Rosalind became serious again, asking, "What about the townsfolk Mama... won't they gossip when they know I am to be married so soon after Papa's death?"

"There is no doubt of that; it had crossed my mind too," said Lilybee defiantly, "But maybe... "

Celia did not wait for her to finish what she was about to say, "That is as it may be, but with all that has befallen this family over the past few weeks, I do not believe your wedding will add much to the gossip. Heaven alone knows how tongues will wag once everyone comes to know that we have been forced to leave 'Fortune's Hand, so the very least of my worries is what will be said about you and Benjamin marrying. We shall just have to wait and see what happens, shan't we?"

"That's the spirit my dear," laughed Lilybee, mightily please that her sister-in-law was at last beginning to exhibit some resilience. Certainly, she would need it to cope with what she had to face over the coming weeks. "And have you thought of what to do about the servants, Celia?" she asked.

"Yes, I have been giving them some thought, indeed I have. Do you suppose they will want to come with us? We have been together for so long… I could not bear to be parted from them. They have been my family… the only family I have known since I first came to 'Fortune's Hand' so many years ago." She closed her eyes and thought for a few seconds. "Let me see, it was when Edmund was born… yes, nineteen years now. How the years have flown, it is almost unbelievable." She paused for thought again. "I'll talk to them this evening after dinner. We'll call them all into the drawing room and tell them what has happened. They shall decide for themselves what they want to do, whether they want to return to North Carolina. They shall have freedom to choose… I think that is the least they deserve after all their years of loyalty and devotion. I cannot bear to think of what I shall do if they decide to leave us though."

*

Before going into the dining room for dinner, Celia went to the kitchen to make her invitation personally. Her heart was heavy as she stepped through the door and felt every eye upon her. "Don't stop what you are doing," she urged, "I have just come to tell you that I should like to speak to you after dinner

this evening... all of you... together... in the drawing room."
She was finding it far more difficult that she had imagined. She
could see the concern on each of their faces, and she tried to
ease their minds. "There is nothing for you to worry about...
I shall explain everything later. Just make sure that everyone
is present. That is all."

As she closed the door, Jassy looked from Joshua to
Maybelle; Clarissa and Clarence looked at each other and
Delilah placed an arm around her son, Tobias, drawing him
close as though to protect him. The rest of the servants were
elsewhere in the house.

"What you s'pose all that about?" asked Joshua. The
women shook their heads.

Clarissa beckoned them with her hand as she whispered,
"I knowed sump'n wrong when I took the tea trolley in...
sump'n no good happened on that trip to New York. You see
if I ain't right."

"Well ain't no good us talkin' 'bout it... we jus' has to wait
an' see what we is gonna be told after dinner... like the
mistress say," said Jassy.

"We is all gonna be told, all of us together, ain't we
Mammy?" queried Tobias, his large black eyes grown even
larger with fright.

Joshua shuffled past him and rubbed the top of his head
ruefully, "That what the mistress say, that what she say
alright."

Again the door opened, this time to admit Amos, followed
by Kingston and Harvest, ready for their evening meal. Six
pairs of troubled eyes turned upon them and Harvest asked,
"What wrong here Mammy... you all looks like sump'n
terrible jus' happened?"

"We don't know yet son; the mistress jus' come in and she say we is all to come to the drawin' room after dinner... all of us together... "

As she was relating what little there was to tell, Grace and Minnie appeared. They were equally intrigued when they saw everyone gathered around, their faces solemn, so Jassy started from the beginning again, finishing with what Clarissa had added concerning the mistress's trip to New York.

"Has Miss Rosalind said anything to you Minnie?" asked Clarissa. Minnie just shook her head without saying a word, but that was nothing out of the ordinary. They had all grown accustomed to her withdrawn silence of late; she had nothing to say to anybody any more.

"Now we only has to tell Beaulah and Bella, when they done servin' in the dinin' room," said Jassy, "And now you all git an' eat, so we don' keep the mistress waitin' after the family done eatin'... we wants to know what it is she gonna tell us... and we wants to know soon."

Not a lot was said during the meal; they were all anxiously preoccupied, trying to imagine what it was the mistress had to tell them. Only Minnie knew with any certainty what the announcement would be, because her young mistress had been unable to contain her excitement as she was dressing for dinner. She had sworn her maid to secrecy before divulging to her that they would all shortly be leaving 'Fortune's Hand', but more importantly, that she and Benjamin were to be married almost immediately, before they left. "Please, please don't say anything to the others Minnie... promise?" Rosalind had begged, "They will all be told this evening, Mama is to call you all together in the drawing room after dinner. She would be so angry with me if she found out that I had already told you, but I must tell someone my happy news... isn't it

162

wonderful that I am to marry Benjamin before we leave. Can you believe it?"

Minnie was stunned, completely unable to believe it, and even worse, hardly able to contain herself at the thought of having to leave 'Fortune's Hand' in the immediate future. What if Run Swiftly should return and find her gone? She could not bear to think of it. Now she was seated at the kitchen table, her meal almost untouched, for she was far too upset to eat, her mind filled with thoughts of her Indian, of how much she loved him. She wondered what would become of her if she never saw him again. She would not want to go on living, she would die of a broken heart, of that she was certain.

*

When she could see that the family had all finished their meal, Celia told Bella that she might clear the table, "And when you return to the kitchen, will you tell the other servants that I shall be waiting for them in the drawing room? They may come in as soon as they wish."

"Yes'm," said Bella with a small curtsey.

All the family were present when the servants came in. They entered in single file and stood in a long, orderly line facing their mistress. Joshua and Jassy first, with their son Harvest and the twins Clarence and Clarissa; beside them Kingston, Amos and Beaulah, then Maybelle and Delilah with their young ones, Tobias and Bella; lastly Grace and Minnie. Celia stood up and stepped a little nearer to them before she spoke.

She clasped her hands together nervously as she began, "You must be anxious to know why I have called you together like this... what it is I have to tell you, and I hope it will not come as too much of a shock... " She paused and looked concernedly from one to the other, then taking a deep breath she continued. "It grieves me to have to tell you that we shall shortly be leaving 'Fortune's Hand'." There was a shocked gasp, and the tidy line crumpled as the servants moved to look at each other, not really able to believe what has just been said. Their mistress sounded apologetic as she explained, "We have no choice, we must leave, but I want you to make your own choice... you may choose whether or not you wish to remain with us, with the family. I think you should know we shall be going down to North Carolina, 'White Lakes', with Mistress Lilybee and you may come with us if you choose to. I hope that you will, because I cannot imagine what I should do without you... but, I want you to think about it very carefully and let me know when you have made your decisions." She finished by saying, "It is just as much of a shock to all of us as it is to you, but it is possible that you may quite like to return to 'White Lakes' once you have had time to consider it... you have many old friends there, who, I am sure, would be happy to see you again." She paused to compose herself; she was overcome with emotion. She swallowed hard and said quietly, "I think that is all... you may go and talk about it together... take a little time before telling me what you have decided."

As she paused, Lilybee stood up and added, "Just one more thing, Celia." She looked at the row of servants and said directly to them, "I think it may help you to come to a decision if I told you that, should you wish to return to 'White Lakes', then it will be as paid workers from now on." There was another shocked gasp. Lilybee smiled. "Things have changed a good deal since you left the plantation... but I hope you will see that for yourselves before very long."

After they had filed out, Celia turned to her sister-in-law, "Do you suppose they will come with us... do you think they will want to?"

Lilybee gave a slight shrug, "I don't know my dear, I really don't know."

*

Thoughts were just as uncertain and confused out in the kitchen, where discussions and arguments raged far into the night. Every one of the servants was determined to have his or her say, and each opinion was given due consideration. The older ones took very little time to make up their minds, that they wanted to remain, which was quite understandable; they were far too set in their ways, and too fond of their mistress to want to leave her after all the years they had been together.

"What we gonna do if we leaves... where we gonna go?" asked Joshua, shaking his head sadly, "Besides, the mistress she take care of us good since we came here, so we ain't 'bout to up and leave her now... no sir we ain't. What you say Jassy?"

"I says Amen to that Joshua... we bin through a lot together, good and bad and the mistress she need us now more'n she ever done... I says we stays." She laid her hand lovingly on Joshua's, on top of the table and smiled lovingly at him.

"I ain't gonna leave the mistress either, not ever," said Beaulah, "I loves her like she my own kin."

Delilah and Maybelle were already excitedly describing North Carolina and the plantation to Tobias and Bella, and Kingston scratched his head and declared, "Well, if my family set on North Carolina, then I guess I is too."

This set them all laughing and gradually the worry and tension eased away. Instead, their mood changed to one of pleasurable anticipation at what their future might hold in store. Only Harvest and Clarence spoke longingly of what it might be like to break free and set off together to see what life might offer them, now that they had the chance. Amos was completely undecided, despite the exciting ideas that Harvest and Clarence were conjuring up in his mind. As for Clarissa, she had no other desire than to go wherever her mammy and pappy chose to go and she became alarmed at her brother's wild notions.

"Why don't you wait and see what it like down at 'White Lakes' now... please? Mammy and Pappy old now, and you knows how they would worry 'bout you if you was off no knowin' where." She looked at her twin and pleaded, "Please Clarence... we ain't never bin parted... what I gonna do without you?"

Her brother dropped his head ashamedly and remained silent. Jassy spoke to Grace, "Don't s'pose you wants to go no place else... you goin' back to 'White Lakes' ain't you?"

"I has to go back. One day Mose comin' back to git me, like he said. I got to be there when he come lookin' for me, I sho has."

"Well you got Minnie now... she be comin' too. I glad for you Grace."

Minnie made no comment, for she felt that her world was falling apart. All she longed for was the one person who could put it back together again, but she knew nothing of his whereabouts.

*

By the following morning, after everyone had had time to sleep on it, the final decision was made. Even Harvest and Clarence agreed to stay with their family, for they felt that the women and older men would most certainly need their help on the long, arduous journey to the South. Jassy was the one to break the good news to Celia and Lilybee whilst they sat at breakfast, and they exclaimed their delight at the unanimous decision. "Please tell everyone how pleased we are that they have decided to stay, Jassy... I cannot tell you how sadly you would have been missed if you had not agreed to come with us. Now, of course, we shall have to discuss the arrangements for our departure, there is so much to be done and very little time in which to do it, but together, I am sure, we shall be able to manage perfectly well. Just let us attend to Rosalind's wedding first, and as soon as it is over, we shall make ready to leave immediately."

"We are fortunate that it will be an ideal time to travel," put in Lilybee, "Before the heat of summer is upon us."

Six

On the day of the wedding, the sun was shining brilliantly from a clear blue sky, although persistent winds still chilled the air. The townsfolk of Asbury turned out to line the route of the procession all the way from 'Fortune's Hand' to the church. Rosalind made a radiant bride and there were gasps of admiration as she stepped from her bridal carriage, eager to meet her groom, and despite her mother's determination to keep the occasion as unpretentious as possible, in an effort to avoid hurtful criticism, she was deeply moved by the number of friends and acquaintances who came to express their good wishes to the young couple. She found it difficult to believe that in all the years she had lived in this small New Jersey town, she had never become aware of just how much its residents sympathised with her and her children, or how much they respected her for her gentility and long-sufferance of her husband, that most hated of men. Now the whole community wanted her to know where their sympathies lay, and she appreciated their warm-hearted gesture.

*

As she sat in the church listening to Pastor James Lawton conducting the marriage ceremony, Celia glanced at Lilybee sitting beside her and smiled happily; she was immensely happy, in spite of all that had befallen her of late. Miraculously, her prayers had been answered, of that she had no doubt; for here she was witnessing the marriage of her daughter to the man she loved. Her beloved son had been returned to her at last, and even more poignantly, never again would she be forced to keep her youngest child, dear little Esther, guiltily hidden away, because the cause of their misery, the one responsible for their years of interminable suffering, had been forever removed from their lives. Even the awesome prospect of losing the family home now occasioned no regret; in fact she was intent upon following Lilybee's worldly advice and taking the God-given opportunity to make a new start. She had always loved the plantation in North Carolina, and now she was looking forward, eagerly, to making it her permanent home.

*

The wedding march sounding forth brought Celia out of her reverie, she watched with pride as Benjamin led Rosalind from the church, closely followed by her maid of honour, Eunice Youngman, and the five bridesmaids whom she had specially chosen. Esther watched over carefully by Eunice's sister Lydia, and the other Youngman sisters, Charlotte, Susannah and Emily. Outside stood all those townsfolk who had not been lucky enough to find a pew inside, so many of them anxious to join in the church service, but now the waiting crowd were shouting and cheering good-naturedly as they wished the newlyweds on their way. Finally they dispersed as the last carriages drove off, but that was not the end of it as far as they were concerned, because this was a wedding of far greater interest than most, and it would be talked of for many a long day, indeed it would.

For a start there was the recent death of the bride's father in the most suspicious of circumstances... and rumours that the son might well be implicated, suffering as he was from strange mental problems. Then there was her broken engagement from Henry Youngman and the mystery surrounding it, but who would blame any young girl for rejecting a man old enough to be her father? It had been said that her father was the instigator of that unholy alliance, but of all people, she had chosen to marry young Benjamin Richmond, the nephew. Now that was something, and look at the trouble it had caused between the young man and his uncle. Apart from all that, his cousins had attended the bride… well it was to be expected after the eldest, Eunice, had been a bosom friend of the Hetherington girl since childhood. Yes indeed, this wedding would be talked about for many a long day, but when all was said and done; there were not many who would point a finger in malice at the happy pair.

*

The reception for the family and guests was a very modest one, but nevertheless it proved to be a truly enjoyable occasion. Celia had invited several of Benjamin's friends, those he had made since coming to Asbury. Then a few of her own, people she had come to know and trust over the years, and once again, all the Youngman family with the exception of their father of course. He had removed himself to New York on the pretext that there was urgent business that needed his attention. In actual fact he had hardly been able to contain his wrath upon learning that his nephew was about to wed the girl for whom he had lusted for so long, and to remain in Asbury whilst their union was actually taking place was more than he could possibly endure. Now all the guests were intent upon savouring the abundant supply of food and drinks, and even the servants out in the kitchen joined in the festivities. Theirs was a double cause for celebration, not only had the young mistress of the house married her beau, but they themselves had just entered a state that, hitherto, not one of them would have believed possible. They had been freed. They had been offered the choice to do exactly what they wanted, for the first time in their lives. They danced, they sang, they hugged one another and they laughed as they had never laughed before. This was their moment for jubilation. Since the mistress had first told them what their future would be, they had been unable to give vent to their feelings, they had had to observe propriety, remain respectfully subdued whilst their dead master was being mourned, even though he merited no sympathy as far as they were concerned. But now, on this glorious day of days, they could celebrate in any way they knew how, and they intended to do just that.

Only Minnie found herself lacking in festive spirit, so when the merrymaking was at its height, she slipped quietly out of the kitchen through the back door, intending to meander down by the river as she had been doing more and more of late. She had no desire to enter into the spirit of the occasion herself, yet she would not cast an air of gloom over it for the others; better that she steal away to where she could think her private thoughts and relive again the precious moments she had spent with her Indian. Strange, she mused, that since the night of his departure, Miss Rosalind had never once spoken of him, had never questioned what had become of him. Since that night a barrier had developed between them, which Minnie found difficult to comprehend. In the past they had always been able to talk to one another, exchange confidences, share each other's secrets. What had changed all that she wondered? She realised that her young mistress now belonged to the man she loved and, of course, he must be her closest confidante, that is how it should be but somehow she knew there was more to it than that. She felt instinctively that their lack of communication was due to something of far more significance. Could it be that Master Edmund had told his sister what he had overheard concerning his father... her father... their father? She could think of nothing else that might have driven such a wedge between them. She knew that nothing would ever be the same between them again, and she was deeply hurt. She wanted to hide away from everyone except Run Swiftly, for he alone could ease her pain, make her life worth living again. She felt the warmth of her tears as they began to trickle down her cold cheeks, and she shivered slightly in the chill night breeze.

"Minnie... Minnie." She heard her mother's voice behind her, calling anxiously. "You git your death out here honey-chile... here, put this round your shoulders. Her mother wrapped a cloak around her as she pulled her close and asked gently, "What you doin' out here by yourself... this ain't no place to be when everyone inside havin' a good time. Why don't you come back in... come now?"

"Ain't nothin' for me to be happy about Mammy; that what I came out here for. I don't want to spoil everthin' for the others."

Grace took hold of her daughter's shoulders and pulled her round to face her. She could not bear to think of her continuing to live in misery because of what she had learned of her father. She shook her, forcing her to look her in the face "Now, you listen to your Mammy, you hear? You jus' gonna have to forgit what I said about who's your pappy... that don't make you no different from what you was before you knowed. I jus' wish I ain't never said nothing... but you knows now and I can't take it back. You remember this though, don't make no difference where you come from... what you is inside is what you wants to be, ain't nobody can change that. He gone for good Minnie, so don't you think about him no more... life gonna be good from now on, you see if it ain't."

Minnie shook her head vigorously, "No Mammy, you don't understand... life ain't gonna be good, not if I has to go from here."

Grace gathered her daughter into her arms and spoke lovingly to her, "You comin' down to 'White Lakes' with me, an' we is gonna wait for Mose to come and git us. I couldn't leave when he took off before, 'cos the Lady Lilybee she need me then, but now she gonna have all her family there with her, so don' make no difference if I leaves. Mose said he comin' back for me, so I gonna be there waitin' when he does. We all be together then, he gonna take you and me up to the North with him and Sunny Blue... we is all gonna make a new life there."

Suddenly Minnie broke down and sobbed, "Oh, Mammy, I'se got a man comin' back for me too... I can't leave, I said I be here when he come lookin' for me... jus' like you told Mose. What he gonna do if I ain't here?"

Her mother was stunned. She asked incredulously, "What you say Minnie... you got a man... who, where?"

Minnie told briefly of how she and Rosalind had found Run Swiftly all those weeks ago, floating in his canoe on the river; of how she had nursed him back to life and of how he had left on the night Gilbert Hetherington had been killed.

Her mother gasped in horror at the mention of the killing, "You tellin' me that this Indian was the one killed Massa Hetherington?" she asked.

"No he ain't... no, no," replied Minnie emphatically, "It some other Indian... I never seen him before... all I know is he in the canoe when Run Swiftly go down to the river. I seen him paddling it and Run Swiftly was sittin' there with him 'cos he bin shot, so he couldn't do nothin'. I ain't told nobody 'bout this before 'cos I don't want my Indian to git the blame. He ain't done nothin', I swear."

Grace could see that she was becoming agitated. "Alright, alright... ain't nobody gonna find out if we don' say nothin', but it ain't safe for you to git mixed up with no Indian... no sir it ain't. Maybe it the best thing we can do is git you away from here before he come back again... if he ever come back again." She shook her head despairingly.

"You jus' like everyone else, but you don't know 'bout Indians the way I does," said Minnie angrily. "He say he comin' back for me and I knows he will, and when he does, I goin' with him."

Grace felt sick with worry, but she knew that her daughter had lost her heart to the man whose life she'd saved. From the way she had spoken of him, Grace realised that she would never be persuaded to forget him. "We best git back to the house now Minnie, but you think about what I jus' said... life gonna be good for you from now on, you jus' see if it ain't."

*

During the following week, the days became more and more hectic for both the family and the servants, with everyone kept busy from morning till night, turning out drawers and cupboards then packing all those things, personal things mostly, that they were able to take from the family home. Although they did not appear to amount to much, even so there seemed to be an endless number of boxes and cases that would need transporting, and Celia was anxious to speak to Benjamin about that operation.

The newlyweds had been staying at 'Fortune's Hand' since their marriage, and as Lilybee had foretold, Ben was proving to be an enormous asset to the family. Both Celia and Lilybee had spoken to him at great length concerning what his immediate plans might be, and much to her delight Lilybee had been successful in persuading him to delay taking any kind of employment in the area, but rather travel with the family down to North Carolina before making a final decision.

"Not only would it be of great benefit to have you accompany us on the journey Ben, but I should very much like you to see our Southern States before you decide where your future lies. Opportunities abound there for anyone with ambition, now that the war is over. There is so much reconstruction under way, so much rebuilding to be done in every sector, so won't you please come and take a look for yourself. I am sure you will not regret it?"

"How could anyone resist such a tempting proposition?" laughed Benjamin affably, "and I thank you for your kind invitation. Yes… yes, I shall be delighted to accompany you. I must admit that it will be fascinating to see more of this wonderful country, and who knows, it may well be that I shall find the South as alluring as you do yourself ma'am, and decide never to return to New Jersey again. We shall see."

Rosalind ran to him and kissed him lightly on the cheek, "Oh, isn't it exciting Ben… I can hardly wait to be on our way, can you?"

"Not so fast young lady, not so fast," teased her mother. "There is much to be done first." She turned to Ben, "Would you go down to the storehouse along the river to find out how much stock is there? Take Amos and Kingston… and maybe Harvest too… they will help you go through everything, make an inventory of sorts… it would be better not to attract too much attention to what you are doing. Oh, and whilst you are there, perhaps you could ask Kingston to take a good look at the wagons, to see if they are in a fit state to make the long journey down to North Carolina. I was thinking that perhaps the servants could make the journey in them, and take the bulk of our belongings too."

"I shall go straight away ma'am. Just as soon as I find the men, we shall be off," replied Benjamin enthusiastically. As he strode to the door he added, "Now my training at Youngman's will serve me well."

Celia smiled as he closed the door behind him. Then a small furrow creased her brow as she asked Lilybee, "I think those wagons of Gilbert's should be substantial enough to take the servants and the heaviest luggage, don't you?"

"Ben will soon find out, I'm sure. You can rely upon that young man my dear... he appears to be fully capable of arranging everything for you, so just leave it all to him. The next priority is booking the stage for ourselves... now let me see, I think I shall take Grace with us, and I daresay you would like Beaulah to accompany you... isn't that so?"

"Oh yes, of course. Kingston can drive us into Clinton first thing tomorrow morning and we shall make all the arrangements then. I think we should try to leave before the bank's deadline if we can. I don't want to be here when they come to take possession of the property, I couldn't bear that."

"Indeed not... that would be intolerable for you my dear, but don't fret, we shall make absolutely sure that we are well on our way long before they set foot on the property." Lilybee patted her sister-in-law on the hand comfortingly, "The sooner we can get you away from all this unpleasantness the better... then you can make a fresh start."

It took very little time for Benjamin to ride to the storehouse on the horse that Kingston had saddled up for him, and the servants followed in a small cart driven by Kingston. The storehouse stood deserted, it had been locked and barred, so the men had to force an entry. Once inside, Ben set to work searching the premises with Amos, while Harvest helped

Kingston to make a thorough examination of the wagons that stood at the back of the building. There were several in a state of dilapidation, completely beyond repair, but they did manage to find two in reasonable condition, plus a third that could also be put to use after a little repair work. The four men spent more than an hour searching and examining whatever stock they could find, before returning to give a report to Mistress Hetherington.

*

After Ben had told Celia of his findings, he suggested that a couple of men from Youngman's workshop might be willing to undertake the work on the wagons. They were very experienced in all manner of repairs, having spent their lives working on Youngman's delivery vehicles.

"Do you think they will agree to repair ours though Ben? Henry Youngman would not be too well pleased if he heard of it."

"They are good friends of mine... one of them allowed me to rent a room in his home when my uncle turned me out. Besides, they would do the work in their own time... he need never know."

"Very well then, I shall be happy to leave the arrangements to you, and I am so grateful Ben. Oh... what about payment... I have no idea what...?"

Benjamin raised a hand before she could finish, "No problem there either ma'am. There is quite a variety of stock in that storehouse and I am sure that the men will be happy to accept goods in payment for their work. There are several crates of brandy and rum that, I have no doubt, would be very gratefully received. Shall I do that... use what is available?"

"Yes, yes indeed… anything you think appropriate. As I have already told you, I shall be only too happy to leave everything to you."

*

So the wagons were expertly repaired and made ready for the long journey south, which would take the servants across the Delaware River into Pennsylvania, then down through Maryland and Virginia before they reached North Carolina. Their excitement mounted daily as they packed what was to be taken, together with provisions for their day-to-day subsistence. Celia asked Benjamin to ensure that anything the servants might need in the way of warm blankets and skins to protect them on their travels, would be provided from the storehouse, and that he did. Then finally came the day of departure.

At the crack of dawn, Kingston, Amos and Harvest went around to the stables at the rear of 'Fortune's Hand', to hitch the teams of horses to the wagons that had stood ready-loaded for several days past. Kingston led the horses carefully from the stables, patting their necks and whispering softly to them. He eyed them over appreciatively as Amos and Harvest helped him to harness them.

"Ain't they handsome?" he asked, grinning broadly, "Massa Benjamin and me done us some real good trade over at Smith's Horse Barn… yessir."

He was referring to when Benjamin had taken him to purchase some strong healthy animals just a few days before, horses that would be able to endure the arduous journey ahead of them, without presenting too many problems. Again he had bartered with the stock from the storehouse, together with some of the older animals that Kingston had charge of, and that he feared would never survive the journey. Happily, they had been able to acquire sufficiently sturdy beasts, that Kingston felt sure would present little or no problems.

When everything was done and the spare horses secured to the back of the wagons, the three returned to the kitchen to announce that it was time to leave. Jassy stepped along to the breakfast room to tell the mistress, and all the family came to say their farewells. There was many a tearful eye in the process, but at the same time joyful anticipation of what the future might hold.

*

While Jassy went to fetch the mistress, Minnie decided to go down to the cabin just one more time. Despite her determination not to leave 'Fortune's Hand', she had finally acceded to her mother's pleas that she travel to North Carolina with the other servants. In truth, there was no other alternative, for she had nowhere else to go. Tears coursed down her cheeks as she sped towards the cabin, her mind filled with thoughts of her Indian. She felt so guilty at leaving him, after having promised to wait, that she was compelled by conscience to leave some indication of what had happened. When he returned, she hoped he would understand how badly she felt; for she knew, without the slightest doubt, that one day he would return. At that time, somehow, he must know why she was not there. In her hand she was clutching a small token, a linen handkerchief embroidered with the letter 'M' which had been given to her many years ago by Miss Rosalind. It had been finely worked, with great love, by her mistress when they were children, Minnie had always treasured it. Now it grieved her to have to part with it, but as she was unable to read or write it was the only message she could leave him, her own personal mark, her initial. She had tied it corner to corner into a small pouch, inside it she had placed a small lock of her hair and a scrap of paper on which she had drawn a wagon, albeit crudely. She pressed it to her heart before placing it on the ground in front of the cabin door. Then she found a suitable stone to place over it, making sure that the tiniest piece could be seen protruding from its edge. She raised her eyes upwards and mouthed silently, "Please God make my Indian find it… please."

When she arrived back at the house a few minutes later, her mother was standing at the kitchen door, she looked agitated. "There you is, Minnie… I guessed you down in them grounds again." She heaved a forlorn sigh, "I sho is glad we gittin' you away from this place, 'cos it ain't doin' no good you frettin' all the time. You jus' gotta forgit everythin' that happened here… now youse gonna start a new life and that jus' what you needs. The others is all waitin' to leave, they gone out to the wagons, so you best hurry else you is gonna be left behind, you hear?"

Grace placed an arm around her daughter encouragingly and they made their way to the stables. She tried her best to raise Minnie's spirits, "I is sorry I ain't comin' in the wagons with you honey-chile, but you be jus' fine. I be waiting' when you git to 'White Lakes'… you be happy when yo gits back there again, I knows you will."

*

Everyone was settled on board the wagons waiting impatiently for the latecomer. Her mother helped her up on the rear of the second wagon, beside Delilah and they started off, very slowly. Kingston was driving the lead wagon, with Tobias beside him; Maybelle and Ella sat on the back, their legs dangling. The second wagon was driven by Amos, with Clarence as his co-driver; then Harvest was driving the last one, with his father, Joshua, beside him and his mother and sister, Jassy and Clarissa as passengers.

The family waved until the wagons were out of sight, then they returned to the house to make ready for their own departure a little later that same morning. "I do hope they have a safe journey," said Lilybee, "and that my letter has the desired effect should they be accosted in any way. There are so many blackguards at large these days... but if they keep to the route we have suggested, then hopefully they should not encounter too much unwanted attention."

"I certainly hope not," replied Benjamin. "To be perfectly honest, I had given some thought to travelling with them myself, to ensure a safe passage in the event that they meet up with any unscrupulous characters."

"Oh Ben... no... we have only just married. I wouldn't want us to be separated so soon. Besides, Aunt Lilybee's letter states quite clearly why they are travelling. It should protect them adequately... of course it should." Rosalind slipped her arm through his and pulled him close, "Don't you know that we need you too?"

There was very little for the family to do for the next hour or so, as the servants had seen to everything before leaving. "I think I'll take one last look over the house," said Celia.

"Yes, do my dear... I shall sit with Edmund until the carriage comes for us. It shouldn't be too long if we are to arrive in Clinton in good time to catch the stage."

Rosalind was suddenly overcome with sentimentality too. She turned to Benjamin and asked, "Come down to the river with me darling... I just want to see it once more before we go?" They walked arm in arm through the trees. "I shall miss this place terribly... we have spent such wonderful times here, wading in the cool shallows during summer, picnicking under the trees with Mama. This is the only home I have ever had... now, of a sudden, I am saddened at the thought of leaving it."

"We'll make a home together soon Roz... one that you will come to love just as much, I promise," said Benjamin. "You shall choose where it will be, and... "

"Sshh... sshh... " cautioned Rosalind, "See, down there by the cabin... look."

Benjamin leant forward, peering intently to where she was pointing. He stiffened when he saw the Indian and placed his arm around her shoulders protectively. They stood watching him, hardly daring to breath. He moved silently, stealthily, around the cabin, crouching, examining the ground around it. He stooped down and picked something up. After looking at it very carefully he lifted it to his face and sniffed at it. Rosalind saw that it was something white, a cloth of some sort. He fiddled with it, as though trying to untangle it. After studying it for several seconds, he looked up in the direction of the house, then slowly began to walk towards it.

"He is coming up here... what shall we do?" asked Rosalind in alarm.

Run Swiftly was certain from his examination of Minnie's token, her message to him, that it had been left only a short time before his arrival. He decided to explore the area surrounding the house, to try and find more evidence of what had happened, where she might have gone.

Benjamin was completely fascinated to see how inconspicuously the Indian could make his way between the trees, without disturbing a single leaf; how warily he trod, with never the sound of twigs breaking underfoot. As he came close, Rosalind gasped aloud. She had suddenly recognised who he was. The Indian heard her gasp and sprang into action, his knife at the ready.

"Run Swiftly, it's Run Swiftly," said Rosalind aghast.

"You know him?" Benjamin was equally aghast.

"Yes, we found him... Minnie and I found him weeks ago, he was almost dead... floating in the river... in a canoe."

Run Swiftly now stood before them, staring into Rosalind's face as she spoke. He put away his knife.

"Minnie took care of him... kept him in the cabin, so that he wouldn't die."

Run Swiftly produced the handkerchief and thrust it forward for Rosalind to see. "Minnie... give this." He handed the token to Rosalind.

She took it carefully and looked at the childish drawing wrapped inside. It touched her heart, for she understood instinctively how much it must have hurt Minnie to leave without being able to say goodbye. She smiled at Run Swiftly and said kindly, "Minnie left a short time ago... we are all leaving here."

He looked puzzled, "I come take Minnie my village. She my woman now."

"She is not here... she has gone," said Rosalind.

"Where gone... she say wait here for Run Swiftly?"

Rosalind began to understand. She remembered how Minnie had spoken of the Indian, how fond she had become of him. Why not, she thought? He was an extremely handsome man. She tried to explain. "She had to go... we all have to go. She did not want to leave you, I'm sure." She felt sorry for him and for Minnie too. She turned to Benjamin, who had uttered not one word, so engrossed was he in listening to their strange conversation. "He could follow the wagons, couldn't he Ben?"

"Oh, er... yes, yes, of course."

"They wouldn't have gone too far, would they?"

"No, I'm sure they wouldn't. They are not travelling very fast." He looked at Run Swiftly, "You could catch up with them... I can tell you where they are going."

Run Swiftly nodded once, and Benjamin slowly explained to him that there were three wagons, carrying twelve black people. He told him they were taking a very long journey south, to North Carolina.

Run Swiftly nodded and grunted enthusiastically when Benjamin mentioned various names of towns on their route. He said proudly, "Run Swiftly scout in war, carry important message for army... go one camp here, go one camp here." He poked his forefinger to one side then the other, to indicate different directions. "Now I go... find Minnie. Go in canoe." He turned back towards the river and disappeared in an instant.

"Do you suppose he will find them Ben?" asked Rosalind. "I do hope that he does."

"I have not the slightest doubt of it my darling, and when he does, I hope with all my heart that Minnie will persuade him to escort the wagons down to North Carolina, for they could not find anyone more able to do so." He drew in a deep breath, "I almost envy then their journey... what I would not give to be with them; what an adventure that would be."

"Now don't go on about that again Ben," laughed Rosalind, "I have told you already that we need you too."

"I know my darling, I know, and I promise that I shall be here for as long as you do."

He crooked his arm and smiled lovingly at her; then clinging tightly to one another, they returned to the house.

Reunions 1866

One

Once Run Swiftly knew that Minnie had gone, the desire to find her overwhelmed him. He soon located where Storm Cloud lay waiting for him on the river bank, and instructed him to take them back along the Muscanetcong as quickly as possible. That was not to prove at all difficult, for they would now be borne along by the fast flow of the river as it wended its way out to the Delaware. As Storm Cloud paddled, Run Swiftly explained why Minnie had not returned to the canoe with him. He spoke urgently, pleading "Must travel fast... must be at Delaware when wagons come."

In response to his desperate plea, Storm Cloud gave one firm nod of his head and thrust the paddle even more rapidly in and out of the water. Aided by the current, the canoe sped along, almost as though it had grown wings. Run Swiftly longed to be able to assist Storm Cloud, but his injured shoulder was still painful, still not properly healed. Nevertheless, he could not wait to see Minnie again; in fact, it was his impatience that had brought him to come looking for her sooner than he should. After returning to his village to wait for his wound to heal, he had realised just how much he missed her, how unbearable it was to be parted from her. His heart had so ached with longing that he had finally begged Storm Cloud to take him to 'Fortune's Hand' to fetch her. At first Storm Cloud had been most reluctant to return; in fact, he had hoped never to return there again after that fateful night when he had killed the man whom he knew was ultimately responsible for the death of his wife, Laughing Eyes. His search had been long and hard, and he had learned much of Gilbert Hetherington before finally taking his revenge.

Since that moment weeks ago in the woods, as Storm Cloud was about to plunge his knife deep into the last of his wife's murderers, the words of his terrified victim had rung in his ears. Over and over again he had heard them...

"It was Hetherington," the man had screamed. At that time the name held no significance for Storm Cloud but yet he could not dismiss it from his mind. Hetherington... Hetherington... Hetherington: it haunted him all the while he remained hidden in the woods, waiting for nightfall; waiting to carry the bodies of Dancing Bear and Grey Wolf back to the canoes. Then, when it was dark, he took them one by one and placed them gently into the craft that lay waiting. He saw that Run Swiftly had left; he knew precisely what had taken place; the signs were there for him to read quite clearly. He saw the blood, much blood. He saw the deep furrows made by the canoe; they told him how weak the injured man had become, that his body had been slumped upon it as he dragged it down into the water, and he hoped with all his heart that his dead wife's brother had managed to survive the journey back to their village.

Great was the sorrow of Chief Running Deer when Storm Cloud related all that had happened on their mission of revenge, for now it seemed that he had also lost his son, but Storm Cloud's shock at discovering that Run Swiftly had not returned to the village, compelled him to set off once more to try and find him. His heart was heavy with grief as he made the painstaking journey along the Muscanetcong, searching diligently for any sign that might indicate what had happened to Run Swiftly. He stopped at the settlements along the river, making his enquiries discreetly, and it was in these places that he learned of the man called Hetherington; came to know of how much he was hated. He heard tell in every settlement of the way in which Hetherington and his men contrived to cheat and rob those with whom they did their trade, and there was much talk of how his murderous crew had recently fought viciously among themselves somewhere in the woods; so viciously, in fact, that not one of them had survived. Apparently, the incident caused little or no surprise, for their drunken revelry was common knowledge throughout the area. By the time the stories of the grizzly death scene came to Storm Cloud's ears, they had grown beyond all recognition, and he marvelled at how successful his cunning had proven, as not the slightest suspicion seemed to have fallen upon the Indians. His search continued, day after day, but he found no sign of Run Swiftly. Storm Cloud remained undeterred; he would not give in. In truth, he vowed not to return to his village, never to face Chief Running Deer again until he could tell him with certainty what had happened to his beloved son.

Then one evening, as night was closing in, just as he had decided to take a rest, he espied a small sheltered inlet on the river bank; an ideal place to pull in his canoe for the night. It was as he looked for kindling to make a fire that he saw the other canoe, the one that he knew Run Swiftly had used. His heart leapt with excitement at the discovery, the first clue to the whereabouts of his missing brother-in-law. As soon as it became dark he explored the area thoroughly, and it took very little time for him to discover the cabin which had hidden Run Swiftly so unobtrusively. He was overjoyed to find him alive and recovering so well, after believing him dead, and the two men exchanged information concerning recent happenings which were of great interest to them both. It was as they were talking that Minnie approached, but they were alarmed to see that she was being watched and followed covertly.

Before she came too close to the cabin, Run Swiftly and Storm Cloud slipped away through the trees, anxious not to be seen by her stalker. As soon as Run Swiftly was able to study the tall, fair haired man from the safety of the darkened woods, he recognised him immediately. That was all Storm Cloud needed; he could scarcely believe how conveniently his evil prey had been presented to him. The moment he heard the name 'Hetherington' issue from the lips of Run Swiftly, the moment he heard Minnie's anguished cry, he moved silently. With unbelievable speed, he emerged from the shadows and struck him skilfully between the shoulder blades. His job completed, he disappeared in the direction of the river, signalling to Run Swiftly to join him without any more delay. To this Run Swiftly readily agreed, but he could not desert Minnie before he had comforted her and made a promise that he would return one day, to take her to his people.

Now, weeks later, the two men were once again negotiating that same stretch of river, this time to find the woman Run Swiftly would have as his own. When they came to the place where the Muscanetcong joined the Delaware, Storm Cloud bore south, precisely as Benjamin Richmond had instructed Run Swiftly to do. They were still fortunate enough to be travelling with the flow of the river as it made its way out to the sea at Delaware Bay, but first it would pass through the town of Milford, where the wagons would have to come to cross over the bridge. When they did, Run Swiftly would be there waiting, eager to see Minnie again, to show her that he had kept his promise.

When they reached Milford and located the bridge, they secured the canoe and hid it on the bank of the river, before going to find a place on the far side from which they could observe everything that drove over it. Later that day their patience was rewarded when they caught sight of the wagons moving slowly across the bridge. They waited for them to roll past, then they followed for a while, careful to ensure that they were not seen. Run Swiftly did not wish to alarm Minnie or those who travelled with her, so he kept watch from a safe distance, waiting until he could attract her attention without causing her too much fright.

Before very long they saw that the wagons were beginning to slow down, then they drew to a halt. Kingston had decided that it was time to take a rest, stretch their legs for a bit; the horses too needed a break. Immediately they had jumped from the wagons, Tobias and Bella chased off into the woods to the side of the road, and Maybelle called after them: "You be careful now... don' you go gittin' lost, you hear?" She looked at Kingston and tut-tutted, shaking her head.

Minnie could see that she was concerned for their safety. "I'll go see what they doin'... make sure they don' go too far Maybelle...don' you worry." She followed the two youngsters through the trees, calling loudly to them: "Wait for me... wait for me... don' you go too far, don' you git lost now." She could hear them giggling; she heard the twigs cracking beneath their feet as they scurried away to hide from her. She smiled at their childish mischief, and joined in their game. Her thoughts returned for a brief moment to the grounds around 'Fortune's Hand', to the times she had played this same game with Edmund and Rosalind when they were small children.

Run Swiftly saw his opportunity and positioned himself between the laughing youngsters and Minnie, then as she approached along a narrow path in his direction, he stepped from the cover of the trees, into her view. Minnie gasped; her hand flew across her mouth as she caught sight of him standing proudly before her, just ten or twelve feet away. He pressed his forefinger to his lips to silence her. They stood transfixed, gazing at each other, neither daring to move, unable to believe that the other was really there. Since he had left 'Fortune's Hand', Minnie had prayed for Run Swiftly every day; many times a day, she had asked God to make him well again soon, so that he could come and fetch her, so that they could be together always. Now, at last, he was here... or was he, was her mind playing cruel tricks? He had been so much in her thoughts, never out of them, in fact, that now she was finding it difficult to believe what she was seeing. Surely she must be imagining it, for how could he be here, in these woods, so far away from 'Fortune's Hand'? It was simply not possible. She had heard Kingston telling Harvest that they were now out of New Jersey, they had reached Pennsylvania. No, it was simply impossible for him to be here. She felt tired, very very tired, for she had been up since the crack of dawn. That was it; of course, it was her tiredness causing strange imaginings. She closed her eyes tightly, then opened them again, fully expecting that the vision of Run Swiftly would disappear, but her eyes grew with disbelief as she saw him walking slowly towards her. Then he spoke: "Run Swiftly come keep promise, take you my people."

Minnie's heart turned a somersault and her legs seemed to have left her as she stumbled unsteadily towards him. "Oh, my Indian... my Indian, is it really you?" she whispered, enfolding him in her arms and drawing him close. She was still finding it extremely difficult to believe what was happening. How could he possibly have known that she would be here in these woods... how could he possibly have found her? All these questions raced through her mind, which was in complete and utter turmoil. "How you come here... how you know I here?" she asked, convinced by now that she was witnessing some kind of miracle.

Run Swiftly took hold of the small leather pouch that hung from a thin strip around his neck. He pulled open the top and produced her crumpled handkerchief from inside it. "Find this at cabin... man... woman... from house say you go long journey south in wagons. Say good I follow you."

Minnie felt elated; God had answered her prayers, there could be no doubt of it. She became aware of two pairs of eyes staring in terror at her Indian. Tobias and Bella had come looking for Minnie, their curiosity aroused by the sound of her voice talking to someone. They stood open-mouthed, paralysed with fear. She smiled and beckoned them to come closer, anxious to allay their fear. "It alright don' be afraid. I knows him, he my friend. This Run Swiftly."

Tobias and Bella stepped towards him cautiously, their fear still apparent, despite Minnie's reassurances, their mouths agape and their eyes as big as saucers. Minnie placed an arm around each of them and led them back towards the wagons. Run Swiftly followed quietly behind them.

A small tremor of fear ran through each of the servants when their eyes fell upon the Indian emerging from the woods on the heels of Minnie and the two young ones, but Minnie was quick to reassure them as she introduced him and explained how she came to know him, and why he was there. Jassy smiled knowingly. "So that what you was doin' out in the grounds at the house, every day and every night... now we knows."

It was not long before they all learned of how Run Swiftly had become a scout for the Union Army in the war, and of how well he knew the country. Kingston produced the crude map that they carried with them, and Run Swiftly tried to explain to them some of the difficulties they might encounter on their journey. The men were all deeply impressed by his knowledge, and Amos ventured to ask if he would agree to accompany them, at least until they reached the border of North Carolina. Harvest and Clarence thought it a splendid suggestion, and urged Run Swiftly to join them. Minnie could see the good sense in what they suggested, and as she was concerned for the safety of them all, she too coaxed him to stay as their guide, just as far as North Carolina. It was obvious to Run Swiftly that these simple, inexperienced people needed whatever assistance he could give them, so he nodded in agreement. "Run Swiftly come... take Minnie people to North Carolina. Then Minnie come my people... Minnie my woman."

"Oh, yes... yes," cried Minnie, "Soon as we gits to the border, when everybody safe, we go back to your village. I wants that more'n anythin'."

So it was settled, with no further ado, and the very first piece of advice that their guide had to give was that they pull the wagons further off the road into the shelter of the woods, so that they could set up camp for the night. He made a sign to Tobias and Bella to help him to find plenty of dry wood, then he showed them how to start the fire. They thoroughly enjoyed this occupation, for they had become enamoured of Minnie's Indian, and were following his every movement. In the meantime, the men moved the wagons, and the women busied themselves preparing the food.

Run Swiftly was much impressed by the extravagance of the meal, but as Delilah pointed out, their kind mistress had made sure that they had ample provisions for their arduous journey. "She jus' about the kindest mistress anyone ever knowed," added Delilah, and everybody agreed wholeheartedly.

When the meal was over and everything cleared away, they gathered together around the fire, which had been generously replenished with the logs that Tobias and Bella had collected. Delilah handed around mugs of fresh brewed coffee, and they settled themselves to rest and talk in the warm comforting glow of the fire. Minnie looked at Run Swiftly sitting beside her, and heaved a deep sigh of contentment. She could not remember ever feeling this happy in all her life. As for Run Swiftly, he sat cross-legged beside her on the thick warm blanket, his back erect, giving an occasional nod of his head as he looked with fascinated interest from one to the other of the smiling faces, glistening like polished ebony in the bright firelight. He too felt deeply content.

Eventually the conversation petered out as one by one drowsiness overcame them, so Jassy, Minnie and Clarissa fetched the fur robes and more warm blankets to bed everyone down for the night. Whilst they were busily occupied, Run Swiftly stole quietly into the depths of the wood, where he knew Storm Cloud had been patiently waiting. He gave their special signal, several whistled notes, softly and unobtrusively. In no time Storm Cloud appeared, without making the slightest sound. The two men spoke quietly together for several minutes, and when Run Swiftly had finished explaining everything to his brother-in-law, they bade one another farewell. Storm Cloud had been entrusted with the message for Chief Running Deer, and he would waste no time in returning to his village with it.

When he returned to the campfire, Run Swiftly could see Minnie watching for him. Her face broke into a smile and she beckoned him to where she had prepared their bed. She was longing to lie beside him once again, as she had done in the cabin all those weeks ago, warming his body back to life with her own. Now, as they snuggled together between the fur robe and the thick woollen blankets, Minnie knew, without doubt, that this was where she belonged. Nothing had ever felt so right, her happiness was complete.

*

The following morning, at first light, the wagons were on the move, and the mood of their occupants was one of joyfulness, coupled with relief that they now had in their midst someone for whom this vast untamed country held nothing that might invoke fear or trepidation. It had come as an unexpected shock on the previous day, when they were suddenly confronted with their own decision making, for they had never before had occasion to do so. Now they could choose for themselves what they might do, or where they might go but this had greatly encumbered them. The initial excitement had soon been replaced by apprehension, their innocent enthusiasm for adventure quashed, as their inexperience of the great unknown became apparent to them. This was their first taste of freedom, of independence, and it was proving to be a heady concoction, which presented a far greater challenge than they could ever have imagined.

Over the next few weeks, however, their guide and mentor was to introduce them gradually to the ways of his people, the Lenape Indians; show them the wonders of this mighty continent of which they stood in awe; this land that had been inhabited by his kind since time began. He would teach them his ancient arts of survival, of how to become as one with nature, so that it would provide for and protect them just so long as they honoured and respected it. They in turn would care to learn, would watch in fascination, marvelling at the skills that his people had shown him, that had been passed down from generation to generation. Run Swiftly was a man of few words, seldom bothering to speak, but he taught by example, and they followed without question. He showed them how to hunt for fresh meat when their provisions ran low, and the men thrilled at the chance to accompany him on his hunting trips, eager to practise what they had learned.

Then in the evening, when they rested around the campfire, he showed Tobias and Bella the crafts of the Lenape; how the women would scrape and clean the furs of the animals that the men had caught, and how they made them into clothing and other useful articles. Delilah and Maybelle thought it very amusing to see Tobias wearing the large fur hat that Run Swiftly fashioned for him, and which he refused to remove from his head, even when he slept at night. For Bella he made a fancy bandeau to wear around her forehead, with a decoration of pretty feathers fastened to the back of it.

Under Run Swiftly's watchful eyes, the group travelled safely, albeit slowly, until they came to the border of North Carolina. Several times they had encountered unexpected problems, and these had been overcome and subsequently forgotten, but they fully realised that the presence of Minnie's Indian had ensured their safe passage, of that there could be no doubt. Particularly when they had been confronted by three arrogant, abusive scoundrels, who had demanded to know their business and where they were headed. It was obvious that their main interest was in the fine wagons and horses. Run Swiftly, who had been riding a short distance ahead, checking the route, returned just as Joshua was producing the letter of authorisation given to them by their mistress Lilybee. When he came upon the scene and stood alongside Kingston, Amos, Harvest and Clarence, eyeing the strangers suspiciously, they immediately became uneasy; their arrogance seemed to desert them. They pulled their horses around without a single word, and left, obviously deciding that the opposition was far too formidable. As they galloped out of sight Kingston, Amos, Harvest and Clarence, each in turn, shook Run Swiftly by the hand enthusiastically and laughed aloud, almost unable to believe that he had despatched the threat so easily. It was fast becoming obvious to them though that their new found freedom would present many such difficulties in the days to come.

Now they were camped very near the border of North Carolina, sadly anticipating that in the morning Run Swiftly and Minnie would be leaving. Their evening meal over, they were sitting around the fire talking of the day's events, and of what they planned to do on the morrow. Minnie asked them to explain to her mother where she was, why she had not been able to return to 'White Lakes' as she had hoped. Suddenly she realised that she would have liked to see her mother one last time, to explain to her why she wanted to go with her Indian and live with his people; but she also wanted to tell her mother how much she loved her, that no matter who her father was, it could never change the way she loved her. She needed her to know that, but now she would not have the chance to say what was in her heart, and she was greatly saddened. As she was speaking, Run Swiftly turned to look at Minnie; he saw a solitary tear escape from her eye, saw it glistening as it fell gently to her cheek, for at that precise moment a charred log had fallen heavily into the heated depths of the fire, bursting into flames and throwing its light on to the faces of those gathered around it. He felt strangely moved by her sadness, and knew instinctively how much she yearned to see her mother one last time.

He looked at the faces of all of them as they sat unusually quiet, and he realised it was because they would no longer be travelling together after this night was over. He raised his hand, Indian fashion, fingers together, palm facing outwards, to draw their attention to what he was about to say, to indicate that it was something important. They all looked at him as he spoke, quietly, haltingly: "Run Swiftly not go north when sunrise in sky, Run Swiftly go with wagons... take Minnie see mother..."

Jassy broke in hopefully: "You means you is comin' with us... you ain't leaving tomorrow?"

Run Swiftly gave one firm nod of his head. "Good Minnie talk with mother first... then go my people." Again he gave a nod of his head. Immediately the mood of everyone changed. Relief flooded over them; not least of all Minnie.

"We sho' is glad you stayin' with us, " said Amos. "Why, don' know what we'd done without you."

"No sir... no sir," the others agreed.

"Anyways, now you git to see 'White Lakes', it sho' a grand place when we all left long time ago," said Joshua.

"Ain't no grand place no more," added Jassy: "Grace, she say nothin' ain't the same no more, not since the war."

They had already witnessed much of the destruction that had taken place in many of the towns along their route, but it was to become more and more apparent the further south they went.

Two

The diminished grandeur of 'White Lakes' was also to come as a considerable shock to Celia as the coach transporting the family turned into the sweeping drive. She remembered with fondness the excellence of the house and its grounds on the last occasion she had visited, and now she found it difficult to comprehend that the war could have brought it to such a pitiable state. Lilybee was quick to notice her sister-in-law's shocked reaction, but she remained silent, weighed down by her own sorrow at all the destruction that had been wrought.

In stark contrast, when they came inside, Celia was amazed to see that it was still immaculately kept. It appeared that the furnishings and accoutrements, everything in fact, had been well maintained and lovingly cared for, and despite Lilybee's recent absence, everything was as she might have wished it to be. The servants too were neat and freshly attired, and the kitchen hands immediately set about preparing a meal for the weary arrivals, whilst the men removed the luggage to the rooms upstairs.

When they finally sat down to eat in the elegant dining room, candles glowing from well-polished candelabra, Celia felt as though she had never ever left. She smiled across the table at Lilybee and said kindly: "This is just as I have always remembered 'White Lakes' dear sister-in-law... it is a place of beauty and tranquillity, and it is as though I have never been away from it."

"Thank you my dear, I am so glad you feel that way about it, for I too have always felt at peace here." She raised her glass and glanced at everyone seated around the table, before saying: "And now allow me to welcome you all to your new home, and I hope that it will give you as much happiness as it has given me."

As everyone murmured their appreciation, Lilybee took a long drink from her glass. She was glad to be home again, and now she was even beginning to feel faint stirrings of optimism about the future; a future she would be sharing with family.

They were all very tired after dinner, and no one seemed the least bit inclined to talk after they had finished their coffee, so it was decided that they should go to their beds. "An early night will do us all good, don't you think? And I am sure we shall feel much better for it in the morning," said Lilybee: "I shall just go along to the kitchen and dismiss the servants, then I shall retire. Goodnight to you all and I hope you will sleep soundly."

As the others climbed the stairs wearily, Lilybee made her way along the hallway towards the kitchen, but before she reached the door she saw Douglas emerging from it. He turned and called back over his shoulder: "Just bring the tray into the library... I shall be in there."

Lilybee presumed he had just come in from wherever he had been, and had asked one of the servants to prepare him a supper tray. "Oh, there you are brother," she said: "I have been wondering where you were. I hoped that you might be here to welcome everybody when they arrived, but I daresay you were with that Clayton man as usual." She could not hide her disapproval.

Douglas looked puzzled. "Welcome everybody... who... have you brought guests from New Jersey. Has Gilbert come with you?"

"Not guests Douglas ... no... and Gilbert has not come either. I have much to explain to you." She breathed a heavy sigh: "Oh, if only you had been here earlier at a more reasonable time. It would have been so much easier. As it is, I am extremely weary; we are all weary from the travelling. The others have retired for the night, and I was just about to do so myself... as soon as I have dismissed the servants. I think we shall have to leave things until the morning... that would be best. I'll speak to you after breakfast... explain everything then." She paused for a moment, placing her hand to her forehead thoughtfully. "I should tell you though that Gilbert is dead."

Douglas turned pale. She could see that the news had shocked him deeply. "How... when did he die?" he asked feebly.

"It was several weeks ago. Dreadful really, he is thought to have been murdered I'm afraid." She waited for several seconds, allowing Douglas to digest what she had said. Then she went on, "But that is what one must expect when one lives life the way he did." She looked at her brother meaningfully. "Now you know why I have always warned you to keep away from Ralph Clayton... why I want to be rid of him. I have never liked the man... you know that. He is completely evil and I fear that one day he too will bring about some tragedy. Look, we must discuss all this tomorrow morning ... it is very late and I really do need to rest."

As she turned from him he whispered hoarsely: "Ralph Clayton is dead too... and murdered, I believe, so your wish to be rid of him has been granted."

Lilybee could hardly believe her ears; it seemed so improbable. Two men whom she disliked so intensely, now dead. She shook her head disbelievingly and said again: "We must discuss all this tomorrow. I am far too tired for it now I shall be off to my bed just as soon as I have looked in on the servants."

Douglas disappeared along the hallway and into the library, where he could steady his nerves with a very large brandy whilst he waited for his supper. The news of his brother's death, so soon after that of his esteemed overseer, had shocked him to the core. To each of them he had given his adulation unreservedly; to him they had seemed indestructible, almost immortal. Now they were both gone from his life and he did not know how he could go on without them.

*

When her mistress left the kitchen to go to her bedroom, Grace accompanied her, and it was as she was preparing her for bed that Lilybee first noticed how downcast her maid appeared to be. "What is the matter Grace?" she asked wearily, "What is it?"

Grace hung her head and answered softly: "It my Sunny Blue Ma'am... he dead."

Lilybee collapsed heavily on to the chair beside her bed. "Oh, no... not another death... what on earth is happening to us?" She looked at her maid and saw how desolate she was. "Oh, I am so sorry Grace ... do forgive me. It is just that I am extremely tired, and my brother has just told me that Mr Clayton, the overseer, is dead too. It is said that if you hear of one death, then you will hear of three. Have you heard that saying Grace? Well now we have our three: my brother, your son and the overseer. Unbelievable... it really is unbelievable."

"It the overseer who killed my Sunny Blue... Massa Clayton. We always knowed he'd do it one day, Mose and me.

That why Mose run away Ma'am, and took Sunny Blue with him."

It was all becoming too much for Lilybee in her travel-weary state. She beckoned to Grace: "Help me into bed my dear... do," she said: "I don't think I have ever felt more tired."

Grace folded back the coverlet and sheet and helped her mistress into the sumptuous comfort of the enormous bed. She plumped up her numerous pillows and made her completely comfortable. "Oh, that is better," Lilybee said, breathing a sigh of relief. "Now my dear, just sit here beside me and tell me how on earth Mr Clayton could possibly have killed young Sunny Blue... surely he should have been somewhere safe with his father, with Mose. I simply cannot make head or tail of it all."

Grace began to relate the story exactly as she had heard it from Mattie and the other servants in the kitchen. "Well Ma'am, seems like when Mose and Sunny Blue run off they jus' keep goin' till they come all the way up to Canada... it take a long long time before they git there, but 'ventually there they was. Now, seems like Mose done real good for himself... he git himself a job in some trading store, and the man owned it liked him real good. Mose and Sunny Blue helped the man build on to the store 'cos the trading was goin' so good. Then after a while, Mose build a cabin so he could bring me to live there too, jus' like he promised. He tell me the night he run off... one day he comin' back to git me. Well, when Mose decide it time to come and git me, the owner of the store he fell real sick, and then he need Mose more'n ever... he need him to run the store. So Sunny Blue say he comin' to git me on his own. Mose he tol' him no, 'cos he not growed up enough to take that long journey alone, but Sunny Blue he say he goin' anyways. So he come to 'White Lakes' one night, and he keep himself hid down in our cabin till daylight, till he see somebody could tell him 'bout his mammy ... where she is, and why she ain't in the cabin no more. When he hear I is up in the North, he git mighty sad, and he don' know what to do. The others tell him to keep himself hid in the cabin and wait till I comes back again... that the only thing he can do. So he wait. Well Ma'am, you knows how youngsters is, not easy for my boy to stay hid when he see his friends passin' by, and the days comin' and goin' and his mammy far away. So he sneak out sometimes, when he think it safe, but them times git to be more'n more, till one time, in the evenin' it was, Massa Clayton see him. He call out... he call out real loud, and the boys was real scared. They knowed they in trouble soon as he see Sunny Blue. Most of 'em run off home, but jus' a few run off and hid, so they knowed what Massa Clayton done to my boy. He up on his horse, like always, with his whip, and he come after Sunny Blue real fast. He bring that whip up and he crack it across my boy hard as he could... then he bring it up again and lash it round Sunny Blue's neck... "

Grace tried to choke back her tears without success. She wiped her eyes quickly with her hand, took a trembling breath, then went on, "He kicked his horse real hard, so it reared up with fright... then it run like the devil was comin' after it. Sunny Blue was dragged alongside, he was chokin'... he grabbed a-hold of the saddle with two hands, tryin' to stay alive somehow. Then Massa Clayton git real mad... he pull that horse to a stop and jumped down on top of Sunny Blue. He was shoutin' somethin' 'bout teachin' him a lesson... and his pappy wasn't gonna stop him this time, then he stood up and he pull the whip away from Sunny Blue's neck. Sunny Blue was jus' layin down on that dirt road... he wasn't movin', but Massa Clayton, he whipped him, and he whipped him, and he wouldn't stop." Grace could not go on. She buried her face in her hands and wept bitterly. Everything was silent. She gradually composed herself and looked up at her mistress guiltily, but her mistress was fast asleep. Grace did not know how long she had been asleep, but it was of no consequence to her. Now she had no reason to continue with her story, no reason to tell her mistress how the other servants dealt with their hated overseer, and for that she was grateful.

She remained quietly seated, going over in her mind what she had been told, dreading the recollection, yet drawing from it a small measure of comfort in that Sunny Blue's murderer had been made to pay for his vile crime.

Apparently, the youngsters who witnessed what happened to her boy had been too shocked, too terrified to move until the overseer had finished his vicious attack. When he had ridden off in the direction of his cabin, once he was well out of sight, they emerged cautiously from their hiding places and nervously approached the lifeless form of their friend. Sunny Blue lay completely motionless, his blood seeping into the dry dusty road. The boys were too horrified to touch his lifeless form, and the smallest of them began to whimper and cry. "Come on... we best go tell Pappy," stammered his older brother. Anxious to escape from the grizzly scene, the others needed no second bidding; they all turned and ran back towards the shacks that were their homes. As soon as their parents heard what had happened, they set off at once to investigate. They too were appalled at what they saw when they came to the place where the dead boy lay. They had all seen what a whipping could do to a victim, some of them had been victims themselves, but never before had they seen anything resembling such brutality as this, and they knew what had provoked this particular attack, why Sunny Blue had been made the scapegoat. The conditions under which they had always been forced to exist had been unimaginably harsh and intolerable, but since the Thirteenth

Amendment outlawing slavery had been ratified, men like Ralph Clayton had stopped at nothing to prove to the negro that his conditions had undergone little change. Since the end of the war the 'Black Codes' had come into force, and these simply replaced one type of slavery with another. The Southern Confederates may have lost the war, but they were determined not to lose their supremacy over their former black slaves. Ralph Clayton had waited a long time to exact his revenge upon Mose and his son, and now he had taken it in full and satisfying measure.

One of the men stooped down and gently rearranged Sonny Blue's body, so that he lay on his back, his arms at his sides. "Somebody go fetch a blanket, so we can move him from here," he said.

One of the women ran off and returned shortly afterwards with a cloth for the body; then the men wrapped it carefully and carried it back to the cabin that Mose had rebuilt for his family. As they went, the group sang together one of the haunting negro spirituals that so poignantly epitomized their years of suffering, and that served to release their pent up emotion, but on this occasion their emotion was not to be so easily quelled. After they had placed Sunny Blue on his bunk, the women cleansed him with loving care, just as his mother would have done; then they took it in turns to sit with him through the night, a single candle aglow, waiting for the dawn of the following day, so that he could be laid to rest in their special little graveyard.

Whilst the women watched over Sunny Blue's corpse, the men set off in a militant group, their anger ablaze, intent upon finding their hated overseer, the perpetrator of this evil crime. He would be made to pay for what he had done. Once and for all they would put an end to his reign of terror. From somewhere they had finally managed to summon up enough courage to do what they knew was right. The hour had come… the final hour for Ralph Clayton.

As they approached his cabin they could see a light through the windows, evidence that he was there. Then when they came closer they could distinguish two men inside; they knew immediately he had a visitor, and knew immediately who it was. Undeterred, they advanced up the wooden steps and across the stoop. Then they struck. That heaving, violent body of men, their anger overflowing, burst through the door of the cabin, their one aim to destroy. All was pandemonium for several minutes, as the cabin filled to its limit. Chairs were smashed, the table and bed overturned as the violence erupted out of control. The biggest and strongest man had by now grabbed the disbelieving victim, and was holding him fast from behind, his enormous arm clasped across his throat, pressing his writhing body painfully against his own. Suddenly an oil lamp was overturned in the furore, catching light to some paperwork that lay in the path of the spilled liquid that had filled its base. As the flames began to leap menacingly, the angry mob hurried out of the door to safety.

At the same time Douglas Hetherington made his escape, terror-stricken, and fearing for his life. He completely ignored the frenzied screams of his ill-fated friend, and fled on his horse before he too received similar treatment. Ralph Clayton was ejected through the door and buffeted from one to the other of his assailants, until he reached the steps. Then he was hit forcefully in the back of the neck and plummeted down the steps, turning a somersault and landing flat on his back on the ground, right at the feet of a very heavily built negro, who promptly stamped his foot on the prostrate form, to make sure that it remained exactly where it was. He glanced up as someone called to him and threw him the whip that Ralph Clayton had always been so fond of using. A roar exploded from the crowd, and the whip rose and fell with vehement force, accompanied by the agonized groans of the recipient. When the groans ceased and the body no longer jerked, the men fell silent. Then, together, the two biggest of them lifted the limp body, upon which had been placed the dreaded whip; they carried it up the wooden steps and across the stoop, and hurled it with all their might through the open door into the raging fire, which would soon destroy every last particle of the cabin that had set the scene for so many horrific ordeals; the place in which so many of their children had been robbed of their innocence. It was fitting that it should be burned, for it was a place that the devil had inhabited.

*

Grace gave a sudden start. She opened her eyes, wondering for the moment where she was. She too had dropped off to sleep, as had her mistress. She felt stiff now from sitting for so long on the upright chair. She glanced at her mistress and saw that she was perfectly comfortable, then she crept quietly from the room and hurried out into the late night. All she wanted now was to go to her own cabin, the cabin Mose had turned into a home, where she could climb into bed and ease away her sadness with sleep.

Three

Not one of the family arose very early the following morning, so breakfast was taken rather late. With the exception of Douglas, Lilybee was the last to arrive, but she felt greatly refreshed from her long sleep. "Good morning everybody, I hope you all slept comfortably... and well," she said cheerily, as she entered the dining room. Everyone murmured a reply and continued eating. "I see that Douglas has not yet put in an appearance," she said: "I want to introduce him to you Benjamin... and Rosalind, of course. He hasn't seen you since you were a small baby. Then perhaps later in the morning he might show you around 'White Lakes'... I'm sure you would both like to familiarise yourselves with the place; come to know everything about it."

"We should find that most interesting Ma'am," said Benjamin enthusiastically.

"Oh, do call me Aunt, young man, you are a family member now, after all."

"I shall remember to do so from now on Ma'am... er... I mean Aunt."

Everybody laughed. They were still chuckling as Douglas came into the room.

"Have I missed a good joke?" he asked.

"No ... not really," replied Lilybee, "Come now let me introduce you to your niece and her new husband."

The formalities were soon over, and whilst Douglas consumed his breakfast Lilybee told him that she had suggested he take Benjamin and Rosalind on a tour of 'White Lakes' some time during the morning.

"Certainly, glad to," said Douglas affably.

"Before you do, might I have a word with you?" asked his sister. "Perhaps you will come to the library when you have finished your breakfast."

"Of course, of course. Shan't be long."

Everybody began to disperse, and Lilybee took herself off to the library to wait for Douglas.

It was not long before he joined her, and she bade him make himself comfortable in a large armchair facing her, on the opposite side of the fireplace. Once he was seated, she explained to him that she had invited their sister-in-law and her family to make a permanent home at 'White Lakes'. Then she went on to tell him all that had happened concerning the murder of their brother Gilbert, and of how he had left Celia and his children without a penny; and even worse, that the bank had seized 'Fortune's Hand', lock, stock and barrel, to pay off his mountainous debts, which in turn had rendered his family not only penniless, but without a roof over their heads. "I had no alternative but to take them in Douglas, but I did it gladly, for as you know, I have always been extremely fond of Celia and the children, and their presence here will give me the greatest pleasure."

"I'm sure, I'm sure," said Douglas: "And perhaps Rosalind's husband might prove of great use in the running of the place."

Lilybee studied her brother for several seconds. Upon hearing of the death of the overseer, she had immediately presumed that now Douglas would shoulder his responsibilities; something to which he had been unaccustomed in the past, but it would seem that he was quite prepared to find yet another substitute to take over the daily tasks that would normally fall upon him.

211

"I should not hold out too much hope of that Douglas, for Benjamin appears to me to be an extremely intelligent young man with lots of ambition, so I think it more than likely that he will be on the lookout for opportunities in keeping with his talents. In any case, don't you think that it is high time you showed some interest in 'White Lakes'?"

"Well things just aren't the same any more, as you know... and without Ralph Clayton there will be no controlling the workers. You have no idea how truculent they have become Lilybee, since their heads have been filled with thoughts of freedom." His expression changed as he said arrogantly: "There are moves afoot though, moves that will put paid to all that."

"What do you mean... what moves?" asked Lilybee. impatiently. Why was it that her brother could always try her patience so, she wondered?

"You don't think that we shall allow the Yankees to dictate to us, do you? I was at a meeting last night... oh, if only you could have been there. That's why I was not here when you arrived. We were discussing the race riots in Memphis at the end of April. You must have heard about them; forty-six nigras were killed. We have to take the law into our own hands. What do those Northerners know about the ways of the South? We are forming a society now... we aim to maintain our authority, our white superemacy... it's called the Klu Klux Klan. It was founded in Pulaski, Tennessee last Christmas Eve, and it's spreading throughout the South. It's the only way we shall keep our control."

Lilybee was horrified. She placed her hands over her ears, crying: "Stop Douglas, stop... I refuse to listen to any more. I shall not hear another word about it in my house, do you understand? Don't you think there has been enough destruction and killing during the war. See what it has done to us, to our land, to our homes… and yet you want it to continue? Why, oh why will you not accept that the time has come for change? We should be thinking of how we can re-build the South, make it prosperous again… how we can restore it to its former glory. Have you learnt nothing of what tyranny and hatred can do? Look at what happened to your precious Ralph Clayton… see what his evil hatred finally did to him?"

Douglas looked at his sister aghast.

"Oh, yes… I have heard what happened to Grace's son," she said, "so it is not too difficult to imagine the repercussions. Now, I am warning you Douglas, I never want to hear another word about secret societies… about punishments or killings. I intend to make sweeping changes here at 'White Lakes'. I shall do everything in my power to restore this land, and I shall do it with or without your help. Our workers will be paid for what they do, and they will live their lives here without menace. My dear Percy realised too late how unjust the system was, that is why he granted Mose his freedom. He made his decision to do what he knew was right… maybe if there were more men of his calibre, then this congressional plan for reconstruction might stand a chance of succeeding."

Douglas was shaking his head defiantly. As he was about to speak, Lilybee leaned towards him: "I know exactly how Percy foresaw what should happen at 'White Lakes'… I still have the letters he wrote to me whilst he was away. As I have just told you, I intend to make changes here, as he would have done, and if that is not to your liking then you must leave."

She stood up and walked towards the door, making it blatantly obvious that she had no wish to listen to any arguments her brother might put forward.

*

Little did Lilybee realise that in less than one week her differences with Douglas would be solved in a most unexpected and propitious manner. It all came about upon receipt of a letter from England; a very important looking letter, that had been sent to her from a firm of solicitors in Lincoln's Inn, London; her father's solicitors, in actual fact. Lilybee took the letter into the library before opening it. She sat at her desk and took up her paper knife. She hesitated for several seconfs before slitting open the envelope; it was almost as though she had a premonition of what it contained. As soon as she had read the first sentence she clutched it to her bosom, not wanting to read on. "Oh, no, no, poor, dear Papa," she sobbed. She sat in shocked silence for several minutes, then she read the letter though she knew she rang for one of the housemaids and asked her to go and fetch Celia and Master Douglas, if he could be found.

Celia arrived almost immediately, and Lilybee handed her the letter without a word.

"Oh, my dear, I am so sorry, so very sorry. I know how fond you were of your father," said Celia, after she had read the sad news. She drew her sister-in-law into her arms, murmuring sympathetically: "There, there."

Lilybee buried her face in Celia's shoulder and wept bitterly. The two women were still clinging together when Douglas came in shortly afterwards. "You wanted to see me urgently?" he asked.

Lilybee turned to him, her eyes reddened and swollen. "Papa has died Douglas... a stroke. I have just received the news from his solicitors." She handed the letter to Douglas, then went and sat down again. "Please, come and sit with me Celia," she urged: "We have to talk about this."

Celia seated herself in one of the small armchairs and waited while Douglas read the contents of the letter. It was quite lengthy, and he read it very carefully, studying certain passages minutely. When he had digested everything of particular interest to himself, he gave it back to Lilybee. "So... he has gone at last," he said unemotionally. "He has certainly lived longer than most do."

Lilybee looked startled. "Is that all you can say... have you no sorrow?" she demanded.

"Well, he was never particularly fond of me, nor Gilbert for that matter, so what do you expect?" he replied sullenly.

"And why do you suppose that was? You caused him nothing but heartache, the pair of you."

"You were always his favourite, you know you were; see; he has even left you the house in London."

"Because he knew how I loved it... and you boys cared not a jot for it; no more did your mother." Lilybee could feel her anger rising, as always when they conversed with one another. "You have your fair share though, don't you?" she asked disdainfully. "You have nothing to complain about, as far as I can see."

The solicitors had outlined the main features of Lawrence Hetherington's Will, and the extent of his wealth came as a considerable surprise to Celia. Her father-in-law had made extremely generous provision for his three children, but as her husband, Gilbert, was no longer alive, then the whole of his inheritance would pass to his son, Edmund, with the stipulation that he take care of his mother and sisters, and provide adequately for their needs. Celia did not doubt for one moment that he would, being of the kind and generous nature that he was.

Lilybee directed her conversation to Celia. "Of course, Edmund will receive his father's share of everything my dear, and I am really delighted. That will amply provide for him for life, and for any family he might eventually have. We must speak to the youngsters, break the news to them without delay." She looked at Douglas with contempt: "And now, with your share of father's fortune, you will be free to go where you wish, and do exactly what you want, which I am sure will suit us both ideally. What will you do? Have you ever thought of returning to England?"

Douglas smiled complacently: "Actually, I haven't, but I am sure you will be relieved to learn that I shall be leaving 'White Lakes' very soon."

Lilybee's curiosity overcame her; she could not resist the temptation to know what her brother was up to now. "Well, what have you in mind ?" she asked.

"I have been informed that there is a fortune to be made from growing tobacco. You would be surprised at how many of our North Carolina slave owners are turning their attention to this most lucrative crop. In fact, I recently met a new acquaintance, and we have talked of setting up together, going into the tobacco trade. He is conversant with all aspects of it and now, with the increased finance I shall have at my disposal, we should be able to get the venture under way much more quickly than we had anticipated. My friend has already found a place that would lend itself readily to the growing of tobacco."

Lilybee could not hide her astonishment; she was deeply intrigued to discover that her brother had even discussed such a venture, although she feared that his acquaintance would not be a particularly desirable character, if his previous choice of companion was anything to go by. "So, Douglas, what has tempted you to try your hand at tobacco growing, might I ask?"

"Well, everyone is talking of how a fellow called Washington Duke came back from the army and started up a small tobacco factory at his farm near Durham Station. He and his sons pack it in muslin bags and ship it all over the country… it's known as Bull Durham, and it seems they have built up a thriving business. Apparently it all started when Sherman's army was camped near their place in the war. The troops came to like the tobacco that was grown there so well, that when they returned to the North they took it with them, and that's how its popularity grew. And they are not the only ones cashing in on it. It seems that there is a family called Reynolds at Winston; they are producing tobacco for pipes and cigarettes, and it is becoming more popular than the old 'chaw'."

"My friend and I are thinking of growing the stuff and processing it ourselves. We'd like to build a factory to manufacture the finished product. It struck me as a fascinating challenge. I can't see how it could possibly fail."

Lilybee decided to be magnanimous. "Well Douglas, I wish you success with your new venture," she said: "But do make absolutely sure that your business associate is completely trustworthy, won't you?" She knew instinctively that he would not be.

Douglas thought it was time to leave. As he reached the door he turned and said: "I would not expect you to approve of any associate of mine dear sister, but your opinion has never deterred me in the past, therefore, I shall simply disregard it as I have always done. Oh, and I shall let you know the exact date on which I shall be leaving 'White Lakes' and I can assure you it will be as soon as I am able to arrange it." He slammed the door loudly as he left.

"He will never change, I'm afraid," Lilybee said with a despondent sigh: "But I'll not waste any more time on him. Let us instead go and find Edmund and tell him what a wealthy young man he has become: I'll send one of the housemaids to find Benjamin and Rosalind too, then we can tell them all the sad news of their dear grandpapa's passing." Lilybee dabbed gently at her eyes and nose one last time as they left the library together. "I still cannot believe he has gone," she said sadly.

Four

The time that her mistress needed to mourn the death of her beloved father, afforded Grace the opportunity that she too needed to mourn the death of her beloved son. She was completely distraught at his loss, and the knowledge that Mose was unaware of what had happened added to her grief. She longed to be able to tell him, but she had no way of doing so, and her frustration at times threw her into such mental torment that she became convinced she would never see her dear husband again either. She had always been an extremely quiet, reserved soul, but now she withdrew even more into her own desolate little world. The other servants did their best to give her what comfort they could, but it seemed that the only consolation she sought was in her visits to their special graveyard, where her boy's body was laid to rest. It was not far from her cabin, and she would escape to it at every available opportunity; during her noon day break, and again in the evening, just as soon as she had dressed her mistress for dinner. Then she would sit by the graveside, crooning softly all the melancholy spiritual songs that Sunny Blue had learned and loved and the sweet sound of her voice would be carried on the still night air, away in the distance to the workers' cabins, where they would be taking their rest.

It was on one such evening, as she sat crooning, that she heard a voice calling her name. It came first from a distance, not much more than a whisper, so that she could almost believe she was imagining it; then gradually growing louder, coming closer; so close that she was forced to turn and see who was calling. She stopped singing immediately she saw Mose, hardly able to believe that he was really there. He came to her and gently pulled her to her feet. "Missy... my Missy," he whispered hoarsely, as his strong arms enfolded her.

Grace clung to him, sobbing as though her heart would break. "Oh, Mose... is yo' here, is yo' really here?" she cried.

"Course I is... didn't I tell yo' I'se coming back to git yo' one day?"

They rocked to and fro in one another's arms for a very long time, then finally Mose took Grace's tear-stained face in his enormous hands and kissed her tenderly; he kissed her eyes, he kissed her cheeks, and he kissed her lips, long and hard. "I missed yo' Missy... I missed yo' real bad," he murmured, as he took her in his arms once again: "And I tells yo' this... we ain't never gonna be apart no more ... never, yo' 'hear?"

"I hears Mose. I missed yo' too... every day, all the time. I never stopped thinkin' 'bout yo'... yo' and Sunny Blue." She turned and looked down at the raised mound of earth that concealed their son's body: "He lyin' here Mose ... here alongside old Isaac, and Angelique, and Blossom Junior, but he too young to be dead. Why it had to happen to our boy... why?" Again her tears began.

"I knows Missy, it ain't easy to understand, 'cos he a good boy. He never done nothin' wrong not to nobody, but we has to git on with our own lives now. I'se gonna take yo' away from this place, up to Canada so we can make a new life together... yo' be happy there, and yo' be free. Ain't that what yo' always talked 'bout... what yo' always wanted?"

Grace gasped. Mose's words had shocked her. "We can't, we can't" she sobbed: "Not without Sunny Blue. We can't leave him here... no, no. He be all alone if we goes."

Mose placed his hands on Grace's shoulders and pressed her gently to the ground. "Sit down Missy, sit down," he said kindly: "I jus' wants to talk to you."

He began by telling her all about the journey that he and Sunny Blue had made from North Carolina to Canada, and of how much they had enjoyed the adventure of it all; how the boy had learned to hunt for their food, and make a shelter when they needed it. He told her what a vast country Canada was, full of opportunity for those brave enough to seek it out. "Every man can be hisself there... ain't nobody gonna tell yo' what yo' has to do. Not like here."

"But we is all gonna be free now," said Grace: "That the law."

"Huh... that might be the Yankee's law, but they ain't down in the South to see if it workin', is they? I had to keep under cover in the day, soon as I git away from the North. I only travel after sundown, 'cos if I don't, man, I finds myself in deep trouble. Too many of them whites ready to pick me up and put me to work somewheres I don't like to be. Why you think I tell Sunny Blue he can't come to git you alone? Then look what happen when he git here. Zac tol' me all about what Massa Clayton done, and how they make him pay for it after, but there a lot more like him around, and they gonna make bad times for us jus' as long as they lives."

Grace nodded disconsolately. "I knows youse right Mose, but I can't leave our boy here."

"No... and he ain't gonna be here. He gonna be with us, wherever we is Missy; that only a body under that ground ... Sunny Blue gonna be travellin' with yo' and me when we goes back to Canada, 'cos that where he wants to be... livin' inside of us, and knowin' we is free... jus' as free as his spirit."

Grace nodded her head several times, turning over in her mind what Mose had said. The idea of going North had always captured her imagination. Maybe they should start a new life... get away from the Hetheringtons, with all the unsavoury memories. She would have some regrets, of course. She would be sad to leave her mistress, but now that her family had come to live at 'White Lakes' she would not feel the need of her maid's company so keenly. She turned to Mose, "Alright I agrees, but we is not goin' till Minnie gits here, and if she wants to come with us, then we all goes together."

"That jus' fine by me, yo' knows how I love that li'l gal." Mose stopped dead, looking thoughtful. He scratched his head, "Listen to me... she ain't that li'l gal no more, is she? Yo' gotta tell me how she growed up... what she bin doing since she gone away. She comin 'back ain't she?"

Grace had mentioned to the other servants that Mistress Celia and her family had come to live with the Lady Lilybee at 'White Lakes' for good, and that all her servants would be returning with her, but she had not breathed one word of what had happened to her daughter at the hands of Gilbert Hetherington. Mose had been told by them what little they knew of the family from Grace, but he had not heard anything about Minnie.

She stood up, saying: "There a lot for me to tell yo' Mose... let's go back to the cabin. Ain't nobody here ever gonna know what I'se got to say, not nobody... yo' has a right to know though, 'cos youse the only pappy she had."

Mose stood up, wondering what on earth he was about to learn, but whatever it might be, he knew it must not be allowed to change their plans; nothing must spoil them, of that he was determined.

They strolled back to their cabin and when they were safely inside, with no fear of being overheard, Grace spilled out the whole sordid tale of what Minnie had suffered at the home of Gilbert Hetherington and of how he had been

222

attacked and killed by an Indian who had sought his own revenge.

Mose was sickened at what had befallen Minnie. He shook his head disbelievingly, his eyes tight shut, his face contorted as though in pain. Finally he managed to control his feelings enough to whisper: "It a good thing that evil man bin killed, 'cos I'd kill him myself for what he done... yes sir, with my bare hands I'd do it, if'n it took me rest of my life to find him, that's what I'd done. After what he done to you all them years ago, I wanted to kill him, but nothin' I could do then... now it different, I knows what it like to be free, to be my own man. I tell you Missy, our life gonna be good when we gits away from this place, we's gonna start a new life, like we jus' bin born again."

Grace nodded. "Yes, youse right Mose, I can see that... we never be happy stayin' here. Best we git right away, somewhere we never has to think about the Hetheringtons again, never again."

*

The next day Grace told the Lady Lilybee that Mose had returned to 'White Lakes', that he wanted to take her to Canada with him, so that they could make a new life for themselves. She told her how sorry she was to be leaving such a kind mistress, but that after all the tragedies of the past it was probably for the best.

Lilybee could not disguise her shock at hearing Grace's announcement, but at the same time she told her that she could fully understand why she wanted to leave. "When do you intend to go Grace?" she asked.

"Jus' as soon as Minnie gits here Ma'am... if you agrees that is. Mose and me, we wants to take her with us."

"Do you think she will want to come with you?" Lilybee had been told about Minnie's Indian by her niece Rosalind; the story had kept the family enthralled during their journey in the stagecoach from New Jersey to North Carolina. Rosalind had also told them of Run Swiftly's appearance just as they were about to leave, and that as Benjamin had given him instructions on how to find the servants and the wagons, he very much hoped that the Indian might accompany them until they reached the end of their journey. Lilybee had exclaimed her delight at his sagacity, and congratulated him warmly. Now she would not divulge to her maid that in all probability her daughter Minnie might not want to go with her and Mose to Canada. She decided that it was not for her to interfere.

Grace was considering what her mistress had just asked her. She had certainly not given too much thought to Minnie refusing; in fact, she did not think that she would. "I's sure Minnie will come Ma'am ... well, sure as I can be. We bin away from one another all them years, we got some catchin' up to do." She smiled confidently.

"Yes... yes, I'm sure Grace," said Lilybee: "It will be wonderful for you to get to know each other again."

*

When 'White Lakes' came into view, Kingston drew his wagon to a halt. The others slowed and stopped just behind him, then they all climbed down and stood in a silent group gazing at the place they had left almost eighteen years before; the place they thought they would never set eyes on again. They could not believe how much it had changed, how run down everything appeared to be. Although Grace had told them of all the destruction throughout the South, it still came as a tremendous shock to witness it in reality.

Nevertheless, they were glad that their long arduous journey was almost at an end, and their excitement began to mount at the thought of seeing all their old friends again.

"Well, come on then. What we waitin' for?" Joshua broke the silence, and they laughed noisily as they clambered on to the wagons and drove on, anxious to get to the end of their journey before nightfall.

As they rode along the dirt road towards the cabins, some children called to their parents to come and see who was arriving, and before they knew it they were surrounded by a crowd of happy laughing faces, shouting greetings and welcoming them back to their former home. They were helped down from their wagons and almost borne bodily, jubilantly, into the long cabin. They could not have received a warmer welcome if they had been heroes returning from the war. Jassy and Joshua stood silently gazing around the long cabin, painfully recalling the old days. "Where's Angelique... I don't remember ever comin' into this kitchen when she ain't here?" said Jassy.

"She bin gone a long time." replied one of the other women.

Jassy nodded sadly: "Yes, I s'pose she has passed, I guess most of the old folks is gone by now, God rest their souls."

There was a commotion just behind them, and they turned to see a group of children gathered around Bella and Tobias, who were giving their own colourful account of the journey from New Jersey in the company of a real Indian. Run Swiftly was sitting at one of the tables over by the door of the long cabin, Minnie beside him. He remained silent, as always, giving an occasional contented nod. Maybelle called to Bella and Tobias and told them to go outside for a while, to give the grown-ups some peace. The children pushed through the door and disappeared, and the women began to prepare some food and drink.

After they had eaten and rested for a while, Minnie told Run Swiftly that she was going up to the house to see Miss Rosalind, to tell her that she intended to leave, to go back North again with her Indian. He walked with Minnie to the rear of the house, then disappeared again when she went inside. He would watch and wait patiently for her to return.

When Minnie came into the kitchen, the first person she saw was her mother. She ran to her and threw her arms around her, hugging her tightly.

Several of the older servants exclaimed their disbelief at seeing Minnie as a grown woman. It was only the older ones who could remember Grace's daughter as a small child, so many years ago. As for Minnie, she could barely remember anyone from her childhood at 'White Lakes'. Grace was overjoyed to see her daughter safe and sound at last, for she had spent many sleepless nights worrying about her. "I's got ta see Miss Rosalind Mammy... I has to tell her that I ain't stayin'," said Minnie: "I's goin' back to the North with my Indian."

Grace was completely taken aback. "What yo' talkin' bout... how you ever gonna find him?" She had hoped that Minnie would forget all about the Indian once she had left 'Fortune's Hand'.

"I don' have to find him Mammy... he came to find me."

Her face was radiant, Grace could see how happy she was, but it did not ease her fear.

Minnie explained exactly what had happened, how Run Swiftly had come after the wagons, and then accompanied them all the way to North Carolina, taking care of them and keeping them safe. "I's sorry I can't stay at 'White Lakes' with you Mammy, but I loves my Indian more 'n anythin' and we wants to be together always."

"Oh, Minnie... I ain't plannin' on stayin' at 'White Lakes' neither. I's goin' with Mose. We is goin' up north to Canada. He done what he said, yes sir... he come back more'n a week ago to git me. All we was waitin'for was yo'. I done tol' him I ain't goin' nowhere till you gits here."

Minnie could hardly believe that Mose had come back. She was delighted at the prospect of seeing him after so many years. She could still remember how much she had loved him... he was her Pappy as far as she was concerned. "Mose... here?" Minnie chuckled happily. "Where is he, I wants to see him?"

"You see him soon enough. He mos' likely back in the cabin, waitin' for me to come home. The family is all in the dinin' room eatin 'right now, so I gits a little time to myself till bed time. Yo' can't see Miss Rosalind till they is done eatin', so yo' can come with me to see Mose if'n yo' wants."

"Yes... yes," agreed Minnie eagerly, "And I's gonna bring my Indian to see him too."

Grace threw back her head and laughed, "Well, that sure gonna make him sit up and take notice."

They left the kitchen together, still laughing, but their laughter stopped a moment or two later when Minnie suddenly remembered Sunny Blue. She asked Grace if he had returned with Mose; she supposed that he must have done.

Her mother stopped and turned to her. "Ain't yo' heard Minnie... my Sunny Blue dead?"

It took Minnie several seconds to absorb what her mother had said. She simply could not believe it. "No... no... he jus' a child. What happened Mammy?"

Grace placed her arm around Minnie's shoulders and led her on towards their cabin, saying: "Don' talk' 'bout it now honey-chile, I tell yo' everythin' 'bout it tomorrow, maybe. We don' wants to spoil your meetin' with Mose now, does we? He gonna be so glad to see yo' again."

Minnie nodded her head; she could not think of anything to say, but her heart was full of sadness for her mother and Mose. She knew how very much they had loved Sunny Blue, what his death must have meant to them.

As they were walking slowly along the path, in silence now, they heard a very distinct soft warbling, as though a bird was whistling low down in the shrubbery to the side of them. "What that?" asked Grace, puzzled.

Minnie smiled knowingly, " It my Indian he bin waitin' for me out here." She turned in the direction of the sound and called: "Run Swiftly... where is yo'?"

Grace nearly jumped out of her skin as he suddenly appeared before them. "This my Mammy... we is goin' to our cabin to see Mose, and I wants yo' to come along and meet him," said Minnie.

Run Swiftly nodded his head deferentially towards Grace. "I come," he said to Minnie.

So the three of them continued along the path in silence together. Mose was sitting outside the cabin watching for Grace as the trio came into view. He stood up and looked with interest at Grace's two companions. Then, as they drew nearer, Grace called to him: "Mose... Mose... it Minnie. She here."

He stood up, his heart pounding in his chest. Minnie ran the last short distance to him and flung her arms around him. His arms enfolded her, and they clung together, their tears falling fast. Neither of them could speak, but no words were needed, their joy overflowed. Finally, they released one another, laughing and crying at the same time. Minnie pulled Run Swiftly gently to her side and introduced him to Mose. He took Mose's hand, as it was proffered, and shook it violently up and down in his own two. They all laughed loudly.

"Come on inside now let me git us some coffee," said Grace: "We sure got some talkin' to do. Mose... yo' light the lamp, will yo'?"

The next few hours were spent reminiscing and exchanging news of what they had each been doing during the years they had been apart. There was laughter intermingled with tears, and many gasps of disbelief at some of the tales that Mose had to tell of his new life in Canada. He and Run Swiftly also spoke of what they had done during the war, and it soon became obvious that their liking for one another was completely mutual, so much so that Mose ventured to ask Run Swiftly if he would like to come up to Canada with him. "There ain't nothin' a man can't do in that country," he said. "Yo' and me could do some good livin', and some good tradin' with the store, if'n yo' had a mind to."

Eventually it was agreed, at least, that Run Swiftly and Minnie would travel with Mose and Grace when they started on their journey to the North. Grace was delighted at the news; now maybe she would have her daughter's company as far as New Jersey, and she could still hold on to the hope that Run Swiftly might one day decide to join her and Mose in Canada. She would say a prayer to God every day, and ask that she and her daughter might be reunited at long last, for He, and He alone could turn her dreams into reality.

When the two women returned to the house later that evening, they left their men contentedly chatting to one another. "I be back as soon as I gits the Lady Lilybee off to her bed Mose," said Grace. She looked at Run Swiftly and said, "And Minnie ain't gonna be too long, 'cos she only gonna tell Miss Rosalind she leavin' ain't that so Minnie?"

Minnie smiled at Run Swiftly: "Yes Mammy... that exactly so," she said.

Miss Rosalind took her maid into the library so that they could talk together in private; it was such a long time since they had spoken to one another. She told Minnie to sit beside her on a small couch, hoping that it would help to create an air of confidentiality. Minnie's eyes were cast down; she could not look at her mistress. The recent revelation as to her father's identity had completely destroyed the bond of love and trust that had always existed between them, and she was painfully aware of it. Haltingly she told her mistress that she wished to leave 'White Lakes' and return to the North with her Indian. She knew it was the right thing to do, for knowing her mistress as she did, she realised that it would be impossible for her to come to terms with the fact that they were half-sisters. Even she had found the knowledge of it unbearably painful.

Rosalind looked at her maid seated beside her, head bowed, and she knew that she would miss her. In a voice barely audible, she asked: "When will you be leaving?"

Minnie hesitated for a moment or two: "Er... I thinks we is gonna leave tomorrow... or the day after that. Run Swiftly and me is a- travellin' with my mammy and Mose."

The news stunned Rosalind. She had accepted that Minnie would eventually leave her, and go off with her Indian, but not so soon. She covered her face with her hands and moaned: "Oh, no... I had not realised... I shall never see you again Minnie, and I shall miss you."

Her shoulders began to rise and fall as she sobbed. Minnie immediately cradled her in her arms, as she had always done since her mistress was just a baby. "Don' cry Miss Rosalind, don' cry." They held one another close for a very long time, sad in the knowledge that it was for the last time. "You got

Master Benjamin to take care of you from now on... he a fine young man," said Minnie, trying hard to console her mistress.

"But you have been with me since before I can even remember, you have always been with me and... and... you are my sister." Rosalind had found it extremely difficult to say what she had just said; she had tried in every way possible to ignore the fact for weeks, but now relief flooded over her, she felt cleansed.

"Ain't no good gonna come of talkin' 'bout that Miss Rosalind," said Minnie emphatically. "That the best thing' 'bout me leavin', we won't never have to think 'bout it again."

"I have always hated my father, you know that Minnie. We all hated him... he was completely evil but I never believed he was capable of such unforgivable sin. Whoever killed him... no matter who it was, did us all a great service. He would have destroyed each and every one of us, so we are well rid of him."

Minnie hesitated a moment before she decided to divulge to Rosalind who was responsible for the death of Gilbert Hetherington. She knew that suspicion had hung over herself, as well as Master Edmund, and she felt it necessary to clear up the mystery once and for all. "I knows who killed him," she said quietly.

Rosalind's eyes were wide with astonishment. "You do... who ... who was it?" she asked.

"It was a Indian... not my Indian... but a Indian who come to find the men that killed his wife. I knows his name... he come from the people of my Indian, but best if'n you don't know who he is. My Indian tol' me the whole story... it mighty sad. Massa Hetherington and his men was real bad to them Indians, Miss Rosalind, they was lyin' and cheatin' when they come to trade... then they killed one of their women and took off with their furs and skins. That why they killed your

pappy, he done got what he deserved... jus' what he deserved."
She gave a satisfied nod.

"Well I never," said Rosalind, greatly relieved that the killer had not been someone familiar to her. "And you are right Minnie... he did get just what he deserved. I am so glad you told me. Now I need never worry over it again."

The two girls chatted together for a while, then bade one another a fond farewell, filled with good wishes for the future. Despite their sadness at having to part, they could each look forward with gladness to the life that lay ahead of them.

*

Minnie was sitting with Mose and Run Swiftly in the cabin when her mother returned very late that night. She came in, her face beaming. "Yo' sure looks mighty happy, yo' must have sump'n real good to tell us," said Mose hopefully.

"I has... I has," laughed Grace.

She sat down at the table opposite Mose, the light from the lamp casting a translucent glow over her face. Mose gazed at her adoringly; she seemed to him to grow more and more beautiful with each passing year. She leaned across the table and clasped his hands tightly. "Guess what the mistress done? Yo' never guess, never," she said, shaking her head and chuckling uncontrollably.

"Well, if I ain't never gonna guess, what yo' waitin' for? Yo' best tell me." Mose was enjoying the joke.

"She done tol' me we can take one of them wagons with a team, and two more horses besides. I can see Kingston in the mornin', and he gonna fix everythin' for us. Ain't that somethin'? And not only that, she gonna give us all sorts of supplies for startin' on our journey.

Mose was duly impressed; so too were Minnie and Run Swiftly. They were all looking forward to their journey with eager anticipation. It was becoming apparent that the trip would prove a really pleasurable one. They talked long into the night, making their plans and deciding upon the best route to take, but finally tiredness overcame them and they went to their beds.

Grace very proudly showed Run Swiftly and Minnie into the bedroom that Mose had built for Sunny Blue, and it was not long before they were all sound asleep.

*

They spent the whole of the following day making the wagon ready and packing it with provisions. Kingston chose the most sturdy beast he could find for their return journey North, then they took to their beds early so that they could set off at first light the next morning. The family up at the house were still sleeping when they left, but they had said their farewells to every one of them the previous evening, amid much laughter and not a few tears. Now it only remained for them to say good-bye to the rest of the servants, who had been their closest friends for the best part of their lives.

All of them stood lining the dirt road to give Mose and his family their heartfelt wishes for a safe journey and a happy life in the North. Harvest and Clarence even ventured to suggest that they might one day up and leave themselves. They had discovered a taste for adventure during the trip down to North Carolina from New Jersey, and Run Swiftly had more than whetted their appetite for life in the great outdoors.

"We be there waitin' if yo' ever decides to come, and there sure is plenty of land for everybody; yes sir… Canada mighty big country," said Mose enthusiastically. He slapped the horses and the wagon started to roll. Grace and Minnie waved from the back until they could no longer distinguish their friends in the distance, and their hearts were light. No longer would they be forced to live a life of servitude, unable to make their own decisions. Now each day was theirs for the taking… they were free.

Grace placed her arm around Minnie's shoulders and hugged her lovingly. Then gently stroking her daughter's abdomen she said: "This chile gonna be the first one born free since our people brought here from Africa. Yo' made your old mammy mighty proud Minnie."

Minnie's mouth fell open in amazement: "How yo' know I's havin' a chile… I ain't told nobody.".

"I knowed it jus 'as soon as I set eyes on yo'. Ain't no way yo' can hide that from your mammy, no way."

Grace threw back her head and laughed loudly; that caused Minnie to laugh, and the sound of their laughter was so infectious that it set Mose and Run Swiftly laughing too, and they hoped the. joy of it would accompany them not just throughout their journey, but for the rest of their lives.

Five

Within days of bidding an emotional farewell to her loyal maid Grace, Lilybee watched the departure of her brother Douglas, in a furore of activity. He spent hours directing the servants who had been charged with the removal and packing of his belongings, and he finally left 'White Lakes' in the late afternoon, with a very curt good-bye. Lilybee watched him ride off haughtily astride his horse, then with an exasperated sigh she went indoors to take her afternoon tea. It was with a twinge of guilt that she admitted to Celia later how very glad she was to see the back of him. The two women had taken to spending an hour or two with one another every afternoon, whilst taking their tea. They would sit enjoying each other's company, idly chatting and exchanging views on any matter that might catch their interest.

Lilybee looked despondent. "I have tried everything in my power to encourage him to make something of himself you know Celia… God knows how I have tried, but unfortunately we have to accept that there are those who simply will not abide by the rules of common decency. I remember telling you many years ago just what calibre of men my two half-brothers were, but even then you knew my dear, did you not, more's the pity? Now I thank God that my papa never came to learn of how Gilbert met his end. At least he was spared that shameful revelation."

"I would have loved to meet your father Lilybee. He sounds to have been a truly fine gentleman."

"I am sure he would have loved to know you, my dear; it would have given him the greatest pleasure, particularly as you bore him three grandchildren... he would have been so proud. Let us not dwell on the past though; we must channel our energy into plans for the future. I have such plans for 'White Lakes'... and perhaps dear Edmund might take an interest at some time in the future. Have you noticed how much he has improved lately, especially since he has returned to 'White Lakes'?"

"Indeed, indeed, but who could not fail to be made well again in this place? I am sure that he will eventually recover; just given the time. Benjamin has assured me that it is possible. He has been so patient with him, and Edmund enjoys his companionship. Rosalind is indeed fortunate in her choice of husband; she could not have wished to meet a finer gentleman."

"I agree... and you will remember I did say that he would be a great asset to this family. Oh, and whilst we are speaking of him, there is something I would ask you to consider Celia. Now what would you think of my asking Benjamin and Rosalind to take a trip to England on my behalf? Don't answer straight away... just give it a little thought. There is so much business to conduct now that Papa has gone, and I could not possibly face such a journey myself, not anymore, but certainly someone has to go and consult with Papa's solicitors on my behalf. I can think of nobody I would rather trust than Benjamin and Rosalind... it is all dependent upon whether or not you agree though, my dear."

Celia needed no time to ponder the question. "What a wonderful idea Lilybee I have no objection whatsoever, why should I? Rosalind will be delighted, I'm sure. She will jump at the opportunity to see England."

"Shall I speak to them this evening, at dinner?" asked Lilybee.

"Most definitely… the sooner, the better."

*

Lilybee's proposition was accepted wholeheartedly by Benjamin during dinner, and Rosalind was convinced that she must be dreaming. How often she had tried to imagine what England might be like, and with Benjamin talking of it continually she had begun to nurture hopes that one day she would visit the land of her husband's birth, the mother country of her own forebears. Now she could not contain her excitement at the thought that she was soon to set off on the trip of a lifetime; she was to cross the Atlantic Ocean with the man she loved by her side. Throughout the meal Lilybee carefully explained what she would have Benjamin do for her. She described in infinite detail all the places of business she required him to visit in London. Of course, he should carry with him a bona fide letter of introduction from his wife's aunt, and she had no doubt of how warmly he would be received when it became known that he had married into the Hetherington family… that he was married to Lawrence Hetherington's granddaughter, no less.

When the meal was over, they all adjourned to the drawing room to continue their discussion over coffee, and it was then that Rosalind threw her arms around her aunt, hugging and kissing her, and exclaiming her gratitude. "Aunt Lilybee, you really are the kindest and most generous lady imaginable. Mama has always spoken of you in the most glowing terms, and now I understand her high regard of you. We shall never be able to repay your generosity, but we shall hold you very dear to our hearts for the rest of our lives... shall we not Benjamin?"

Lilybee was blushing profusely at her niece's enthusiastic reactions. "Oh, the exuberance of youth," she said laughingly, but her delight was obvious. She took her niece's hands in her own and looked intently at her, speaking seriously, she said: "You, my dear, have never really had the opportunity of seeing the Hetherington family in a particularly good light, much to my regret, but I want to remedy that. From now on I hope with all my heart that this family's reputation will remain honourable; that you and Edmund, and your children's children, will be proud to speak the Hetherington name. My two brothers besmirched it, but it is to you, the future generation, that we shall look to see it restored. You will fully appreciate my meaning when you begin to circulate in the world that was your grandfather's. He was held in the highest esteem by everyone with whom he associated. Regretfully, his sons were incapable of emulating his fine character, but that is no longer a matter of concern. Now it is your time to show the world that you truly respect its old values, and when you meet some of your grandfather's former friends and acquaintances, I am sure you will heartily agree with what I am suggesting."

"After we have dealt with the most urgent of your business Aunt," said Benjamin: "I should like very much to take Rosalind on a visit to my own family. My mother would appreciate the opportunity of meeting my beautiful wife, and I am sure that Rosalind too would love to make her acquaintance. You cannot imagine how grateful I am for what you are affording me with this trip. I really am overwhelmed by it."

"On the contrary Benjamin, you are doing me a great service by undertaking to go on my behalf, and please enjoy it to the very full. Once my immediate business has been attended to, then you should simply set out to make the very most of your visit. My father's house, or mine as it is now, will be at your disposal, and you may remain there for as long as you wish. The housekeeper and the servants are to be retained, so you might just as well enjoy the comforts they so readily provide. To be honest, that is the only regret I have in not undertaking the trip myself... I shall not have the chance to see that wonderful house in Chelsea... my former home. I hope you come to love it as much as I do. Oh, and you must give my very warmest regards to all the servants."

So the arrangements were made, and plans put into operation, and three weeks later Lilybee, Celia, Edmund and Esther, as well as several of the servants, stood on the sweeping drive of 'White Lakes' to wave farewell to Benjamin and Rosalind as they departed in the pony and trap driven by Kingston. Harvest followed in another conveyance piled high with their many trunks and cases. "Enough luggage for a whole regiment," laughed Celia, when she saw what her daughter was taking with her. "Have a wonderful time," she called.

"Yes yes... enjoy yourselves," joined in Lilybee.

Everybody waved until they saw the vehicles turn out of the gates on to the road, then they went back into the house, sadly aware that young Miss Rosalind's bubbly presence would be sorely missed during the weeks and months ahead.

Six

"Shall we take tea out on the veranda, my dear?" asked Lilybee.

"That would be lovely," replied Celia.

"You go on out then; I shall join you in a few minutes... I'll just go and fetch the letter that came this morning from Rosalind; I must read again how much she is enjoying New York. I'm so glad they have had to wait awhile for their ship to England, it has given them time to enjoy all the wonders that city has to offer. I remember our trip there together many years ago; how we enjoyed it." Lilybee purposely avoided any mention of their most recent visit, but a few months ago. She was sure that neither of them would ever have any wish to recall that miserable event.

As Celia made her way out on to the verandah, Lilybee disappeared in the direction of the library to fetch Rosalind's letter. It was then that she saw a visitor being admitted at the front door, an unexpected visitor, someone she had almost given up hope of ever seeing again. She gasped with delight, then flung open her arms in an enthusiastic welcome.

In the meantime, Celia had seated herself in one of the large comfortable armchairs; she was gazing into the distance towards the river. She heaved a contented sigh; she felt at peace, as she had always done since her first visit to 'White Lakes'. She smiled dreamily as she recalled what Lilybee had just said. Yes, their trip to New York all those years ago had been wonderful. It was the most memorable occasion she had ever known in her life. She allowed her thoughts to drift pleasurably, thoughts filled with fond memories of Ian Forbes.

There was a sound behind her, no doubt the tea was arriving, but she would not let it intrude upon her reverie. She remained gazing into the distance, the pleasure of her thoughts reflected in her expression.

"How beautiful you are Seeley O' Malley... even more beautiful than the last time I saw you."

It was his voice. Or was she imagining it? She was almost afraid to look around; she did not want him to disappear, to find that he was merely a figment of her imagination.

He took her hand from where it was resting on the arm of the chair, he lifted it to his lips and kissed it lovingly. She saw that he was standing before her, he was real... she could see that he was real. Her heart began to pound. "Ian... Ian how... how?"

He pulled her gently to her feet and into his arms. He would have the rest of his life to explain how he had come there, that was not important. He silenced her by placing his lips upon hers, and he kissed her in a way she had never been kissed before. He kissed her with passion that sprang from the depths of his love. Then he held her close, murmuring: "I have waited all my life for this moment Seeley... I love you. I have loved you from the first moment I saw you."

"Oh, Ian, I love you too," whispered Celia. She was so overcome with happiness that she could hardly speak. They stood together, their arms wrapped around each other, unable to believe that nothing, nobody, could ever come between them again.

Lilybee instructed one of the servants to take the tea on to the verandah for Mistress Celia and her guest, then she returned to the library so that they could be alone. She smiled a satisfied smile, pleased that her efforts to contact Mr Forbes had been so successful. She had written to him when she and Celia were in New York attending to business matters several months ago, and her letter had finally found its way into his hands. Now she was so thankful that they had managed to keep in touch with one another over the years, albeit intermittently, for somehow she had always known, somewhere deep inside, that one day she would be instrumental in bringing the two of them together. She had known it, without a shadow of a doubt, because she had never seen two people more destined to spend their lives as man and wife together.

Bibliography

American Civil War: A Complete Military History, Douglas Welsh.

Encyclopedia of American Facts & Dates, 9ᵗʰ Edition, Gordon Carruth

Longman History of the United States of America, Hugh Brogan

The Civil War & Reconstruction, J.G Randall & David Donald

Historical Atlas of New York Eric Hamburger

The Making of America, B.W. Beacroft * M.A. Smale

The Native Americans (An Illustrated History)

The Oxford History of the American People, Samuel Eliot Morrison

The Pelican History of the United States of America Hugh Brogan

Pictorial History of Shipping & Emigration

Readings in American History, Fouth Edition. Volume 1: Pre-Colonial through Reconstruction.

The United States of 1865, Michael Kraus

Rise of the American Nation, Third Edition. Incorporating *History & the Social Sciences,* Mark M Krug, Lewis Paul & Merle Curti.